AMONG
THE LIVING

AMONG THE LIVING

TIM LEBBON

TITAN BOOKS

Among the Living
Print edition ISBN: 9781803365947
E-book edition ISBN: 9781803365954

Published by Titan Books
A division of Titan Publishing Group Ltd
144 Southwark Street, London SE1 0UP

First edition: February 2024
1 3 5 7 9 10 8 6 4 2

This is a work of fiction. Names, characters, places, and incidents either are the product of the author's imagination or are used fictitiously, and any resemblance to actual persons, living or dead (except for satirical purposes), is entirely coincidental. The publisher does not have control over and does not assume any responsibility for author or third-party websites or their content.

Tim Lebbon asserts the moral right to be identified as the author of this work.

A CIP catalogue record for this title is available from the British Library.

Printed and bound in the UK by CPI Group Ltd, Croydon CR0 4YY.

For Howard Morhaim, my agent and friend.

ONE

Dean stared into a darkness that no human had entered for at least thirty thousand years. The shadows appeared solid, bearing mass and viscosity, rather than simply being an absence of light. It was as if they hunkered down in defiance of the long days and short nights experienced at this time of year on Hawkshead Island. They held the weight of history. Or maybe it was just the cold of the dawn playing tricks on his mind.

"Looks like a good place to tie on," Lanna said. She pointed at a spur of rock to the left of the narrow fault in the ground as she shrugged a coiled rope from her shoulder.

"I'll give you a hand," Dean said.

"Hmm, promises."

Dean rolled his eyes and glanced back over his shoulder at the Stallion. Emma was climbing down from the high cab, and she caught his eye and smiled. She didn't smile like that very often. That caused Dean's paranoia to kick in. Maybe it was quiet laughter. Maybe she'd heard Lanna creep into his tent the previous night. Not that it mattered. Lanna made no secret of their occasional trysts, passing jokes in front of the others without embarrassment. They'd slept together a few dozen times over the years, and Dean took her lead on what any of it meant. *Just a bit of fun*, she'd say. He definitely agreed with her that, yes, it was fun. But sometimes he'd find himself wishing it could be a little more. Today he'd planned to talk to Lanna about things, find out what their future might hold. Emma's smile cooled that thought.

"How're things, Wren?" Emma asked. Wren claimed he'd picked up the nickname on a South American expedition a decade ago, but Lanna said she'd heard it was what his mother used to call him. Six feet and four inches of gruffness and sharp edges: naming him after the UK's smallest bird gave him a Little John vibe.

"Ready to rock and roll!" Wren said. He was at the Stallion's open rear doors, prepping the four identical backpacks that they would wear down into the caves. Each one was loaded with tech and worth about ten grand.

"Hey!" Lanna said, punching Dean's arm. "Dreamer!"

"I don't dream," Dean said.

"Sure you do. Everyone dreams." She waved the rope at him, and he went to help her tie it around the rock spur. "You were mumbling in your sleep last night."

"I needed a leak."

"You were saying, 'Just cut the line'. Something like that."

"Huh." A cool thump hit Dean's stomach. Cold pulsed through him. *Just cut the line*. He grabbed the end of the rope and scrambled up and around the sharp rock. "You must've made me delirious. Raised my heart rate."

"Raised something." He caught her eye and he wondered yet again. *Really? Just a bit of fun?* But the moment to say something had come and gone. Maybe his lack of confidence meant he'd lost too many opportunities to make things more than they were.

They tied the rope around the rock, taking turns to hold on and lean back to test its strength, then threw the coiled end down into the impenetrable darkness of the narrow fracture that formed the cave mouth.

"Okay, come grab your packs, guys," Emma said, and Dean and Lanna headed over to the parked Stallion, light from their head torches dancing before them. It was a large vehicle, the best that money could buy for an expedition like this, with six chunky-tyred wheels almost as tall as him, independent suspension rods as thick as his thigh, a sealed rear compartment with thick solar-panelled walls and roof, and reinforced windows, which would have slept four comfortably if it wasn't so packed with kit, and an elevated cab where Emma usually drove and Wren rode shotgun. It was designed for the most inimical terrain, and they'd used it in places far worse than this.

Somehow, though, Hawkshead Island felt more desolate than anywhere Dean had ever been. He'd visited deforested regions of the Amazon on several occasions, the vast Siberian steppe, and a scattering of remote Antarctic islands exposed by melting ice, but this place sang of solitude and whistled with a constant gentle breeze that originated from unknown places, heading nowhere. The terrain was harsh and rocky, marshy and unpredictable, nurturing a dozen ways to kill them, but it wasn't only that. Dean thought the feeling was more to do with his memories of being a child in Boston, when harsh winters and hot summers brought real distinguishable seasons. He'd loved it most when it snowed, especially those winters when a storm dumped thirty inches over a weekend, because that had meant a few days off school and endless fun outside with his friends. A fresh new world, a pristine landscape for a while. As the covering melted, revealing the old familiar ground underneath, his heart would sink back towards a less exciting normality.

Hawkshead Island had been smothered with snow all year round for millennia, but that was no longer the case. Large patches still remained, but wide swathes of landscape now showed through. Temperatures had risen, hovering above freezing for most of the year. This was a changing place, and the island's desolation was painfully obvious.

They took turns shrugging on their caving helmets and packs, and letting Wren ensure they were all a perfect fit.

"You're putting on weight," he said as Dean shouldered his pack.

"Easy living," Emma said.

Dean laughed. "Screw you."

"Wren's right," Lanna said. "You are developing love handles."

There was a moment's uncomfortable silence. Then Lanna caught his eye, wriggled an eyebrow. Wren chuckled.

"Jesus, guys," Dean said, smiling.

"Okay, gang, let's hustle," Emma said. Wren locked the Stallion—he called the vehicle his baby, and however remote their expedition he was always paranoid that someone would come along with the desire and know-how to hotwire a million-dollar piece of kit and steal it—and walked up the gentle slope towards their chosen cave. The Stallion's big lamps were programmed to stay on for half an hour, lighting their approach and descent into the system. They had sent down a remote-controlled drone that Emma piloted with aplomb, and they'd zeroed in on these caverns as the most likely source of rare earth minerals.

After that, Dean had sent a simple, anonymous message with these coordinates. He didn't know if Bethan had received them. He didn't know if she would come, and when she might arrive. If she did, he had no idea how it might be between them. But whatever happened, he knew that in sending her that message he had taken a step away from this world that had never really been his.

What they sought was worth a fortune, and their small team was renowned for its success rate. In the right circles, at least. It wasn't exactly legal, and the moral side was something that Dean used to put into a solid mental box and set to one side. Once, huddled in a one-person sleeping bag, sweat still sticking them together as their heartbeats and breathing started to slow down, he'd tried talking to Lanna about this. They were on a rocky South Atlantic island where penguins watched their every move and wind drove freezing rain against exposed skin like bullets. She'd laughed at him, then fallen quiet. He had fallen asleep waiting for her to say something profound.

"Follow me, I've got the map!" Wren said. He had a small screen attached to his wrist on which he could call up the virtual 3D map of the caverns made by the drone. It wouldn't be a complete map, but it would show the general lie of the land. "A tight wriggle to start with, so feet first. Twist to the left, then it opens out. It's a scramble down a steep slope to the first cavern big enough to stand in. Hold onto the rope all the way. I'll guide you."

"Don't get stuck," Dean said, and Wren grinned. He was a big man and had been on a fast track to semi-pro football when a shoulder injury finished his career. He was always the first of them to venture into narrow spaces. If he could make it, they all could.

Wren grabbed the rope, backed up to the narrow cave mouth, and eased his way in and down. As the darkness swallowed him, Dean experienced a twinge of claustrophobia. *Am I really following him in there?* he thought, and he frowned. He'd never felt like this before. He'd been caving since he was a kid, and it was usually heights that got to him more than enclosed spaces.

"Don't wait up," Wren said, and his face and upper body were swallowed by the darkness almost too soon, as if greedy shadows had closed him off from the rest of the world.

"Comms on," Emma said, and they each tapped the communications unit curved over their right ear. It transmitted their voices through bone conduction, leaving their ears free to detect any localised dangers. They started calling their names so that the others could check that the systems were working.

"Wren?" Emma asked after a pause.

"Balrog," Wren growled, and then he said, "Whoops!"

"What is it?" Dean asked.

"Slippery. Rocks oozing moisture. Muddy. Be careful on the way down. You can start heading in now."

Dean stepped forward before Emma or Lanna could move, keen to get on with this. He didn't like the unfamiliar nervousness, and knew that the best way to subdue it was to confront it head on. The more he thought about things, the more troubled he became. Just like his problem with Lanna.

"What is it, Dean?" Lanna asked.

"Huh?" Dean grabbed the rope and stood at the cave mouth, facing his two teammates.

"Dunno. I thought I heard you sigh."

Wren laughed, and Dean heard it echoing up from behind him as well as through his comms.

"Just wind," Dean said, and he started easing back into the cave mouth. Darkness drew him in and down, cooler even than the cold air outside. The atmosphere in the cave was utterly still, like a held breath, and he gripped the rope hard as he descended. The powerful light from his headlamp washed across the sloping floor beneath his feet. Wren was right, it was slippery and muddy, and his teammate's footprints were already being washed away as Dean added his own.

"I'm in the cavern," Wren said. "Whoah."

"All good?" Emma asked.

"Yeah. All good. It's beautiful."

Dean smiled at the wonder in Wren's voice. *Letting your mask slip there, big guy.*

"We're heading down," Lanna said. Dean felt the rope above him tighten and then vibrate as the other two started descending after him.

He slipped a couple of times, easing his weight and grip on the rope to keep himself upright. Then he saw his own shadow splashed ahead of him and felt Wren grab his waist, easing him down the last slippery slope into the larger cavern.

Dean turned to thank him and then saw what Wren had seen.

"Wow," he said. The cavern wasn't huge, but one end was taken up with a pool of water, a sheen of retreating ice an inch below the surface casting a ghostly glow upwards when his light fell upon it. It silvered the cavern's uneven walls and low ceiling. Gentle ripples passed across the water, perhaps from their footsteps on the cavern floor, or maybe from something that had just ducked beneath the surface.

Stop that shit right now! Dean thought. He smiled at his overactive imagination.

"Told you," Wren said. "But look this way." He tapped Dean on the shoulder, and he turned and added his light to Wren's.

At the other end of the cavern a wide crack split the wall from floor to ceiling, offering them a way deeper into the system. They'd guided the drone in that direction the day before, but none of them had appreciated the full detail of what they were seeing. The fault they had just descended, this cavern, and the tunnels leading off it had been clogged with ice for many millennia until the permafrost started thawing forty years before. That melt had sped up during the past decade: as the ground thawed so had much of the surface ice, creating routes for the passage of warm air from above that accelerated the melt even more. Now, sculptures of ice clung to walls and hung from ceilings, some of them ragged where they'd cracked and fallen away, others smooth and shimmering where water flowed across their surface. The ice was dark and dirty in places, a deep emerald green elsewhere, and here and there it seemed to swallow the pure white light from their headlamps and glow as if lit from within. It illuminated the whole cavern.

"Amazing," Dean muttered, and then he felt Lanna nudge against him and grasp his hand. He'd been so enraptured with the scene that he hadn't heard Emma and her complete their descent. She squeezed, and he experienced one of those sublime moments of overwhelming peace, wholeness, and presence that rarely lasted more than a few seconds.

They stood together for a while, just looking around and taking it in. Their combined headlamps set the cavern on fire. It was as if the icy cave relished this first touch of light in many millennia. Perhaps it was the first time ever.

"Okay," Emma said at last. "Let's move on. Wren?"

"Yeah." He tapped the display on his small wrist screen, and as he turned the image followed his movement, perfectly synchronised with their surroundings. "This way."

They headed off into the cave system, feet splashing in mud, thin thermal jackets protecting them from most of the chill. It was colder down here than up in the open air, but their suits were designed for such environments. Lanna tied the end of a ball of strong wire-threaded string to the rope they'd left hanging down from above. The reel was attached to her belt, and as they moved off she rested one hand there to ensure the string played out behind them.

Wren went first, as usual, then Emma followed behind him. She carried a probe which she used to tap the walls, pausing now and then to check the readings.

"Anything?" Dean asked after a while.

"Traces," she said.

"Maybe just picking up minerals in the meltwater," Lanna said. The walls dripped and flowed, and they splashed through mucky water that streamed in the direction they were heading, sometimes shallow, sometimes up to the shins of their heavy boots. There was probably a series of subterranean waterways ploughing through the melting permafrost, carving new channels or following old routes that had frozen thousands or millions of years before. It was something that always worried them in situations like this: as the team geologist, Dean was supposed to put their minds at rest. *Yes, sure, the tunnels are safe*, he'd say, but they all knew the truth—they were taking their lives in their hands.

That was why they were never keen to go too deep.

These tunnels, illuminated by bright splashes from their helmet lamps, were ancient natural architecture revealed as the deep soul of the ground itself began to thaw. Billion-year-old rock existed on a different timescale to puny people. One day these tunnels would cave in, change, erupt, just as someday a tree would fall. That didn't stop a person from touching it or walking by. Dean's trust in his surroundings, his awareness of risk and its mitigation, came from his understanding of geological timescales.

Those timescales had been upset, and sometimes accelerated, by the thaw, potentially causing flash floods, ice-weakened cracks and faults in the seemingly solid surroundings, and cave-ins. Plenty of stuff here was ready to kill them without a second's warning. Dean felt the weight of this place ready to drop and crush them flat.

They moved onwards, erring down, and ten minutes later he realised that they'd passed the last of the strange ice sculptures. They'd been reducing in size and frequency, catching light and reflecting deep, old colours and suspended dirt. Now there were no more.

"This is it," he said. "We're past the point where ice formed down here."

"Ground's still slick," Wren said.

"A century ago these caves would've been mostly dry."

They were in a wider passage, the floor uneven, several tall dark cracks slashed upwards into the ceiling. Some of these faults would provide routes deeper into the cave complex. Emma edged closer to one wall and ran the probe up and down, and a series of loud uneven crackles echoed around the chamber.

"Okay," she said, checking the digital readout. "Okay! This might be a good place to start. Dean, check it out."

Dean moved beside her and shone his lamp across the surface. The powerful light reflected from the dampness there, a thousand glimmering drips, and it was far too bright. He flicked it off.

"Aim your lights left and right," he said. "Not directly at the wall." The others did as he asked, and he pulled a small, weaker penlight from his belt. He stepped in closer and ran his gloved hand across the surface. He shook away the moisture and leaned in, moving the torch slowly left and right, up and down. Plucking a knife from his belt, he pressed its point against the wall... and stopped.

"What?" Emma asked.

"Hang on." Dean took a couple of steps back and lowered his penlight. "Am I seeing things?"

The others turned and their lamps splashed from the wall again, too bright for detail.

"Just penlights," Lanna said, and Dean heard something in her voice.

"You see it?" he asked.

"Maybe." She turned off her headlamp and took out her own smaller torch, and the others followed suit. The cave became much darker, shadows crowding in from deep cracks in the walls and scampering across the ceiling as if trying to avoid being seen.

"Come on, rock boy, what is it?" Wren asked. "Signs of cerium?"

"Paintings," Emma said, and Dean let out a deep breath, relieved that it wasn't just him.

"Holy shit," Lanna said. "How old?"

Dean shook his head. His heart beat faster. He was trying to comprehend, compute, but all sense left him as he attempted to understand just what they were looking at.

"Not just paintings," he said. "Carvings. Images carved deep into the rock, then dyed or painted in somehow. Otherwise they'd have eroded away by now."

"So how old?" Emma asked, echoing Lanna.

"Don't know." Dean played his light back and forth across the uneven cave wall, trying to establish the extent of what they had found. He was no archaeologist, but sometimes his own expertise crossed with different disciplines that all explored and investigated Earth's history. He'd been more immersed in such things during his time with Bethan, and he often found himself missing that. Sometimes, he mourned it. She'd always told him that his work was in the realm of aeons as opposed to millennia, but he still experienced the power and deep history of what he was viewing right now. If anything, it made the caverns feel that much older.

"*Don't know*?" Wren asked, an edge of impatience in his voice. "You're the one with a rock degree, why don't you—"

"Thirty thousand years?" Dean muttered.

"That's impossible," Emma said. "How'd you figure?"

"These caves were frozen solid, shut off from the outside world, tens of millennia ago. I dunno, they might even be sixty, seventy thousand years old. Even older."

"There were people doing shit like this that long ago?" Wren asked.

"Sure," Lanna said. "There are cave paintings in Indonesia that are maybe fifty thousand years old."

"But there's good trace in these walls, Emma?" Wren asked.

"Readings certainly look promising."

Dean stepped closer to the cave wall and turned around. "You're joking, right? These carvings and paintings themselves are probably priceless."

"We can't take them down and sell them, can we?" Lanna asked.

Dean ignored her and looked to Emma. She stared at him, grim-faced.

"I mean, what are they even supposed to be?" Wren asked. "Is that a person? What the fuck's happening to their head?"

"Emma," Dean said, "These tunnels go deeper."

"We don't go deep unless we have to, you know that. And we're not archaeologists, Dean."

"The next chamber. That's all. We can't just—"

"Dean!"

He blinked, paused. His usual stance was to give in, but not here. He *couldn't* back down here. "We can't just tear this down, Emma. Besides…" He turned and examined the wall again, running his hand more carefully across the surface. He felt carved runnels that he'd previously thought were natural faults, marvelled at how old they were, tried to imagine the last hands that had felt across the rock like this. He wished he could see with their eyes.

"Besides, what?" Lanna asked.

"Don't like the look of these faults," Dean said. There *were* faults, but he didn't think they were that bad. He wasn't lying. Just massaging the truth. "Deeper, maybe we'll find somewhere easier and safer to excavate for samples."

"Huh," Emma said. "Okay, next chamber, and that's it. Wren?"

Wren consulted the map on his wrist screen, turning slightly left and right to orient himself. "Yeah, got it. Maybe ninety feet that way. Tight squeeze, then it opens out into a much larger chamber. That's as far as the drone went, and maybe that's the place."

Emma nodded, and Dean sighed with relief.

"That's it, though," she emphasised. "Deep enough. There's too much meltwater here for my liking. Remember Patagonia."

Dean could hardly forget. They'd been trapped in a cave system for three days after a flash flood, with no one aware they were down there. It was only Emma's brave swim through flooded caves, with no knowledge of their geography, that had found them a way out. Dean had suggested the attempt, Emma had taken it on. She'd said it was because she was the best swimmer, but they all knew the truth. She felt responsible for them.

As the others headed off towards a narrow, low fault at the end of the cave, Dean took a last look at the paintings.

Touched by only his light they were given more shadow, more texture, and they jumped out in sharp relief. He breathed in the wonder of what he saw. To the left, a huddle of shapes that might have been people, a dozen or more squatting or crouched down. They were tall, with spindly limbs and large heads. To the right stood another figure, an object in its left hand that might have been a weapon, and something in its right hand that resembled a drooping plant or several individual lengths of rope. Standing above this scene, and somehow set behind it by the way it was carved and coloured, a much taller figure on three propped limbs. A tree, perhaps, with a thick trunk. Or maybe a strangely shaped cloud emitting three streams of lightning down at the prone people.

Between the standing figure and group of people, another shape sat in a strange attitude, and Dean couldn't get Wren's comments out of his head. *Is that a person? What the fuck's happening to their head?*

"Dean, keep up," Lanna said in his coms. "We'll take pictures on the way back. Maybe we'll leave an anonymous tip somewhere if this cave doesn't work out."

Dean glanced back the way they'd come, wondering if and when Bethan might arrive. There were no questing lights, no sounds of anyone else within these caves. *Maybe she knows it's me and won't come at all*, he thought.

He switched on his helmet and pack lamps and headed after the others.

They entered a narrow, twisting route, splashing through the thick, muddy water. It got even deeper the further they went, and a couple of times they had to crouch down and crawl on hands and knees, pulling themselves through a long, narrow section that was almost too small to fit through. Despite their waterproof clothing and gloves, Dean felt the bite of cold slowly freezing his fingers. Their helmets scraped on rock, and he had to grasp on and pull, pushing with padded knees and the steel toecaps on his boots, taking deep breaths to try and settle his fear and his beating heart. Wren grunted and swore up ahead, and Dean knew the big man wouldn't do anything he considered too dangerous. They often took sensible risks, but always balanced against potential outcomes. They did this for the money, but none of them was reckless. That was why they worked well as a team.

Just as Dean was beginning to think they'd have to turn back and start excavating into the walls of the painted cave after all, Wren's voice rasped in through their comms.

"Holy shit, guys. I think we've found Dean's life models."

"What?" Dean said. "What do you mean?"

"Jesus," Emma said.

"Oh my…" Lanna's voice faded away into a deep intake of breath.

Dean sped up his crawl and reached out when he saw Lanna leaning down for him. She grasped his hand and helped him up and out from the muddy crawlspace. He knocked his helmet on the low ceiling of this new cavern, and his light flickered a few times, adding a strobe effect to the scene that awaited them.

The cave painting they had left behind, come to life.

Come to life in living death, Dean thought, and the idea, though accurate, sent a chill right through him.

"Okay, I am officially spooked and ready to get the fuck out of here," Lanna said.

No one replied. Dean was ready to follow her. Yet fascination took him another few steps forward.

"Dean…" Emma breathed. "Stay back."

"It's okay," he said.

"How the fuck can this be okay?" Wren asked.

"Because they're old and dead," Dean said.

"How old?" Dean wasn't sure if that was from Emma or Lanna. Their voices were low, whispered, as if afraid to cause echoes that might have touched the strange tableau.

Afraid that *they* might hear.

"Very," Dean said. He took a step closer and turned his head, splashing the bodies with light.

And their eyes open because it's the first light to touch them in thirty or fifty thousand years—

He hissed at his spooked thoughts, making the others jump.

"They're just like those paintings," Wren said.

The cavern was larger than the one with the decorated walls, the ceiling towards the centre higher, and the air here felt dry. A stream tinkled into a crack in the ground and echoed away further, deeper, into hidden places they'd never see. The air smelled dusty, not damp, a scent that Dean associated with deep age.

The bodies were higher up, untouched by the flowing water, on an elevated section of the cavern floor. A dozen or more sat huddled together, so close that they looked like one large, confused tangle of limbs and merged torsos, heads drooped or resting on each other's bony shoulders.

The remains of ropes encircled them, individually and also as a mass. The scene was confusing, but Dean could see that the bodies were mostly mummified, skin tight across skulls and drooping from arms, hanging in swathes across torsos, and still hidden in places behind the remains of clothing. Eye sockets were empty, mouths hung open to display a few yellowed teeth. Hair clung on where scalps remained, though there were places where the skin had dried and crumbled, taking the hair with it. Clumps of it settled in the hollows between bent limbs, dark as the shadows that haunted this cavern's deeper places.

Every skull bore a puncture wound. Some were small, no more than a finger's width, while others had cracked and crazed around the impact point.

"Tied up and killed," Dean said. His words echoed away to nothing. He wondered if their screams had disappeared into the same hollow places beneath the ground, or whether this had been something else. Something none of them here, now, could understand.

Dean made out a dark spread on one body's bare shoulder which might have been a tattoo. The same body wore a necklace made from delicate shells on a thin leather thong. Another corpse clasped a round clay bowl in one hand, finger bones twisted through a hole in its side. Elsewhere, a shredded cloak held memories of a faded, wispy colour.

"So old," Emma said.

"Yeah," Wren said. "Like, when does a mass grave become archaeology, you know?"

Dean knew what he meant. Yet even so old, their presence here felt like a transgression.

"This one's different," Lanna said. She was standing by two more figures, the taller of which seemed to be seated and slumped on a high rock, leaning forward onto a thick metal spear. It punctured the body's chest and exited through its back, metal barbs down its length caught on ribs and spine.

"Suicide?" Emma asked.

"Maybe," Dean said. It was a haunting display, but his focus was drawn again and again to the figure between the seated speared body, and the huddled mass of bound corpses.

"Now that is pretty fucking bizarre," Wren said. "Is it… a kid?"

It was difficult to tell. Definitely a person, the corpse seemed compressed down, legs tucked beneath the body that crouched to the ground, arms hugging itself tight, head

What the fuck's happened to their head?

curved down beneath the torso. An impossible position, unless the neck was broken or completely severed.

"It looks ritualistic," Lanna said. "Like a sacrifice, or something."

"Who knows?" Emma said, and then her probe started ticking and crackling. "Hey!"

Dean glanced back to see Emma at a far wall of the cavern, checking back and forth across an area low to the ground.

"Well, that sounds hopeful," Wren said, his voice lighter.

"Good readings," Emma said. "Dean, take a look."

Dean took another glance at the ancient bodies, mummified and dried and playing out their strange last moments forever. Then Lanna grabbed his arm and leaned in close.

"Let's get working and get the fuck outta here," she whispered. She knew that the others would hear through the comms, but it still felt like it was just between them. She was so close that he could smell her breath, her scent, and he was glad for that.

Emma and Wren were already taking the heat wands from their backpacks, checking that the trailing wires were clear and preparing to fire them up. The wands were just part of what the hi-tech packs contained, tools designed to gently heat ground that might still be frozen solid to make digging and extraction of samples easier. They were only hand tools, and as such their effectiveness was limited to very small areas. But the minerals they sought were rarely found in large concentrations, and this expedition was simply to gather samples. They made their money from selling location information. The larger-scale mining operations that might follow were always in someone else's hands. As such, they didn't need a large amount of a good quality sample to make their trip worthwhile.

And if Dean was reading Emma's excited probe's chattering correctly, they might have found what they were looking for.

He stepped in closer and examined the cavern wall. It was mostly solid rock, but down closer to the floor there was a layer of looser sediment, maybe three inches thick, that exuded a heavier, saltier water. He scraped with his knife and a curl of sand fell away.

"This might be it," he said.

"Okay, get to work," Emma said. "Wren and Lanna down that end, me and Dean here. You know what to do."

They all knew. They had done this before. But never while being observed by the dead.

Dean crouched down close to the ground and shone his headlamp at the wall, while Emma fired up her heat wand and aimed it at the layer of sediment. She prodded it forward for a few seconds, then drew back. The burst of heat washed over Dean, surprising him, and he flinched and blinked to moisten his eyes.

"You're too close," Emma said. "Ease away."

He shuffled back and she passed the wand across the wall again. The sizzling echoed around the cave, repeated from a few feet away where Wren and Lanna were doing the same. Dean took a blunt bladed tool from his belt and scooped along where the surface had been heated, drawing out more of the loosening sandy sediment. Emma swept the wand again, he took another scrape, and they repeated this process a dozen times until there was a small mound of excavated material on a smooth part of the cave floor.

Dean reached around and took a small device from the side pocket of his rucksack. He switched it on, and even though he'd done this earlier he initiated a quick diagnostics check to ensure all readings were accurate.

"Warming up in here," Wren said.

"We've only been doing this for five minutes," Dean said, but Wren was right. The air in the cave seemed to be agitated. A breeze breathed through where there had been none before, carrying a skein of mist so thin and slight that it might have been dust across his eye.

"We got anything?" Emma asked. She sounded impatient. Dean checked his device to confirm that the diagnostic was complete, then rested its series of five metallic probes on the small mound of debris. Its screen flickered to life as it analysed, and moments later the results were displayed in a small chart.

"Top notch," Dean said.

"Okay, good shit," Emma said. "Let's clear out what we can in an hour."

Dean shrugged off his pack and pulled out a selection of folded plastic sample boxes. Lanna did the same. They worked smoothly, filling the boxes with the residue they'd filter and refine later in the Stallion, clicking them shut, and stacking them to one side. His device showed impressive traces of rhodium in each scoop, and he glanced left and right along the wall, starting to wonder just how rich this deposit might be to whomever came after them with proper mining equipment. The amounts they were removing now were minuscule; it would take industrial mining and refinement to make this site profitable.

Which is exactly what Dean wanted to avoid. If Bethan came, as he'd hoped, she and her associates would do everything they could to ensure this place remained untouched. The cave paintings would help, for sure. They might even get UNESCO involved.

Dean glanced back over his shoulder. The bodies were shadows now, with the team's lights concentrated on their work. As his headlamp moved, so did the spidery silhouettes cast by the bodies. He tilted his head left and right, making them dance, and wondering once again what had happened here, and when, and why. It was haunting and disturbing, but he also relished the mystery. He liked the idea that not everything could be known and explained, much as the soul of the land often kept its secrets close. Sometimes the past should remain buried.

That pile of corpses, tied up and bound together, each bearing a head wound. A sacrifice or an execution.

The dead person seated on their own, slumped forward onto the propped metal spear. A suicide or a murder.

That crouched, huddled figure that sat between them.

"Hey, Dean, keep in the moment," Emma said, slapping one gloved hand against his leg.

That's the biggest mystery, he thought, and he shone his light at that strange shape.

"What's that stink?" Lanna asked.

"Dunno," Wren said. "Maybe those bodies have decided…"

They saw and realised, all at the same time. Dean's heart thudded in his chest, and he heard Emma's indrawn gasp, and Wren muttering something under his breath. Lanna dropped the sample box she'd been holding.

The crouched corpse had changed, and it wasn't an effect of the light, or a shifting shadow, or even that their being here had perhaps disturbed the air or ground.

It had *moved*. The head was up, still facing down at the floor but lifted from its previous impossible position beneath the body, a few strands of clotted hair swaying as if tasting at the gentle breeze their presence had caused.

On that breeze, the stench of something old, rotten and rank.

A thin limb encased in leathery skin shifted and braced itself against the ground, and with a crackling, snapping sound it exerted pressure.

In a confusion of boiling shadow and panicked, flickering light, something began to shift.

What the fuck's happened to their head?

Something wet.

TWO

"This isn't what we agreed," Bethan said. "A Ford Xtreme, fully charged with solar backup array, freeze-dried rations for a week, water purifier, camping kit and climbing ropes and winch. Three thousand dollars for eight days. And you told me you'd advise us on routes and recent terrain changes, and give us info about the other team. Instead... that?" She nodded at the vehicle parked close to the dock. She was amazed it still ran. Actually, strike that—she hadn't seen it moving yet. "For fuck's sake."

"Hey, the advice and info I can still offer," Frank said. He was old, weather-grizzled, skin like faded leather. He might have been Goyo's twin, except Goyo had a long grey ponytail. And more than an ounce or two of honesty and honour. "But my brother needed the Xtreme to travel along the coast to his wife's parents' place, and you know what it's like here."

"Brutal," Bethan said. "I hate this fucking place already."

"Family comes first." Frank glanced over his shoulder at the small coastal town of Joyce Sound, then back at Bethan, as if one look could encompass everyone he knew in the town, and how community bound them tightly together. He raised an eyebrow. "You always swear so much?"

"Only when somebody fucks us over."

"Come on, Bethan," Goyo said, touching her shoulder. Always the calming presence. He never raised his voice, never broke out in anger, and sometimes that drove her mad. It levelled her, too. When they were out in the field he was the order that tempered her occasional penchant for chaos.

"Goyo, it was agreed—"

"But things appear to have changed." Goyo nodded at the old Land Rover Discovery. Alile was walking around it, kicking tyres, shading her face at the window to look inside. She looked back at Bethan and Goyo, mouth twisted in an *I dunno* expression.

"What's the mileage?" Bethan asked.

"Round the clock," Frank said.

"How many times?"

He shrugged, and a smile ghosted his mouth. Damned if the fucker wasn't enjoying this.

"Listen—" she said, and Goyo was there again, his voice holding her back. She'd been about to take a step towards the big man, with no idea what might follow. Anger often made her run off at the mouth, and sometimes she acted without thinking. And she knew it wasn't really anger at Frank. He was just a good guy looking after his family and community, and they were a bunch of strangers come here to do things he had no idea about. To him, Bethan and the others were just like the team they were following.

They were *nothing* alike. But Frank wasn't to know that.

It was *them* she was angry at, and it was a familiar feeling from other places, other journeys.

"We'll take it," Goyo said. "I used to drive one of those things back in twenty-two, maybe twenty-three. Decent vehicle. Rugged."

"It's thirty years old!" Bethan said. "Look at it!" The Discovery had certainly seen better days. It might have been black, once, but the harsh environment of Hawkshead Island had abraded it so much that several repaints had overlaid each other, and now it was matt green, blue, and swathed with patches of rust brown. The windscreen had a crack zagging down from one top corner to the bottom centre. One rear window was missing and covered with a heavy seal skin folded and screwed roughly into the chassis.

"It'll get you where you want to go," Frank said. "Especially with the free advice and maps I'm throwing in."

Bethan bristled. Was he kidding? "Free?"

"It's fine," Goyo said again, and though his voice was gentle, she saw the look in his eyes. *Save it for other battles*, it said, and she knew he was right. She sighed, then offered Frank a weak smile.

"Sorry. Been a long journey. Free advice and maps, and a decent hot meal before we head out, and it's a deal."

Frank held out his arms. "You think I'd let you go without a meal? Look at you. You're all wasting away." He chuckled. "Got bottles of my homebrew we can share, too, while we go over the maps. I call it 'Old Bastard'."

"Apt," Bethan said.

"Did you do that for the other team?" Goyo asked. Bethan's flush of anger rose again—at what the team they pursued was here to do, the carelessness they carried like a bad smell, their greed—but she knew this was best left to Goyo.

"How'd you know the *Kelland* doesn't belong here?" He nodded at the modern vessel anchored offshore, white and gleaming. When none of them said anything, he shrugged and smiled.

"They were up their own, for sure. Sailed in, took their beast of a truck off the boat, acted like they owned the place. Asked me a few questions, bought some fresh supplies then headed inland. Can't have been in port for more than three hours."

"You get their names?"

"One I spoke to, the one in charge I guess, named Emma. The others didn't mix with anyone but themselves. That's all I know." He frowned. "Take it you and they ain't the best of friends."

"They're illegal miners," Bethan said. "Prospectors. They find a rich source of what they're after and others will come, rip the island apart."

"They told me they were researching permafrost melt." Frank looked surprised, and perhaps upset he'd been fooled.

"Researching to make dollars," Goyo said.

"You the authorities?"

Bethan shook her head, held his gaze.

Frank considered, then nodded. "Come on. I'll pop a cork on some Old Bastard. Table at the Spacey Jane, good food, quiet corner where we can talk."

"Thanks, Frank," Goyo said.

"So you're paying that three thousand in cash, right?"

Bethan snorted and took a few steps back towards the dock and the cold sea beyond. She absorbed the smell of the little fishing port, the sound of several boats bobbing tied to the dock, their colours revealing the care they were given by the townsfolk. She had great respect for people like these, still existing out on the boundaries of civilisation, and knew it was they who saw the changes in the world more than most. She also noticed the signs of how those changes were affecting them. Out among the moored boats were the remains of several buildings protruding above the waves, wood rotting as they were taken down into the rising seas. Beyond, the ugly modern boat the other team had arrived on looked out of place, riding the waves of the modern world.

"Alile!" Goyo called, and their companion waved and came to join them.

"We're really going in that?" she asked Bethan as they drew close.

"Yeah. Sure. Goyo used to drive one."

"Goyo's like a hundred years old."

"And wise with it," Goyo said, from where he and Frank had started walking on ahead.

"Sorry," Alile said, "didn't know you had your hearing aid in."

Goyo gave them the finger over his shoulder, and they followed him and Frank from the harbour and into the small town huddled at the edge of the world.

The Spacey Jane had just opened for lunch and they were the only clientele. Frank spoke quietly to the tall old woman behind the bar before guiding them over to a table in the far corner. The owner brought four large unlabelled brown bottles and a corkscrew, glancing curiously at her new customers, and Frank went about opening them. It seemed almost ceremonial for him—serious face, deliberate actions—and by the third bottle Alile was unable to hold in her giggles. Frank raised an eyebrow, then slid the first bottle across the table to her. He fell still, silent.

Alile's smile faded into the quiet. Everyone was watching her. Bethan knew she wouldn't like that, but Alile weathered it well. "Oh. Okay."

Frank's stern expression twitched, just for a second, and Bethan wasn't sure Alile had seen it. Tall, fit, she hardly ever drank. She looked after herself as much as she looked after the wild she loved so much. Bethan knew she was simply doing this to humour their host.

Alile picked up the bottle, sniffed, then took a swig. Her eyes went wide and started watering, and she placed the bottle gently back on the table. "Smooth!" she croaked. "Tasty. Really, really nice!" She glanced at Bethan, eyes wide and watering.

"See?" Frank said. "Don't judge by appearances." He started chuckling.

Bethan and Goyo grabbed their bottles, and Frank raised his and gave a toast. "May the road rise ahead to meet you, and may your enemies be defeated in the mirror behind."

Bethan lifted her bottle. "If that thing makes it onto any roads."

Frank smiled and they all drank, and Bethan closed her eyes as the potent brew hacked its way down her gullet and spread warmth through her bones. She wondered where Frank brewed it and how, and decided it was probably best she didn't know.

"Talking of roads, gimme a minute." Frank went to the bar, reached over and returned with a folded map, which he opened and spread across the table. He sat down with a groan. "Okay. Roads. There really aren't many."

"Just around the island's coastline, I guess?" Goyo asked.

"Wasn't always the case. See this one here? 'Til three years ago it would've taken you most of the way across the island to the north coast. Hundred twenty miles across, and I've done that journey in four hours."

"'Til three years ago?" Alile asked, her voice still hoarse.

"Landslips. Couple of methane eruptions, and the whole southern portion of the road has come apart as the ground beneath weakens. Some of it's sunk, some has…" He shrugged. "Moved. The whole place is changing. Used to be just the sea was rising, now it's the land beneath us trying its best to move us on." He looked sad when he took his next drink, and Bethan felt bad again for giving him a hard time.

"You seem to be doing okay here," she said.

"We adjust. We're rebuilding, adapting, doing our best to handle the changes. It's our home. But it's tough here. Always was. Hell, when I was a kid it was polar bears and frostbite I had to worry about, and where the next meal was coming from. Now, lots of kids grow up, head off to Canada or further afield where they think it'll be easier."

"How old is this map?" Goyo asked.

"Eight years. Way out of date."

"Can you tell us where we need to go?"

"Huh." Frank scratched at his bald head, riven with wrinkles. "Where're you from, friend?"

"Originally, a small village in Colombia. Life there fell apart when I was a kid and illegal loggers settled in. Lost my parents. I've been drifting ever since."

"Where?"

"All over. Lots of places."

"Guess I meant, drifting with who?"

"Greenpeace. Extinction Rebellion. I was an early member of Immediate World Action, left when the killings began. I never stay for long. I don't do joining any more. Politics always gets in the way of real change, however small the organisation."

"So you lost your home forty years ago."

Goyo grinned, and the smile broke apart his grizzled face and touched every part of him. Bethan was used to it but it never failed to give her comfort, even peace. She knew so much more awful stuff about Goyo's past that few other people would ever hear—his mother's rape and murder at the hands of those illegal logging gangs, his wife's death from pollution-linked cancer at thirty, bringing up his son on his own. These and a dozen other reasons meant he might never feel the inclination to smile again. But he kept his balance in the present and made the most of things. *The past and the future are a waste of energy,* he'd say, and even if deep down his history still haunted him, he did his best to never believe in ghosts.

"You're too kind," he said. "I'm seventy-two."

"You look younger."

"I've had a good life. Travelled a lot, seen the world. I like animals, nature, and maybe three people. But my real love's plants."

Frank laughed. "Don't look like a flower kinda guy."

"Plants rule the world, most people don't realise that. They keep us and sustain us, feed us and give us the air we breathe. They're the foundation we build everything on."

"And we're undermining our foundations," Bethan said.

"Exactly." Goyo nodded. "We have been for a century or more."

"Pollution," Frank said.

"And global warming," Alile said. "Acid rain, species depletion, deforestation. Genetically modifying crops means there's no diversity anymore, and less resistance to disease."

"I can see it's your passion," Frank said. "All of you." Bethan thought it wasn't only their similar age that gave Goyo and Frank a sense of mutual respect. It was their understanding of their world, and how it had changed in their lifetimes.

"Go into a forest on a quiet day and you can hear God thinking," Goyo said.

"Huh. Didn't mark you as religious, either."

Goyo only smiled. Bethan knew that was a deeper, more complex conversation.

"Sounds to me like you all know how things are changing. On Hawkshead Island that's an ongoing process. We lost a husband-and-wife trapping team last year to a methane geyser, twenty miles inland. Just six months ago a landslide took out half the town's cattle when they were grazing a mile from here. Only found one of their bodies. It's like the island swallowed them up."

"Permafrost melt," Alile said.

"I'm not stupid," Frank said. "Know what it is. Been happening for decades, but these past few years it's all sped up. And don't think that's just an old man's perception of time."

"That's why we're here," Alile said.

"You gonna freeze our island again?" he asked, taking another drink.

TIM LEBBON

"We try to stop people damaging the land even more," Bethan said. "Back in the real world I'm a lawyer, specialising in climate justice."

"And I'm a journalist," Alile said. "Among other things. I write about the changes I see when we're on these jaunts, effects on indigenous communities. My contacts ensure what I write gets out there. But when we're here…"

"Activists," Frank said. "Met your kind before. Good intentions but without a clue."

"We're different," Goyo said. "We know what we're doing."

"Huh. So these illegal miners, exactly what're they out here looking for?"

"Rare earth elements," Alile said. "The shit they use in microchips, tech, magnets, car batteries. They're just the prospectors—the advance guard. If they find what they're looking for, they take enough to make themselves lots of money, then they sell the location and info to bigger concerns. You'll see a more sustained illegal mining set-up coming in. That's bad enough, but it's what else they might release that causes the real problems."

Frank eyed Alile, and to begin with Bethan thought he was just being a guy. But she saw his brows furrow as he thought, and his gaze was beyond Alile, somewhere much further away.

"Huh. Rare earth stuff. So when you find them, you ask them nicely to stop?"

"Something like that," Goyo said. Same tone, but his brevity spoke volumes.

"Okay. Well. Janice is cooking the best meal you'll have this side of the North Pole. So while she's doing that, let's take a look at this map, eh?"

"You know where the other team went?" Alile asked, her eagerness apparent.

Frank looked at her bottle. It was still mostly full. Alile picked it up and glanced at Bethan as she took another mouthful.

"Uh. Well, that woman Emma asked me certain questions, and I gave her certain answers, and putting 'em together with what you've told me, I got a pretty good idea of where they might be." He leaned over the table and smoothed the map, then plucked a pen from his shirt pocket.

Bethan was growing to like Frank. She liked much less what he told them over the next twenty minutes.

When their meal came it was as good as Frank had promised. Eager to leave, they ate quickly, and he and Alile conducted business over the Discovery while Bethan and Goyo waited outside, soaking in the sun even though they'd had to shrug on their thermal overshirts. Alile and Frank joked and laughed over by the vehicle, and it was no surprise he had fallen for her charms. Everyone liked Alile. Bethan hoped she'd negotiated a good discount.

"Tough job," Goyo said.

"All the best ones are." Bethan felt relaxed, probably due to the effects of a lunchtime beer of indeterminate strength.

"Think he'll be there? This is the sort of thing he—"

"I don't know or care," she said.

"Right. That message came from someone, Bethan."

"I'm not looking for him, Goyo. None of what I do is ever about him. And why the fuck do you think I *would* want to see him again? He thinks I'm a murderer."

"Fine. I'm sorry."

She shook her head, sighed, and walked along the street towards the shore, and the old Discovery that would soon be taking them inland. She passed colourful wooden buildings, a couple boarded up but most of them obviously lived in, used and well loved. There were a few shops, a church, and the largest of the buildings seemed to share use as a school and medical centre. She smiled at the townsfolk and mostly received smiles in return, though also a few curious frowns. She wished Frank had more to tell them about the other team, but he'd only dealt with the woman. Even so, he'd given them a pretty good guess as to where they might have been headed.

All she had was the mysterious email she'd received from one of her unnamed contacts—*Hawkshead Island, team of four, gone digging.* That, and a date.

Now that they knew for sure the team was here, Bethan was excited for what came next.

And if Dean *was* part of the group, she'd confront that if and when they met.

"Just cut the line!" he shouts. He's only just behind her, but Bethan can hardly hear him. The big generator ninety feet to their left is screaming, filling the air with whines and grinds of pain as its inner workings start to break down.

I did that! Bethan thinks, and she's so surprised it even worked that the sheer danger of what they're doing hasn't even settled around her. People shout and run around the site in a panic, while she and Dean hunker down behind a storage container and large fuel tank. *We can't be seen*, she'd said as they'd made their way here, afraid for their careers and the judgement of family and friends. But now that thought seems so foolish and naive, the concern of someone in the distant past, not just a day ago. Bethan has become a different person. Today she has moved from protest to direct action, and it feels so good.

"Just cut the line!" Dean shouts again, and she looks back at where he's sheltering behind a prefab plastic storage unit. His voice is almost swallowed by the cacophony of the malfunctioning generator and the agonised screeching of things breaking.

She grins and gives him a thumbs up. He shakes his head and points at the huge fuel tank to her left. One of the supply lines hangs on rusted hooks and trails away from them, snaking between buildings and across rough ground to the dying generator. It's one of six that are scattered around the site, servicing the fracking machinery that has been torturing and raping this land for the past six weeks.

Online protests have done precisely fuck all, Bethan said five days before. *I can file injunctions and sanctions and sue them as much as I like, but they've got better lawyers earning five times as much as me, and they've got me tangled up in legal circles while they keep drilling and filling their tanks and bank accounts. So what, do we actually fly out to Alaska and wave placards? Do we go there and…*

She drifted off. Focused on a point just over Dean's left shoulder. *We go there*, she said.

Now they're here, and it feels good. It feels… fucking… *great*! Bethan is beginning to understand her future. It doesn't involve placards and expensive lawsuits that get bogged down in red tape and court decisions that take months, while these people suck the soul out of the land. Seven years ago in Canada, a whole town went up in a methane explosion caused by over-fracking. Over a hundred dead. The inquest is still ongoing.

Fuck that shit, this is immediate action, she thinks, and she turns away from Dean because she can see that he still has doubts.

She doesn't. Not anymore.

Shouts reach her, and she crawls forward and peers around the edge of the huge fuel container. The site is in turmoil. The main fracking rig is still and silent, shut down as soon as the big generator malfunctioned after their sabotage, but everywhere else is movement, panic, and chaos. Three people are gathered at the screeching generator, but sparks are flying from it now, and smoke, and she can see flames licking along one side. They can't get close enough to shut it off. The cutting of a cover, the snipping of a few wires, it's amazing what little it took to cause this. The snippers in her pocket did more in ten seconds than years of high-level legal campaigning and protest.

Two other people are running towards the fuel container she's hiding behind. They look terrified.

"Bethan!" Dean shouts, his voice just one of many. "Cut it!"

She turns and hurries back towards him, risking exposure between the fuel tank and storage unit, but it doesn't really matter anymore. Even if someone does see them, they'll have more to worry about.

"Time to run!" she says as she reaches Dean, and she pushes past him and heads for the hole they cut in the perimeter fencing seventeen minutes earlier. She can see him saying something else but she shuts it out, focusing only on getting away from here. She's on fire. She's *enlightened*, and a rush of energy bursts through her, a flush of revelation and realisation at what she has to do. This has all been a long time coming. Her new friend Goyo has dropped hints at his own darker past when it comes to climate activism, but she's always just listened and let it pass her by, wilfully blind to the truth he's been subtly hinting at every time they met.

Now, after this, she and Goyo need to talk *real* truths.

"Bethan, this is more than we agreed—we were just going to break stuff!" Dean is behind her, crouched down as they both dash for the fence.

"Can't you hear that?" she says. Loud whining, grinding, cracking and crackling, and the shouts of flustered people as they try and bring their immoral money-spinner back online. Thinking ahead five days or years, instead of five decades or a generation, or beyond the time of their death. Their panic is a hymn to everything she wants, everything she craves. "That's what broken sounds like!"

As they reach the fence, the generator explodes.

Within that fire, that chaos, that rain of shrapnel and flame, three lives come to an end.

And Bethan's new life begins.

Her head was being tapped, tapped, and she thought it was Dean trying to wake her, though she couldn't remember being struck by something and passing out at all. That was all wrong. *We ran and got through the fence and got out of there,* she thought, and she opened her eyes and lifted her head away from where it was vibrating against the Discovery's side window. Alile smiled at her in the rearview mirror.

"How long was I asleep?"

"Twenty minutes," Alile said.

"I think our friendly Frank's Old Bastard was wine strength rather than beer," Goyo said. "Alile's probably way over the limit."

"I think my internal organs have melted, and I only had three swigs," she said. "Doesn't matter. We'll probably end up crashing anyway. You might have driven one of these babies a century ago, Goyo, but it wasn't built for places like this." Her tone was calm as always, her demeanour chilled, but her voice was tinged with real concern.

Bethan leaned forward between the front seats and stared ahead. The terrain here was harsh and mostly untouched, even this close to the coast. There were buildings here and there, most of them unused and tumbled to ruin. Practical rather than aesthetic, they were built square and solid against storms, with shuttered windows and low-pitched roofs. None appeared large enough for permanent habitation, and Bethan guessed they were shepherds' huts or storm bothys, shelters for anyone caught out in the open. The landscape was wide and wild, low hills sweeping off to the horizon in every direction, grassland giving way to scrub to the north and east, scree slopes climbing a steeper, higher hill range to the west. Further east, a river wound down towards the sea, carved deep into the land, banks sheer and recently formed.

Way ahead of them was a range of snow-dappled hills, streaks of white in valleys and crevasses untouched by the sun. Some of that snow and ice might be decades or centuries old, compacted and pushed down by fresh fall after fresh fall. Now, it was slowly melting away, in sympathy with this summer's polar sea. The ice cap had been measured at only two hundred miles wide this year, down from around six hundred miles a few decades before, and in places it was so thin that to attempt a traverse would be suicide. In mere decades, Bethan knew that she would be able to sail to the North Pole.

"It's amazing how they stay here and adapt," Bethan said.

"Frank and the townsfolk?" Alile asked, and she sounded surprised. "What choice do they have? Their ancestors have been here since before recorded history. They're tough, they live with the land."

"And change with it," Bethan said.

"Right. This is their home. They'll hold onto it as long as they can. If everyone upped and left, they'd just be…" She glanced sidelong at Goyo, who was looking out of his window at the passing landscape.

"Adrift," Goyo said. "Look over there." He pointed. At first Bethan thought it was a spread of snow remaining lower down on the plain, sheltered from warmer winds by a ridge of rocks perhaps.

"Steam?" Alile asked.

"Cold mist, I think," Goyo said. "Steam would rise and disperse."

"Not a geyser, then," Bethan said.

"No. Just the land breathing out as it thaws."

It was a haunting image. The idea that the land had a heartbeat, a rhythm, was something she was very at peace with. The concept of the land breathing out really hit home, because any slow breath might be its last.

Goyo had Frank's map on his lap, folded to their location, and he spread it across his knees and traced his finger north from Joyce Sound towards the coordinates he'd marked only after leaving the town behind.

"About thirty, maybe thirty-five miles," he said. "Road runs out soonish. Then we'll see how much off-road this old beast has left in her."

"Shit," Bethan said. "They really did screw us over, didn't they?"

Alile laughed. "I'm starting to like it. It's responsive. Really light steering for such a unit. And I like an engine you can hear."

"We're climate activists driving a fucking diesel monster across a land that's already changing," Bethan said. "I don't know whether to laugh or..." She trailed off.

"Hey, what's that?" Alile said. They'd both seen the same thing.

"Sinkhole," Goyo said. "Ease back, Alile. Don't get close. It could expand in a flash."

The road they were rolling along, already cracked and crazed and potholed, disappeared a few hundred yards ahead, its jagged edge dropping into a dark hole that looked to be ninety feet across, perhaps more.

"How far have we come?" Bethan asked.

"Ten, twelve miles," Alile said.

"Going to be a long drive," Bethan said.

"It is," Goyo said. "But at least we're not on foot. Alile, let's head around. Give it a wide berth. That thing spreads, we'll disappear like Frank's cattle. Bethan, I'll keep watch ahead while we move; you keep an eye on the hole."

"For what?"

"In case a tentacled monstrosity emerges ready to eat us." Goyo chuckled, but with little humour.

Alile steered them off the rough road and onto the rougher natural skin of Hawkshead Island, and the Discovery groaned and grumbled as it started to bounce and lurch.

"I feel sick already," Bethan said.

"Watch the hole," Goyo said.

"Watching the hole. Watching the hole."

They passed the deep, shadowy sinkhole and found that the track beyond was degraded to such an extent that it was just as easy driving off-road. They entered a spread of low-lying mist that Goyo suspected masked a dangerous change in the landscape. He was right. It was only Alile's skilful, patient driving that hauled them out of the first area of marsh, Alile cursing under her breath, their left wheels skidding and spinning, windows splashing with fresh dark mud as she guided them up and out. The four-wheel drive saved them, and Goyo jumped out and walked on ahead, testing the ground and guiding them on like an old-fashioned funeral procession. They made two miles in an hour, then reached an area of raised land which seemed to be surrounded on all sides by boggy ground. The mist had lifted, at least, and the early evening sunlight scattered small rainbows across the landscape. Clumps of low bushes sprouted here and there, and Goyo paused now and then to examine the undergrowth.

They ended up backtracking half a mile and finding a safer route, and soon they were on higher, firmer ground, leaving the rainbows behind as evening brought a deeper mist from the marshes.

"Even two decades ago that would have been solid, safe ground," Goyo said.

"It looks lush, though," Alile said.

"Lush with plants that mostly weren't there before. That's no bad thing—everywhere changes, over time." He said no more, but Bethan could see that he was troubled. He'd tell them why in his own time.

After they'd covered about eighteen miles the sun set with a slow, dazzling display cast through clouds of moisture hanging in the air above the distant range of hills they were heading towards. At this time of year it would dip below the horizon for just a few hours, and that gentle setting meant the sunsets and sunrises would often be magnificent. This sunset also cast three columns of blazing white light closer to them, surrounded by haloes of colour twisting and writhing like giant snakes in the low-hanging clouds.

"Geysers," Alile said.

"You're sure?" Goyo asked.

She glanced at him, smiling. "Doubting me, old man?"

"Nope, not at all. I know you have a degree in geysers."

"What I have is an inquiring mind and the patience to research the places we're visiting. It's called preparation."

"Then they're geysers."

"Probably thrown up by methane release," Alile said. "And three in a line like that suggests a fault. We should steer well clear." She edged them off their route, full-beam headlights illuminating the ground. She drove no faster than ten miles an hour, watching for obstructions, uneven surfaces, or smoother spreads of grass or stripped ground that might indicate more marshland.

It was difficult to know what to watch out for. Bethan had never been anywhere that was changing so actively, moment by moment. While there was beauty in the sunsets and the lush plant growth taking advantage of a more welcoming, unfrozen subsoil, she also found it frightening. She respected nature, held it in awe, but it was a strange feeling being afraid. She didn't like it. Alile was always most prepared out of all of them, but none of them had deep experience of a place like this. It was as if the land was waking, groggy and grumpy from a long, dreamless sleep.

The puncture was inevitable, really. The Discovery jerked and jarred, then Alile brought them to a halt. As she turned off the engine and the three of them jumped from the vehicle, Hawkshead Island hit them in the face.

Such scale and silence. Such rawness. Bethan gasped but said nothing. It was terrifying; it was almost sacred. Until now, hunched behind glass with the grumble of the Discovery's old diesel engine and the creak of its arthritic suspension as a soundtrack, they had not experienced the true reality of the land.

Bethan let out a slow breath, and with her next inhalation she caught a subtle, acrid chemical scent on the air. Beneath that was the familiar smell of rotting vegetation, common in marshy areas, and something almost sweet that she couldn't identify. Not rot, but something else. The perfume of unseen blooms, perhaps.

The quiet and stillness was a shock after a couple of hours in the Discovery, but as her senses adjusted she realised that it wasn't completely silent. A gentle breeze blew across the landscape, rising and falling like secrets whispered from afar. There was also something else, and to begin with Bethan thought it was her own pulse in her ears.

"Are those... drums?" Alile asked.

Goyo turned his head, trying to place the source of the soft booming sounds.

"Something in the ground," he said. "It's almost sub-audible. Like a vibration."

The wind was a cold breath against their car-warmed bodies, and they shrugged on their coats and zipped them up.

"Let's see if we can plug this," Alile said. "If not, we'll have to use the spare."

"You start," Goyo said. "I'm just..." Bethan assumed he was going for a leak as he walked away from them, but he went further than necessary, shining a torch across the ground before him. As Alile set up a small lamp so they could inspect the punctured tyre, Bethan saw Goyo reach a low spread of shrubs and a few hardy trees. He reached out and touched some branches, ghostly in the harsh light from his torch.

After a few minutes they'd managed to plug the puncture and reinflate the tyre. Goyo returned, silent and clearly preoccupied.

"What is it?" Bethan asked as they climbed into the cab and set off again.

"A tree I didn't recognise. And some of those shrubs... at least three species I don't know. That means their seeds have been frozen for tens of thousands of years, maybe hundreds of thousands, underground and dormant. They belong to the past. They're history. And because of human activity it's becoming their present again."

"But that's pretty amazing, right?" Alile asked.

Goyo grunted. "I love how you see the upside." Then after a long, thoughtful pause, he said, "Makes you wonder what else might be thawing."

"Your many-tentacled monster?" Bethan asked, but it wasn't funny. They could both sense Goyo's concern. He'd talked about his fears enough times before.

"Smaller monsters, and nastier," he said. "Try virus size. Could be anything here, from tens of thousands of years ago or more. *Anything.*"

"And that's why we do what we do," Bethan said. "Giving a shit because others don't."

Goyo nodded but said no more. She didn't like his silence.

It took them another five hours and two more punctures before they estimated that they were approaching their destination. They travelled through Hawkshead Island's short night, and dawn came two hours before they arrived, the rising sun casting another riotous display through skeins of mist. They passed a low, marshy plain pocked with sinkholes and witnessed one open up less than a mile from them, the venting gases catching the dawn sun in a chaos of shattered rainbows. They navigated through a low range of hills where landslides had scarred the previously smooth landscape with sharp new ridgelines, crevasses and rugged tears in the ground. Skirting far around a boiling lake spitting steam to the sky, the dazzling phosphorescent waters were beautiful and daunting. In places the vegetation was almost defiantly lush, spilling across the ground like a slow-motion flood, smothering the landscape with joyous abandon as if released from some sort of incarceration. A variety of grasses, shrubs and trees seeded themselves anywhere there was soil. Alile paused their vehicle a dozen times to take photos, and Goyo observed with his usual calmness and patience, and sketched in his notebooks, noting the names of species he knew and leaving a blank space beneath those he did not. Even through this calmness, Bethan knew that he was on edge. His energy was different; he was buzzing, not settled. Wired.

As they approached Frank's best guess at the other team's location, Alile slowed the Discovery and crept along the base of a hill, keeping to cover where she could. Some of their previous encounters with illegal prospectors had turned ugly, so she knew to be cautious. Though, apart from a few piles of rocks and some gentle ripples in the ground, there was little to shield their arrival.

After circling for an hour, they emerged from behind the shoulder of a low hill and spotted the gleam of a vehicle in the distance. As they drew closer, three figures appeared in the early morning light gathered at the expensive-looking truck's open rear doors. Bethan could see that something was amiss: it was evident in the peoples' movement, their agitation. It was in their tense expressions as they turned to watch these strangers arrive.

She leaned forward between the front seats, but Goyo had already seen Dean.

"Ah hell," he said. "Be calm, Bethan."

"You know me," she said.

Goyo grunted.

Alile cut the engine, and the three of them sat for a while in the sudden silence.

THREE

"Just who the fuck is this?" Emma asked.

Dean had seen one of the figures behind the windshield, and even from this distance he knew who the fuck this was. And however he'd expected he might feel—knowing that this moment was coming, waiting for it ever since they'd disembarked at Joyce Sound and started their journey in the Stallion—that had been changed by recent events.

Everything had been changed.

At least the new arrivals had broken Dean, Emma and Wren's argument. *We have to go back and find her!* Dean said, and Wren shouted *No way, did you even* see *those fucking things?* and Emma replied *We stay here, take stock, and prepare before we go back down there.* Now, perhaps things had changed again.

What have I brought her into? he thought.

The battered old Discovery had come to a stop fifty yards away. It was splashed with mud, which only added to its faded, rusty colour scheme, and one of the front tyres appeared to be low. Their trip in the Stallion had been difficult and dangerous enough; travelling across Hawkshead Island in that old banger must have been traumatic.

"Saw that old thing back in Joyce Sound," Wren said. "Locals come to keep an eye on us?"

"I paid them enough to stay uninterested," Emma said. "This is someone else, and we need to keep them away from this." There was a nervous shiver to her voice, a slight tic in her left eye. She was trying to hold it together.

Dean had never seen her like this. Emma was their rock.

"Whatever this is," Wren said.

"This is nothing," Emma said.

"They might be able to help," Dean said. "Lanna's still down there somewhere, injured or lost or trapped."

"And we're going in to find her!" Emma snapped. "But we don't need strangers. We know what we're doing."

"You telling me you *know* what that was?" Dean asked. "What happened down there?"

"It was *nothing*," she said again. "Stupid panic, and we'll bring Lanna out, but we've got to do it sensibly, safely. It was *nothing*. Got it?"

Nothing doesn't smell or sound like that. Dean's mind flashed back to the deep cavern with the grotesque tableau of ancient bodies. That crouched figure, that corpse, shifting and twisting and *expanding*. Wren shouting at them to keep their lights still because the writhing shadows were freaking him the fuck out. Lanna stepping closer, hers the only light beam that remained focused, trained on what was happening at the centre of that cave. The deformed head tilting to one side as if it was too heavy, and then lifting on a neck that sounded like it was full of broken glass.

Running, tripping, falling, shouting. And then the scream.

Dean took in a deep breath, held it, then slowly exhaled as the Discovery's doors opened. Three people got out, and he felt a thump low in his gut as past and present finally collided.

Bethan stood with two other people beside the vehicle. One of them was Goyo, who he'd met a couple of times years ago. The tall woman he didn't know. They stared at Dean and his companions, and for a moment he wasn't even sure Bethan recognised him. Then she took a couple of steps forward, and she was looking right at him, and she was frowning.

"Oh shit," he said, even though he'd known she was coming. He had sent her the anonymous message, partly to back him up if he'd been unable to prevent his team's exploitation of this place. But the main reason was that he missed her, and he thought it would be easier to talk through stuff in the field, doing what they'd always done, than over the phone. After so long, he wasn't even sure she'd agree to come if she knew the invitation had been from him.

On the back of what had recently happened, bringing Bethan and her companions here suddenly felt like the worst idea he'd ever had.

"What?" Emma asked. "Who are they?"

"That's my old partner, Bethan," he said. "I told you about her."

"You told us she was some sort of activist," Wren said.

"Well. Yeah."

"That's just great," Emma said. "What the hell are they doing here? Did you fucking tell them?" She unslung her backpack and propped it against one of the Stallion's tall wheels.

"Of course not!"

She tugged something from the pack's zipped side pocket and held it down by her leg.

A pistol.

"Emma, what the hell!" Dean said.

Emma glanced at Wren and Dean, then took a few steps towards the other group. She kept the gun by her side, casual, but very obvious about it being on show.

"She's cool," Wren said. "She knows how to use it."

"That's what I'm afraid of."

"This is a private site!" Emma called out.

Bethan's tall companion lifted a phone and started photographing or filming them.

The gun looked so alien in Emma's hand that it changed her whole bearing. She felt like a stranger to Dean now. Or perhaps that was still shock, and the terror of what they'd fled from and were now preparing to return to. Down into the darkness.

"We're just looking around," Goyo said. He looked calm and kind, but Dean knew that appearances could be deceiving.

"Look around somewhere else," Emma said. "It's a big island."

"Nice truck," the woman with them said. She was athletic, tattooed, obviously at home in the outdoors. She was smiling, and it looked genuine. "What's that worth, half a million?"

"And then some," Wren said. Emma stiffened but didn't look back at him and Dean. *She wants to handle this in her own way*, Dean thought.

"You made that amount yet from the stuff you're stealing out of the ground?" Goyo asked.

"Oh, okay," Emma said. "It all becomes clear. So, what, you film us and upload, maybe send footage to whatever authorities you think might help?"

Goyo shook his head. "We don't concern ourselves with authorities." A loaded comment that hung in the air between the two groups.

Dean kept trying to catch Bethan's eye, but she now seemed to be looking anywhere but at him. He took a couple of steps to one side, and the tall woman with Bethan aimed her phone towards him.

"We'll just blow the cave," Goyo said.

"Very responsible," Emma said. "So what have you got in the Discovery?"

"Enough," he said. He didn't say enough of what.

"Emma," Wren said softly, and she waved her free hand at them. *Stay back. Stay out of it.*

"You can't blow the cave," Dean said. He felt the heat of Emma's gaze. Her anger. But he didn't glance at her. She suspected that he'd brought them here and he couldn't change that, and really it didn't matter now. Lanna was still down there, and she should be the priority. Not what they'd come here to mine, nor this group that had come to stop them, nor his history with Bethan, wired with potential like a spring between them. Bethan caught his eye and he said, "We lost one of our team down there, and we're heading in to bring her out."

"Lost?" Bethan asked. Dean hadn't heard her voice in six years, apart from on old clips. It sounded somehow sadder, though that might have been the distance between them and the crisp air of this dangerous place. It might have been his own pumping adrenaline. Fear heightening his senses.

"What happened?" Goyo asked. Beside him the tall woman still filmed, scanning her phone left and right.

In the distance a bird called out, shrill and excited. Much further away there was a rumble as something stirred deep beneath the surface. Dean wondered if it was below them, involving Lanna. He thought of her the night before last, warm in his embrace.

"We were down in a cave system, a few hundred yards in, and there was some movement. Something wrong."

"We ran and Lanna got left behind," Emma said. "Cave-in. We were just preparing to bring her out."

"It wasn't a cave-in," Dean said.

Emma rested her free hand on his shoulder and squeezed. "You mind shutting the hell up about our business?" she said into his ear, loud enough for everyone to hear.

"Our business?" he replied. She blinked at him, and he could see that neither of them was anywhere near in control. His own shock was still raw and open, and the guilt at leaving Lanna behind poked at the fresh wound.

"What did you find down there?" Goyo asked.

"Bodies," Dean said. "They were really old, like ancient. And a load of weird paintings on the cave wall."

"How long ago since you left her behind?"

"Sounds like you're blaming us," Emma said, and her gun-arm shifted, just fractionally.

"Emma?" Dean muttered. "Really?"

"How long?" Goyo asked again.

"An hour," Dean said.

"And you're only going back in to find her *now*?" Bethan asked. "Fucking hell, she could be lying under rocks with a broken leg."

"It wasn't a cave-in," Dean said again. "We've been debating how to—"

"That body was fucking *moving*!" Wren said behind them, and Dean sighed, because that was it, the truth, out in the open and spoken at last. And the truth was what they all needed to confront. However ridiculous and unbelievable, there was no escaping what he thought he'd seen happening down there, and Emma's and Wren's shock meant that he wasn't alone. It had been an hour, yes, but an hour in which shock had grasped them tight—shock and terror—as they tried to make sense of what they'd seen, arguing about it, preparing themselves, each of them wanting to be the one to make a decision.

"Body?" Bethan asked. "Moving?"

Goyo came forward towards them, and the woman kept filming, stepping to one side so that she got them all in frame.

Emma didn't lift the gun. Dean was glad for that. He hadn't even known that she was carrying it in her rucksack, although he'd been aware that she had one in her kit in the Stallion. Wren carried, too. Their activities had always been on the shady side of legal, and Emma's need for the two of them to carry weapons was something that had never been discussed openly. This was the first time he'd ever seen her bearing it in a threatening manner. It made the whole situation even more unreal.

"How was it moving, Dean?" Goyo asked. His voice was low and level.

"Just… weirdly," Dean said. "I mean, it was dead but moving, you know? We were out of there."

"And the paintings?"

"Old," Emma said. "None of this is anything to do with you."

Goyo looked them up and down.

Dean shifted uncomfortably beneath his scrutiny. "What?" he asked.

"Goyo, she's got a fucking gun," Bethan said.

Emma glanced down at her hand, almost as if she'd forgotten she was holding the weapon. She slipped it into her belt.

Goyo turned and headed back towards the Discovery. "I need to close that cave," he said. "I've been shot before, a long time ago, I can't say I enjoyed it. And I don't relish the idea of being shot again. But that's what you'll have to do to stop me."

"You are *not* closing the cave!" Emma said.

"Goyo, Lanna is still down there!" Dean said. "Now you're here you can help us—"

"We didn't come to rescue clueless illegal miners," Bethan said.

"Really, Bethan?"

The groups were silent for a time, the only sound Goyo opening the Discovery's rear hatch. It creaked.

"You have no idea what you've encountered down there," Goyo said.

"And you have, old man?" Wren asked.

Goyo stood by the open trunk. He wiped a hand across his face, and it was the first time Dean had seen him anything other than calm and composed. And that terrified him.

"No," Goyo said, "other than it can't be anything good. And that's why the cave has to be closed." He hoisted a backpack from the trunk and slung it over one shoulder.

"No," Emma said. This time when she pulled the gun, she clicked off the safety and pointed it.

"Oh jeez, Em," Wren said.

"Emma," Dean said, but he wasn't looking at her. He was watching Bethan, because in his head this was more her sort of world. What happened in Alaska obviously hadn't stopped her. If anything, it had given her even more drive.

She stared right back at him, giving nothing away. Then she stiffened, shifted her attention past him, and at the same time Wren said, "Holy shit."

Dean turned around.

Lanna stood close to the cave mouth, the rope they'd tied around the rock together clasped in one hand. She'd lost her helmet and rucksack, and she was bleeding from a gash in her scalp, the blood matting her hair and soaking the left side of her face. Despite these injuries she appeared still, calm, and totally in control, glancing at each of them in turn as if assessing the situation, taking in the scene. She wasn't even squinting.

She looked at Dean and away again without a blink.

When she saw the strangers—and Emma still aiming the gun in Goyo's general direction, even though she was half-turned and looking back at Lanna—her eyebrows rose in surprise.

"Lanna!" Wren said. "Are you a sight for—"

Everything about her changed. Her eyes fluttered, her lower jaw dropped, her brow furrowed, and all composure and presence flittered away. She staggered, and her body went limp as she fell to her knees, then slumped forward onto her face.

Dean's first thought as he ran to her was that the faint was a sham.

Something about the way she landed, he thought. *Too soft... too slow.* She'd folded to the ground, not fallen.

"Stay away!" he heard Goyo shouting, but Dean didn't know who he was shouting at, or why, and right then he didn't care.

Lanna rolled onto her back and sat up again, without using her hands. This time when she looked at him she was wretched, bleeding heavily from an horrific open wound above her left ear, eyes flushed and red with blood, and as she put her left hand up to her face she said, "Oh, Dean, it's taking me." Then her eyes rolled back in her head and she jerked once, hard, her whole body stiffening as if electrocuted. He heard the crack of something breaking.

Bone, he thought. As he drew close to Lanna, there was a shout behind him.

And a gunshot.

FOUR

She's been missing down there for an hour, Goyo thought. She wasn't wearing a helmet or pack so had probably lost her lights and torch, and he wondered what had really happened, and whether they'd actually abandoned her in the caves, leaving her to find her own way out in the dark.

He hoped that wasn't the case with Dean attached to the group, but then he hardly knew the guy at all.

What Goyo *did* know was that he needed to get down into that cave to assess the situation for himself. Nothing he'd heard or seen made him feel positive about any of this, but now that the woman had emerged, he had a responsibility to find out as much as he could.

Blowing up the cave entrance, burying what might be down there, was no longer good enough. A blocked cave could be excavated.

He started towards the woman with the gun.

"Goyo!" Bethan whispered, but he was moving now, thankful for his inherent fitness. He had more than seven decades under his belt, but he wore them lightly.

He jogged past the Discovery, ignoring Alile as she reached for him, her fingertips whispering across the back of

66

his shoulder. He was focused on the woman who Dean had called Emma. She still held the gun, but she had half turned to see the emergence of her team member from the cave, and now it was pointed down and to the left. He came at her from the right, and it was only in the last couple of seconds that she heard him.

She started turning back towards him, bringing the gun up to bear again, and he had to believe she was intending to shoot him. Even if she hadn't been before—if it had been a bluff, and even with all his years of experience in such loaded and dangerous situations he honestly could not be sure—the shock of him running at her might shift the balance.

He really had been shot before. He'd told the truth about not caring for it.

Goyo had already shifted the rucksack so that it slung over one shoulder, and he let it fall down his arm, grabbed the strap, and swung it in a wide arc. It struck Emma's gun hand and knocked it to the side, and when she fired, the bullet ricocheted from a rock with a haze of sparks and fractured stone. The report shocked them all but he carried on, knowing he could not afford to pause. The gun fell from her hand, and he used his momentum to knock her from her feet. She went sprawling across the wet wild grass, grunting as her breath was knocked from her.

Goyo kept his footing. He picked up the gun and held it down to one side, shrugging the pack back onto his shoulders.

Emma glared up at him, but by the time she found her footing and stood she appeared more contrite.

"I wouldn't have used it."

"Fine," Goyo said. "Go see to your friend."

Emma backed away towards the fallen woman. She appeared to be out cold, and Dean and the big guy were kneeling beside her, attending her as best they could. Goyo's concern could not be for her, or them, or even himself. It stretched far beyond any of them here. For years he had feared a situation like this. Travelling, searching, preparing for it, and hoping with every cell in his body that it would not arrive.

His only aim now was to discover if it had.

As he edged towards the cave, Goyo was conscious of the weight of the gun that he'd tucked into his jacket pocket. It felt ridiculous, but there was also a comfort to it. He'd fired guns before, but never at anything alive. He knew how to handle them. It gave him a sense of control that was probably way out of place, but which he grabbed onto as he approached the cave.

"Hey!" someone shouted from the mining group. He thought it was the big man, not Dean.

"Goyo!" Bethan's voice.

He answered neither of them because there was nothing to be said. If he came back out, perhaps then he would be able to explain why he was doing what he was doing. But not right now.

He reached the cave and pulled a head torch from the waist pocket of his rucksack. It was small but powerful, and it lit the cave's throat as he grabbed onto the rope that led down into the darkness.

"Careful," someone said. It was Dean. That gave Goyo pause, but only for a second.

Panting from exertion, sweating, he eased down into the opening, watched the world disappear as he descended. Just before his view was completely cut off, he caught Bethan's eye from a distance. She looked serious and worried. They'd talked enough about what the melting permafrost might reveal, and she knew his real purpose as he travelled with her and Alile. Plants, yes. But also more.

Dean had said they'd found bodies and weird cave paintings. The old bodies troubled Goyo, because even though the air in the caves had been frozen and dried for centuries or millennia, they might still be in a state that presented a threat. Their claim that a body had moved was patently absurd, probably an illusion caused by their shifting head torches.

But it was the paintings that concerned him more.

He'd seen warnings to the future before.

He climbed down, seeing the other group's boot prints in dust on the wall and mud on the steep slopes. When he reached the first chamber he let go of the rope and turned to look around. His head torch forced back the darkness, shadows hunkering down in cracks and corners. He stuck out his tongue, sniffed the air. He tasted damp and smelled age. He heard the trickling and tinkling of water nearby and echoing from further away. He'd been in places like this many times before, but there was something different about this cave, something off. Maybe it was its deep, dark history that had recently been disturbed by people.

Blood was spattered on the ground underneath the rope he'd just used to descend. Lanna had sustained a head injury somehow, and he leaned closer to look at one of the splashes, wondering if that blood was now contaminated. He headed deeper, following the most natural route through caverns, tunnels and cracks in the walls. He saw blood spatters here and there, and the scrapes and signs of recent disturbance. Sixty feet in he came across an abandoned helmet, the headband red with blood, light smashed. He surmised that she'd hurt her head somehow, then put the helmet back on before losing it again.

Goyo checked the weight of the gun in his pocket. Still alien, still a comfort. He sensed no threat down here yet, but there were deeper caverns to explore, darker places to see. He sniffed at the air as he went, wondering what he might be breathing in. He had long ago come to terms with the fact that his travels, his fascination, and especially his fears might mean he was inviting his own death closer. He'd much rather do that than exist standing still and not caring.

He thought of Nathan, his son. He hadn't seen him in three years, simply because of distance more than anything else. He was a paramedic in France, where he'd moved soon after leaving university. Despite the infrequency of their visits, they maintained a close relationship. Those times they saw each other were all the more precious.

He froze, up to his ankles in ice-cold filthy water, and shone his light past dripping rock walls and into secret crevasses. There would come a time when he saw his boy for the last time, and he wondered whether that moment had already been and gone. They'd parted at an innocuous airport cafe, sharing a hug and a promise to call each other soon. 'Soon' often stretched out, but the love and affection remained. It was a precious, valued thing, and behind virtually everything Goyo did, the dangers he put himself in and the threats faced by the world, was concern for his son. Nathan and his partner were edging into middle age now and considering adopting, and Goyo relished the idea of becoming a grandfather.

He was down here to make sure Nathan still had that choice. A million Nathans around the world, making a million decisions that would change their lives for the better. Goyo had never bestowed any grandiose aspect on his purpose, but his fears had taken him all over the world to see things most people never would.

No one should have ever seen this, he thought, and the idea became so firm that he almost turned and made his way back out. He did not, though. He needed certainty, not just a feeling. If he closed up this cave now, he'd always wonder, and always fear it being uncovered again.

And he had to know what had happened to Lanna. He remembered her eyes after she had emerged from the cave and before she had fainted, so filled with intelligence and purpose. What might have caused that? What ancient disease or contagion, born again from ground frozen for so long? Perhaps it was nothing more than a knock on the head, confusion from emerging from darkness into light. He hoped. He would pray, if that had ever been something he found value in.

"Nothing," he said, and his voice echoed away into darkness.

He moved on, and soon he came to a long, low cave where he glimpsed the first of the cave paintings. He paused, breath held, and for a moment after catching sight of them he aimed his head torch elsewhere, looking at damp black rock and shadows that hid away from his light, preserving that brief, calm moment between not seeing and seeing, not knowing and knowing. He gave himself a few more seconds of peaceful present before turning back to the paintings. He examined the images with a sinking heart, focusing on the strange shape between the gathered seated figures and the one, taller likeness of a person. The crouched figure looked strange, twisted, almost not human at all. Contorted with pain, perhaps. Writhing with ancient agonies. Behind them all, the taller shape made no sense to him, but perhaps it had to those who had carved it so long ago.

"Oh, Nathan," Goyo said, a whisper that echoed and winnowed its way deeper into caves and crevasses.

He looked around the cavern, wondering where the bodies were that Dean had spoken about, and the others had been carrying in their frightened gaze. He saw scrapes on the damp rock, a few signs that the team had gone deeper, and he followed.

He could smell the mustiness of decay now, a sweet scent not of fresh rot or recent death, but something much older. If there was anything else carried on this dank, still air he had already breathed it in. He crawled through a long, low, narrow tunnel, worried that his backpack would snag and he'd be trapped there. As he pushed through, he thought that this might be a good place to set off the explosives he had in the backpack, if he deemed it necessary.

"But there's her," he said, thinking of Lanna. He'd been stupid. He should have insisted that she was isolated before he came down here. His voice was swallowed by the rock, muffled so much that he almost didn't hear his own words. This new world swallowed them whole.

In the next chamber he found the bodies. He also saw the lines of excavation in the cave wall, narrow veins that the mining group, including Bethan's former friend, had scraped and chiselled out. Fresh scars in this place of old death.

He skirted around the edge of the strange display of ancient dead. He guessed they must be twenty thousand years old, perhaps as old as forty thousand, dried and mummified down here in cool air, now disturbed by the melt and warmth of this changing world. If Alile had come down with him she might have more of an idea of their origins from their size, the shreds of material still evident here and there on their mummified bodies, and the dark glimmers of small decorative stones around limbs and necks that might have been jewellery.

It was the body in the middle, crouched down on its own, that grabbed his attention. The way its limbs were propped like a dead spider's legs. The weird sense of movement even though there was none, as if it rested coiled with potential. The strange stench emanating from it.

When Goyo saw how its head was opened up like a dried, broken flower, he felt the whole world pivot on the moment of this single, dreadful discovery.

"Oh, Nathan," he said again, and he knew that their last moment together was gone forever.

FIVE

While Goyo was down in the cave, Lanna died. There was no noticeable moment between her last breath and silence. She simply faded away, going from something to nothing. When Wren announced her death, Dean sighed and Emma leaned on the Stallion. It was as if they'd been waiting for this ever since she had emerged from the cave.

Her death made every moment Goyo was away from them seem to stretch out into an endless held breath.

"He's been gone a long time," Alile said.

Bethan glanced at her watch. She'd done so twenty times in the past half an hour. Alile had moved the Discovery closer to the cave, and they stood beside it, taking advantage of the sun. Even with the rise in temperatures, this far north the air was still cold, the breeze adding to the chill. Their thermal jackets kept them warm, but the sun on their exposed skin felt good.

"Almost an hour," she said. "He'll be careful. He knows what he's doing."

"But do they?"

Dean and his companions had carried Lanna's body into the shade cast by their huge Stallion and covered her with a blanket. Dean had looked their way a couple of times, but Bethan and Alile kept their distance.

She looked at her watch again. The world continued to hold its breath. Bethan was eager for it to breathe again. A calm exhalation, she hoped. Not a grunt of anger or pain.

Twice the woman who appeared to lead their group—Bethan had heard them call her Emma—had approached the cave, then turned and come back again, looking as if part of her wanted to follow Goyo down, but most of her couldn't face it. Initially Bethan had feared Emma would go after Goyo, and if that happened she wasn't sure what she'd have to do. Try to stop her? Hold her back? She wasn't a fighter, and the woman looked like she could handle herself.

She resented that Goyo had decided to go off on his own. There was no overt hierarchy in their group, but Goyo was the oldest, the wisest, and both she and Alile looked up to him because of everything he'd seen and done. Bethan was too headstrong to feel a real sense of abandonment, but she hated that he had decided to act without discussing the situation with her and Alile. She'd always known that he was along for the ride, but she also knew that they were stronger together. She'd believed that he had known that, too. They had come here together, and they should have remained so.

"She was a good person," Dean said from where he knelt beside his dead companion. "Sent money home to her parents."

"I'm really sorry," Bethan called to Dean. He watched her for a beat, then turned back to Lanna. Something about Dean's attitude to the dead woman told her that they'd been more than partners on this expedition. She wasn't sure what she saw—his look, his mannerisms—or whether it was some deep, subconscious hangover from their damaged friendship, a misplaced jealousy about who he might be with. She hadn't thought she could care anymore, but she would never pretend that her relationship with Dean wasn't complex.

"What if he finds what he's looking for down there?" Alile asked, and it was everything that Bethan had been asking herself.

"Quarantine," Bethan said. "I guess."

"For us?"

"Probably. Maybe the whole fucking island."

"But her head's all bashed up," Alile said, nodding towards the others. "Skull fracture. Bleed on the brain, that's all. Seen it before."

"She still made it out of the cave, seemed to know what was going on."

"You saw what she was like," Alile said. "The sudden bleed from her ear, and the way her neck twisted. Head injuries can mess you up." She exhaled and grabbed Bethan's arm. "Come on, we should keep busy. Leave them to their grief." She pushed off from where she'd been leaning against the Discovery, heading for the trunk.

"I still worry. He looked really determined."

"He's confused, Bethan. Don't you think? If he wasn't he'd have taken me with him. Cave paintings, old bodies, I'd have more idea about them than him."

"Because you did an anthropology degree a decade ago?"

Alile shrugged. "I read. Keep up with things. Got a good memory. Want something to eat?"

"Really?" Bethan asked. "No, not hungry, not right now. I'm going to check on them." As she started towards the other group, crossing wet ground churned into mud by their vehicles, Alile said something she didn't hear. She was probably trying to stop her. Bethan wasn't sure why she'd decided that now was the time to go and see what was happening with the others.

Maybe because the land's held breath was becoming uncomfortable.

She heard Alile jogging to catch up with her, and they reached Dean and his group together.

"We're really so sorry," Bethan said.

"Yeah, right," Emma said. "One less bad guy for you to worry about, right?" She looked sad, but her eyes kept flickering back towards the cave.

"It's not like that at all."

Emma snorted but said nothing more. Bethan caught Dean's eye but he looked away again, down at the body covered with a blanket. The big man, Wren, sat with the dead woman's head in his lap, as if he didn't want to let her touch the cold damp ground.

"So did you find much of what you were after in there?" Alile asked.

"Yeah. Left it all down there, though."

"When you ran away from the bodies," Bethan said.

"We didn't run away."

Dean stood and stretched, close to Bethan. He didn't correct Emma, but the strained silence that hung after her statement spoke volumes.

"How long to get down to the chamber you found and back out?" Alile asked.

"If he went that far, he should be out again soon," Wren said.

Bethan looked down at the dead woman again. One hand was exposed from beneath the blanket, and one booted foot, and a curl of her hair flickered in the breeze. Bethan imagined contagion with every inhalation. If there was something down there, they had all been exposed. Goyo knew what he was looking for, and his actions and the expression on his face as he'd descended into the mouth of the cave indicated that he had found at least part of it.

Bethan shivered, not only from the cold. She remembered a dozen conversations in hotel rooms, on flights, and around campfires where Goyo had talked about the fears that kept him moving from place to place. It wasn't only losing his home at a young age that had turned him into a wanderer. It was the things he had seen. He'd told her about a place in Brazil where six prospectors had emerged from a never-before-explored remote ravine, pleading for help from the locals. Two of them had been suffering an illness that caused them to swell until their skin split and burst, and the others had all been showing early signs as well, limbs expanding and hot. The locals had killed them, burned their bodies, and buried their remains beneath piles of rocks. That place had been pronounced out of bounds, and three villages and all their inhabitants put into quarantine for six weeks. No one outside knew. Nothing had spread, not even news of what had happened. Goyo had dug deep to find out about it.

The world has to be lucky every time, Goyo had said when he'd told her this story, sitting beside a campfire in the north of Greenland, *and any of these new nasty diseases only has to be lucky once.*

Goyo was far from a lone crusader. Governments, health organisations, corporate entities, other groups like theirs: many people knew the potential risks of runaway climate change and permafrost melt exposing something terrible. That was why Goyo was part of their small group. His fear was that illegal activities would circumvent caution. Many people knew of the dangers, but not everyone cared.

"Maybe we should wrap her a bit better," Bethan said.

"You're not getting anywhere near her," Dean said.

"Okay then, not me, but you guys. You know, just make sure she's—"

"She's only just fucking died!" Dean said, glaring at Bethan. "She's not even getting cold yet! She's our friend, so kindly get lost and let us..." He trailed off a little, his voice lowering, shoulders sagging. "Just let us have a moment, yeah?"

"So how *did* you find us?" Emma asked. As if that mattered now.

"Frank," Bethan said. "Old guy back at—"

"I know who he is. None of us told him where we were going."

"You asked him some advice about the island though, right? His family's lived here for countless generations. He knows every hill and hole in this place. Even those just being revealed. He pointed us to these caves as the most likely place you'd be."

Emma didn't seem convinced, but she looked down at Lanna's covered corpse and said no more.

"Goyo's back," Alile said, her voice still calm and level. Bethan wished she had her friend's laid-back attitude.

Alile pointed past the front of the Stallion towards the cave. The rope snaking down into the cave mouth was taut, shivering, and moments later Goyo appeared framed in the opening. He squinted against the sun, hand raised to shield his eyes, and Bethan saw him taking in the situation.

She nodded to him, and he nodded back. But his gaze settled on Dean and his group.

"Oh. I'm sorry," Goyo said.

"So did you see them?" Emma asked. "The paintings and those bodies?"

"I did." Goyo's voice was low as usual, but Bethan detected an edge. At the same time she noticed that his backpack was missing. She glanced at Alile, saw that she had noticed too.

"And?"

"Like you said, just a few old mummified bodies," he said. He strolled towards them, casual and calm. "Interesting cave paintings. I took some photos. I know some people who'd love to get in there to see them."

"Yeah, well, that's not gonna—" Emma began, and Goyo pulled Emma's gun and pointed it at the group.

"Goyo," Bethan said, but she saw his face, and knew that no one could do or say anything to change whatever course he was set on.

Dean and Emma stood facing Goyo. Wren remained seated, Lanna's head still nursed in his lap.

"She's definitely dead?" Goyo asked.

"About half an hour ago," Wren said. "Why are you aiming that gun at us?"

"You need to get away from her," Goyo said. "She's dangerous."

"Dangerous dead?" Emma asked.

"Humour me," Goyo said.

"Goyo, what did you find down there?" Bethan asked.

"You're insane," Dean said. "She's dead and gone, and you're—"

"So you won't mind if I pop a couple of bullets into her head, just to make sure."

"Goyo—" Bethan began.

Emma took a few steps towards him.

Goyo looked past her, gun still aimed, his face very calm and set, and Bethan thought, *He knows exactly what he's doing, like he's waiting for—*

"What the hell?" Wren shouted. The blanket was moving. Wren shuffled back, dragging the blanket away from the woman as he went, and they all saw what was happening to her head.

A gunshot blasted the world apart, and the land let out its held breath with a scream.

The bullet struck the prone woman in the upper leg and she jerked, both arms twitching. It might have been the force of the shot causing that movement. Might have been. Goyo did not let that distract him. He fired two more bullets into her chest. It was the first time he had ever shot anyone. He felt calm, almost serene, but he knew that was the distance of delayed shock, holding his self away from his actions, his body and soul. He hoped he could fend it off a little while longer. There was more he had to do.

"What the fuck, Goyo?" Alile shouted.

Bethan stood beside her, staring at him but silent. *She knows what the fuck*, Goyo thought. *She's always known.*

"Move away," Goyo said to the dead woman's friends. Her head was deformed, the skin around the injury on her scalp stretched and pulled taut, as if something inside was trying to get out.

Oh no no no, Goyo thought, and as he aimed at her head, her eyes—half-open, rested and at peace—rolled to look at him. He could see that they were both flushed red with blood.

Goyo blinked, trying to shake the impression that she was staring right at him with her ruined eyes. He fired once more, a bullet in the temple. Her head jerked, then slumped to the side. Still. Silent. She faced him, one eyelid closed in a lazy wink. Her blood-filled eyes were too wet and shiny, as if made from glass.

"Oh, Goyo!" Bethan said, her voice high with shock and fear.

Emma came at him, fast and silent, and he turned the gun her way. He didn't know if he could shoot her, but he was also determined to finish what he'd started. He was glad when she skidded to a halt, hands up, fury nestled in her eyes.

The big man reached for the side pocket of his cargo pants. Goyo twitched his aim a few degrees towards him and shook his head. He glanced at Dean. *Maybe they're all armed*, he thought. *And isn't shooting them all for the best?* It was an errant thought, given life by a part of him he was still holding in check. He tried to shove it to one side.

"Don't, Wren," Dean said.

"She was already dead," Goyo said. No one answered. Their shock at what he'd done begged only silence. "You know that. Right?"

"Maybe she just seemed dead!" Dean said.

Wren said nothing. He looked down at Lanna's corpse then back at Goyo, and Goyo could not read him.

"Everyone stay away from me," Goyo said. The distance was fading from around him, the buffer of shock at what he had done flittering away, and he felt a quiver starting deep in his chest. When he was younger he'd used to meditate, imagining a deep well of light, wellbeing, peace, expanding from his chest to fill the world. He could not find that light now. Now, there was only darkness and dread.

"What did you find down there?" Bethan asked again.

"Stay away." He looked down at the dead woman, at Dean and the big man standing beside her, and blinked. *I'm sure*, he thought. *I'm as sure as…*

Everything he'd seen down there made him sure, but not certain. He could not afford the time certainty would take. *Maybe I've been dwelling on this too much, for too long. Maybe it's stirred my senses, made me see and smell things that aren't really there.*

It was too late now. Whether she'd been dead or not when he opened fire, her brains were on the ground. Her blood was spattered across the short scrubby grass and the churned soil, and whether that blood and brains were infected with a deadly contagion or not—

I'm sure but not certain—

—he had to continue with what he had begun. He could not stop, because if he was right he still had more to do, and if he was wrong then they would see him as a cold-blooded murderer. His life had moved on. He had to flow with it.

The ground pounded with a single hard thud. A few seconds later a rumble growled beneath and around them, and Goyo's vision blurred for a second or two. The air seemed to shimmer, as if a heat haze had settled over this cool, bright place. A cloud of dust and grit spewed from the cave mouth. He had no idea whether the charges he'd placed had blocked the route down to that cavern. He was no explosives expert, but he'd done his best.

He nodded at Alile. "Keys," he said. She hesitated for only a beat before lobbing him the Discovery's key fob. He edged sideways past the Stallion and towards the Discovery. He kept his eye on them, gun aimed at the ground before him.

He aimed at the Stallion's big front wheel and pulled the trigger. The bullet *thwacked!* from the thick rubber wall and whined off into the distance without even marking it. He didn't waste another. He knew what he had to do. *To be sure*, he thought. *To be certain.*

"You're fucking insane," Dean said.

"I hope he is," Bethan said.

"What's that supposed to mean?"

Bethan looked down at the body, the brains and blood, and Goyo knew she was remembering all those conversations they'd had about what really scared him.

"I mean if he's not insane, then we're all in a load of trouble."

Dean reached for the dead woman, not quite touching. He held his hands above her, moving them back and forth as if there were some invisible field preventing him from going any closer.

"You should all keep away from her," Goyo said.

"Or what, you'll shoot us too?" Wren asked. His voice was calm, level, and Goyo thought, *He knows... he knows she was dead before she started moving.* He climbed into the Discovery's cab and kept the gun in his hand as he pressed the ignition button. He looked out the side window at Bethan and Alile and hated the shock on their faces. They were watching him like he was a stranger. The others *were* strangers, and they saw only a madman.

"I hope I am insane," he muttered, but he knew that was not the case. Deep history had come back to bite, and he only hoped he was acting fast enough to ensure it remained history.

He stomped on the accelerator and the automatic gearbox jumped and rattled, the car threatening to stall. He steered in a wide circle, away from the group of friends and strangers huddled around the dead woman, avoiding rocks as he picked up speed. He turned back the way they had come, following their recent tracks compressed into tough grass and soft soil, and he looked in the rearview mirror, watching them watching him go.

Maybe they thought he intended to keep going.

When he reached a relatively flat piece of land he steered right, trying to maintain speed while avoiding any wrinkles in the ground that might damage the vehicle. Bouncing in his seat, the Discovery creaking and groaning around him, Goyo swung around until he was following his own tracks back towards the cave, the people and the Stallion. He pressed down on the gas.

Dean and his group started dragging the dead woman aside, but Bethan and Alile watched as Goyo roared towards them. They knew his intention was not to run them down.

Maybe I should, Goyo thought, and for a few seconds he had the chance to twitch the steering wheel to the right and mow down both friends and strangers. But the idea was never real. He could not shoot living flesh, he could not mow down these people, even with everything he thought he knew.

Instead, it was the Stallion that grew in his view. He steered with one hand and reached for the seatbelt with his other, flailing for it but keeping his aim true. He might have no second chance at this. He grasped the belt, felt down until he found the buckle, pushed his arm through and pulled it across his chest, and clipped it home just a few seconds before the speeding Discovery slammed into the Stallion's side.

Glass smashed, metal crashed and crunched, and as Goyo was flung forward in his seat he was struck in the face, a loud, ear-splitting hiss smothering all other sounds of destruction.

The Discovery's engine roared, emitting a high whine. Goyo's body felt as if it had been bent over backwards, muscles spasming. His eyes watered and blood flowed from his injured nose. He tried to move but could not. He was pressed back in his seat, and he feared he was broken and shattered, bleeding out in the ruins of the Discovery, and he could only hope that he had succeeded in crippling the Stallion too. Then he heard a low, gentle whisper of escaping air, and the pressure on his face and shoulders lessened as the emergency airbag began to deflate. He blinked his eyes clear and saw blood spattered across the shrinking bag.

The Discovery's engine was still grumbling high and loud. Goyo reached for the gears and slipped it into reverse, pressing on the gas as the bag finally slumped enough to give him a view of what he had done. The windscreen was smashed into a haze of cracks and swathes of it were missing, enabling him to see past the vehicle's crumpled bonnet to the Stallion. The bigger vehicle was dented and scratched around its front end, and its wheel was gashed and deflated. But Goyo thought it could probably still move.

He coughed and blood hazed the air before him. Something stabbed into the right side of his chest, and he guessed he'd bruised or cracked a couple of ribs. He looked through the passenger side window, still somehow whole, and Bethan was approaching. She held something in her hand that might have been a gun. Behind her, Wren knelt on one knee, one hand to his face. *Well done Bethan, taking that from him*, he thought, and he shook his head at her. *But I'm not done yet.*

Goyo stopped the reversing Discovery thirty yards from the Stallion and slipped it into drive again, slamming his foot on the accelerator.

The second impact was not as powerful but its results were more violent. With the protective air bag now deployed and deflated, Goyo flipped forward and smashed his already bleeding nose against the steering wheel. He cried out loud, the pain centred in his face spreading with the splash of his blood. The engine grumbled but continued, and the stench of spilled diesel filled the cab, cloying and sweet. The dashboard was cracked in several places, the door pillars deformed. Steam erupted in a hiss, dispersing to the air outside the crunched vehicle and fading away.

Goyo wiped his eyes, groaning at the pain from his ribs and bloodied nose. Most of the shattered windscreen had now fallen away, and through his blood and pain he could see the front of the Discovery buried in the Stallion's wing. The larger vehicle's wheel was fully deflated and torn, and the passenger door had caved in.

Not expecting anything to happen, Goyo moved into reverse and eased on the gas, and the Discovery rolled back, engine rattling and screaming but still somehow under his control. Back at Joyce Sound he hadn't wanted to sound like an old man by saying they didn't make things as good as they used to, but he thought that now. He even managed a smile as he let the Discovery roll to a stop and dropped it into drive one more time.

"Goyo!" Bethan shouted. "There's—"

Goyo pushed his foot on the accelerator and aimed the vehicle's smashed nose towards the damaged Stallion's front end. The stench of diesel was stronger, and just as they met for the third time he smelled burning.

The collision was not so great, but Goyo was thrown into the steering wheel, his injured ribs screaming, eyes watering, and through the crunched merging of already broken metal he heard the soft, unmistakeable *whooph!* of igniting fuel.

He unclasped his seatbelt and reached for the door handle. It came off in his hand, the door remaining closed. He clicked off the central locking, but there were no lights on the dashboard now, no sign that any of the Discovery's electrics were still working. Smoke rose from the wrecked engine, seeping from around the crumpled and cracked bonnet and pouring into the cab through the shattered windscreen.

Goyo tried to move but his left foot was trapped, held fast by a fist formed from the Discovery's broken body.

"Goyo!" someone shouted, and he wasn't sure if it was Bethan or Alile, or both of them. He shouldered the door but it didn't budge. Even unlocked, it would have been wedged in its deformed opening.

"See it through," Goyo said, not sure who he was talking to. "See it through."

He felt heat. The flicker of flames caught his eye and he leaned forward, looking out through the smashed windscreen and down into the engine compartment through the crumpled bonnet. The fire spread. He felt heat touch his feet, his legs. He tugged again, but his foot was held fast.

Goyo had been close to death before, but never as close as this. A form of low panic began to take hold. He looked at the Stallion, tried to assess the damage, hoped that it was as crippled and finished as the Discovery was.

As he was.

"See it through!" he shouted this time, looking through the smashed passenger window and catching Bethan's eye. She was close, but smoke started to billow, carrying the bitter scent of melting plastic, burning fuel, and the promise of death.

Goyo looked for the gun and saw it spilled into the passenger footwell. He reached for it, but flames gushed through from the engine, catching onto the carpet and singeing hairs all along his hand and arm. He flinched back, and as he did so he felt some give around his ankle. He rocked left and right, leaning hard, and then his foot popped free.

"Goyo! I'm going to—"

Something exploded, a heavy thud that gave fuel to the flames.

He felt rather than heard a solid impact against the door, and as he leaned right and left again the door opened and he fell, gasping in a breath that went from cool to hot as everything became fire.

SIX

Flames dance. Sparks fly, flirting with a million other stars. The heat is fleeting, comforting, and touches their primal hearts.

"Does nothing scare you, Goyo?"

"I'm not a robot."

"I've wondered," Alile says, and she laughs. She stokes the fire and drops on another chopped branch.

Bethan leans back against her rucksack, comfortable and content. They've hiked over twenty miles, drawing water samples from three tributaries of the Amazon and taking photographs of several areas where pollution is painfully evident. The samples will link the pollution to Ark Industries, a company they've been gathering evidence against for over a year. Whether it will lead to any significant repercussions, none of them can know. But Bethan takes comfort from being out here with her like-minded friends, and for now she can rest and drink and talk with them in the knowledge that at least *they* are taking action. Others around the world had made efforts as well, in small ways like them, and large-scale like the establishment of the Virgin Zones. Even with worsening climate change continuing to smash them in the face—the devastating yearly wildfires in Europe, the American farming belt suffering so much from drought that some had taken to calling it the Desert, floods and famine in India—far too many people still chose to do nothing. There were the doubters, but worse in Bethan's mind were those who chose to ignore it.

Alile's question is prompted by the last sample they took that afternoon, and Goyo stepping calmly from the river as an anaconda drifted past close enough to touch his boot. Bethan swears it was fifteen feet long and as thick as her thigh.

Goyo leans forward and smiles as he passes his hand slowly through the feisty campfire's flames, back and forth. Bethan breathes in, searching for the scent of frizzled hair but finding none. She's never figured out how he does that.

"If I was a robot I'd have fried circuits by now," he says.

"Sure, with rough whiskey and rougher women," Bethan says.

"Whiskey never broke my heart."

It's a familiar exchange, and that familiarity provides another comfort for them all. They're singing the same song, performing a familiar dance, and they know each other well enough that the singing and dancing never grows stale.

"What about you, Alile?" Goyo asks.

"I asked first." Goyo shrugs. She laughs and takes a small swig from the bottle of whiskey they're passing around. She's never been a big drinker, but she does it to please Goyo. He always brings them rough whiskey.

"Okay, well… spiders," Alile says, looking around at the darkness held back by the campfire. There's moonlight and starlight up through the scant canopy, because they've chosen the clearing of a decade-old illegal logging site in which to camp. Just beyond, and all around, the dark wall of the night-time jungle begins.

"Fuck me, you definitely chose the wrong hobby," Bethan says.

"Jesus, it was the size of a kitten." Alile shivers, the others laugh. Bethan knows that she's remembering the spider she found in her walking boot one morning the year before. Goyo assured her it was mostly harmless as he shook it out and shooed it away, but Alile insists that it still haunts her dreams.

"It's the little ones that are most dangerous," Goyo says, taking the bottle from Alile. "Consider Bethan."

"Fuck you?" Bethan suggests.

"So what else?" Goyo asks. "Because, spiders. A cheap get-out. Fear of spiders doesn't surprise anyone. It's like fear of heights. Give us something more. Something that'll tell us more about you."

"More about me," Alile says. She sits back against her pack, looking up at where sparks from the fire flicker out and smoke disappears into the night. "You know everything there is to know about me, and then some."

"I seriously doubt that," Goyo says. "You never really know anyone but yourself, and I'm even a stranger to myself most of the time."

"Okay. Enclosed spaces."

"Fuck, another easy one," Bethan says. "Buried alive."

Alile doesn't reply, and though she's still looking at the fire's sparks and smiling, Bethan knows she's thinking deeper. Maybe she's searching for something more, or wondering how to say what she wants to say.

"Mint."

Goyo grunts, swigs and passes the bottle to Bethan. They never wipe the neck.

"My mother used to tell me, when she was back home and the food was running out, that they'd sometimes chew wild mint to make it seem like they were eating something. It never took away the hunger, but…" She shrugs. "Made it feel better for a while. So I don't like mint. Don't eat it, hate the smell, don't even like seeing it growing. I've been lucky, never known hunger like my mother and sister did, because they always made sure I didn't. I guess I hate it for them."

"Is that the same as being scared of it?" Goyo asks.

"Yeah," she says. "It is."

"Mint," Goyo says, as if considering the word for the first time. After a pause, he says, "Bethan?"

"She asked you first," Bethan says. "I mean, it's obvious you're not afraid of anacondas—"

"It was the branch of a tree."

"My ass it was."

"Talking like Yoda now?" he asks, and Bethan takes a while thinking about what he means. He likes those old *Star Wars* movies, and still can't believe it when she says she hasn't seen them. She has, of course, but doesn't want to give him the satisfaction. She thinks he'd like being called Chewie a little too much, though she'd more likely pin him as Obi-Wan.

"Okay," Bethan says. "As it seems you think you're in charge, which I have to say is some macho bullshit right there, I'll go next."

Goyo chuckles and sips some more whiskey.

"Heights," she says. "Yeah, boring."

Goyo spits whiskey across the fire. It flares briefly, yellow then blue then gone.

"Shit, spiders and enclosed spaces, now heights. Leave something else boring for me, eh?"

"Haven't finished," Bethan says. "Puppets in kids' shows. Not all of them but a good proportion. Remember an old show called *Lazytown*? Spooky as fuck. I think they're designed to frighten away adults. It's like a conspiracy... messages to kids we aren't allowed to hear. Weird thing is, I'm only afraid of these things in dreams. You've seen me, I can climb a tree with the best of them, and remember that cliff in Patagonia?"

"How can I forget," Alile says. "Saved my ass."

"Nice ass to save," Bethan says. "And find me an old episode of some kids' show now, and I'll happily watch those fucking puppets gurn and dance and sing to each other all through the night while you two snore and fart to dawn."

"I do not snore," Alile says.

"But if I nod off and dream of climbing that cliff, I always fall in my sleep, and I've never yet hit the ground 'cos—"

"Hit the ground in your sleep, die in real life," Alile says.

"Right. I'm afraid of those dreams of heights, because I'm always worried I'm going to hit the ground."

"And puppets?" Goyo asks.

"In my dreams it's always me they want, not the kids," Bethan says. "It's like... something's after me. The consequence of something. And if I slow down or fall, the puppets will catch me, or I'll hit the ground, and that'll be it."

They sit silently for a while, drinking, comfortable. A knot pops on the fire. The jungle mumbles and reverberates with the usual night sounds, scratching and calling, growling and rustling.

"So," Alile says eventually. "You can't get away with this, Goyo. Not fair. Tell us what scares you or I'll boil your robot balls on this campfire."

"Fry my circuits." He tries to make himself more comfortable, but Bethan thinks it has the opposite effect. Like the very idea of telling them something is an act to fear.

They finish the whiskey, and that's enough drink for the evening. Goyo's had at least half of it. They're warm and settled, and something about the night, the fire, the liquor, the sense of safety with each other gives Goyo that extra push he's always needed. He's talked to Bethan about his fears before, but always in passing, obliquely. Never like this. He's never been so plain.

"What scares me most is the idea of a disease emerging from the deep past and coming to kill us all." The fire spits and night creatures call out, the hunters and hunted. Flames and animals, impartial and unknowing. "There's precedent. In our history, there have been contagions that might have wiped out the world, if they'd had the means to spread. A valley here, everyone dead and the disease with nowhere to go. An island there. Now the world is smaller, we're all interconnected, and they'd *have* that means. Six degrees of separation has become four. Tell me a tale of a computer programmer in Stockholm and give me long enough and I'll find some way I'm linked to them by a handshake, a flight, a drunken kiss, sharing a glass in a bar. That gives disease a route to spread without any natural boundaries to slow it down. What use is a wide river now? A mountain range? An ocean? Hardly anything."

"It's happened," Bethan says. "We've had Covid-19, and more recently Broughton Haze. Science finds a way to combat them, and the science has accelerated."

"It has," Goyo says. "But what really, really scares me is an intelligent disease. One that uses its host to spread, and rides on its host's intelligence. It'll happen. It *has* happened."

"How do you mean?" Alile asks. "You're scaring me, now."

Goyo sighs and looks to the sky.

"No fucking way," Bethan says. "You've started so you'll finish."

"I suppose I must. You know I have your back in all of this..." He waves his hands at the storage bags they've been lugging around with them. "All this climate activism. It's as important to me as it ever has been to you because it's been the driver of my life since I was a child. Like millions of others, I'm adrift because of what we've done to the planet. But really, I'm looking for signs of something worse."

"An intelligent disease," Bethan says. "Well, that sounds utterly fucking terrifying. So please explain."

"Show me a bacteria that can do crosswords and coding, and I'll be as petrified as you," Alile says. No one laughs.

"There are stories of some sort of contagion on a South Pacific island sometime in the seventeenth century. There are a few written accounts, mainly put down by those who heard second-hand stories. These are unreliable on their own, but I've researched them, and they're often independent, and separated by continents and oceans. Mostly carried by word of mouth. Anyway. Those places are still pretty isolated now, even with all the help they're receiving to combat the rising sea levels. Back then, if there was contact it was intermittent, and only with neighbouring islands. The islanders called this disease Deadeye, because in its final stages it swelled the brain fluid enough to bleed through and flood the eyes with blood. Horrible enough, but it's the accounts of how it spread that are most horrific. It infected the brain, riding on the victim's thoughts and actions, until it started steering them. It took control of them so they became its puppets. Some of them died quickly, ensuring that they stayed close and infected their families and friends. But others lasted longer, sometimes days. Long enough to sail to neighbouring islands."

"Looking for help?" Alile asked.

"Looking to spread," Goyo says. "The infection steered them and drove them that way."

"You're saying the bacteria took control and made them sail to other islands to spread their disease?" Bethan asks.

"It's unproven." Goyo shrugs. "It was a long time ago. But it's terrifying enough, even if it's only ten per cent true."

"Wait," Alile says. "I've heard about this. Ants, right? Some sort of fungus takes over their brains and kills them and turns them into zombie ants, right?"

"Er, fucking zombie ants?" Bethan says. "You can shut down that shit right now."

"She's right," Goyo says. "Or sort of. Zombie fungus is its more dramatic name, but if you really want to know it's called *Ophiocordyceps unilateralis*. It's a fungus that infects an ant and can steer its focus and direction. It encourages it to climb a blade of grass, for instance, to just the right height—about ten inches, let's say—and the right attitude—the north side of the grass—so that when the ant dies and the fungus grows out of its head and spores, it's at the optimum height and direction for the spores to spread."

"That's, like, science fiction," Bethan says. "I guess these things are the size of cars, too?"

Goyo chuckles. "Normal size ants. And no, it's science fact. It's the name that makes it sound more scary than it is. It's just nature."

"So the fungus controls the ant's brain?" Bethan asks.

"That's the strangest thing. It's thought it takes control of the ant through its muscles. There is no trace of the fungus in the ant's brain. It literally steers the ant."

"But you're not talking about that," Alile says.

"The Ophiocordyceps fungus itself possesses no intelligence. Not in any way that we understand. It's pure evolution that has driven it, and the ant, to experience such a relationship. I'm talking about something far worse."

He tips the bottle, remembers it's empty.

"I've had plenty of time to think about this, how it might work, and really it's not at all unfeasible. An intelligent disease spreads into a person's brain and slowly takes control. It possesses purpose and guile. Its purpose is to perpetuate itself, spread all over. Its guile... those infected might not even understand they have the disease. It might make them aggressive and strong, if that's needed. It might sustain them, maybe preserving a spark of life in bodies kept in hibernation for years. It might even fool them. Manipulate their minds, make them believe they're not even infected at all. Maybe that's what happened with Deadeye."

Bethan looks at Goyo across the fire. She likes to think she knows when he's joking, which he does quite often. This does not feel or look like a joke.

"Thanks for the fucking nightmares," she says, hoping for a smile. She receives none.

"So how did the South Pacific disease stop spreading?" Alile asks.

"It ran out of hosts," Goyo says. "Everyone on those islands died. Seven islands, nine thousand victims. Over time, the bacteria died out."

"If they all died, how did anyone know about it?"

"Just one witness survived."

"Ah," Bethan says, "the famous 'only survivor' plot twist."

"It's just how it is," Goyo says. "She saw what happened, retreated from her friends and family and neighbours, and lived in a small cave on one of the islands until everyone else was dead. The accounts come from her, though they were scattershot and incomplete. She survived long enough to see the first new settlers arrive on the islands three decades later."

"She lived on her own for that long?"

"On purpose, to ensure she wasn't infected. She'd seen what it did to people she loved, how it made them drones for its own spread, so she stayed alone for the rest of her life just in case she'd been infected too."

"For the rest of her life?" Alile asks. "You said she stayed there until settlers came."

"I'm guessing that's when she checked out," Bethan says.

"She fought them off to begin with, standing on the beach and shooting arrows at them. When she ran out of arrows, she threw rocks. But the island was beautiful, bountiful. And, unusually for back then, the settlers were also caring. They didn't want to harm this woman. They thought she might have been a castaway, so they wanted to hear her story. They waited until night fell, then went ashore quietly in three boats."

"Did they kill her?" Bethan asks.

"No. She heard them coming, set a fire on the beach, and threw herself into the flames. They rowed ashore in the fire's light."

"Holy shit," Bethan says. They stare into the flames of their own fire for a while. "But the disease was gone? The settlers weren't infected?"

Goyo shrugs. "I guess so."

"Long way away," Alile says. "Long time ago. Few records. Could have been anything. Maybe the islanders died of some mundane infection, fled to other islands to try and escape, spread it accidentally. And she went mad on her own and made up the story."

"Sure. Entirely possible. Other stuff I've heard is from even longer ago. The fever that an Aztec city caught from a family group of spider monkeys roaming far from their usual foraging grounds. They thought it was some sort of demonic possession. The hunters on the Siberian steppe driven mad by some disease, tying themselves onto horses and dying, decomposing, rotting in place, riding their freed horses for years while they wandered and fed and bred. There's more, stories ranging from barely known fairy tales to almost-accepted histories. But what if the causes of some of these stories are far from vanished? Frozen into glaciers or Antarctic ice, for instance. Hidden at the bottoms of lakes that are slowly drying up due to drought. Buried in permafrost that's starting to warm and melt. Borders, boundaries, rivers, mountain ranges, even oceans… none of them are barriers anymore. There's no natural containment for anything that…" He sighs, deep and heavy, and Bethan hears something she doesn't like.

"Goyo? There's more, isn't there?"

He stares into the flames. "That's what I've heard. The stories, the rumours, the crazy fucked-up histories." He looks up, staring at both of them for a couple of seconds. He rarely swears. "But there's also what I know."

"And what's that?" Alile asks. Her voice is soft, and Bethan thinks it's because she doesn't really want to hear.

Goyo shakes his head, smiling a little. He looks confused. "I've always tried to explain it away."

"Goyo…" Bethan says.

"Even in my dreams."

"Goyo!"

He sighs, stares into the flames. "Twelve years ago, I spent some time in Siberia. Small town, just north of the Arctic Circle. Remote, desolate, hard people living off a hard land. There was a trapper, came into town one day, everyone knew him and recognised him, but… that time, they all saw something wrong. I went to bed one night to the sound of drinking and music from the town bar. Next morning, the trapper was dead, and I woke to the stink of him and seven others burning on a fire at the edge of town. That stench of cooking flesh… I'll never forget it. I asked what had happened, and the town mayor took me to one side, made me promise to not tell anyone about what I'd seen. 'That was not Leonard,' the mayor said to me. 'Leonard was inside, but that was someone else.' And he used a word I couldn't quite translate, but which I think meant 'clay man'. He'd been working in open land where permafrost melt had produced a sunken valley and thrown up all sorts of things. Even an old mammoth corpse, starting to rot again. In the space of one evening, he'd come to town and given whatever he carried to seven townsfolk."

"Maybe it was a fight," Alile says. "A feud."

"Three of the dead were children," Goyo said. "One of them a baby. That man, Leonard, or whatever he'd become… he'd gone around town picking on those who were alone and infecting them. The town was grieving. The mayor sent me on my way." He shivers and shakes his head. "Four weeks later, the Russian air force carpet-bombed that town from the map, along with three miles of land all around. Blamed it on insurgents. I've told you rumours and old tales from history, but that's my own story. And I… I know I'm right." Fear would have been fine, because each of them has learned to confront their fears. But in Goyo's voice now is hopelessness. "History's bad news beckons. Bury me alive. Drop me from a plane. Give me spiders and mint any day of the week."

They fall silent, thinking on what Goyo has said. Alile feeds the fire some more. For once, they take no comfort from its warmth and light.

SEVEN

The air smelled of smoke, melting plastic, burning rubber, the rich tang of blazing diesel, and a powerful loamy warmth as the surrounding ground was scorched black. But it was the stench of roasting flesh he would remember forever.

Goyo looked like he should be dead. Maybe he would be soon. Dean's shock held his fury at bay, but he wasn't sure the same could be said of Emma and Wren.

Where the fuck did he get that strength? Dean wondered again. It had seemed unreal, watching Bethan and Alile drag their bloodied friend from the blazing cab, seeing him stand and push them away, his clothes smouldering as he staggered to Lanna's body, picked her up, and then stumbled back to heave her into the conflagration.

Why did none of us stop him? Lanna had been lithe, thin, and Goyo was undoubtedly a strong, wiry man. But it had seemed to happen so quickly. Shock could do that, Dean knew, compress time so that an event felt like a single moment, not a series of connected incidents.

This all felt like a terrible nightmare.

Wren moved first. He stepped in and punched Goyo, one solid strike at his bleeding face that dropped him like a shattered mannequin. He held his fist ready to punch again, hesitated, stepped back.

Dean looked at the burning vehicles. Flames roared, metal distorted, plastics thudded and cracked. A tyre burst, a convulsive boom that sent a breath through the flames, setting them dancing to another song.

He breathed in through his mouth, not wanting to smell, but he tasted the cooking flesh instead. He looked once again at Lanna's body. Goyo's throw had been strong, and she'd landed on the Discovery's bonnet where it was crumpled against the Stallion, before sliding down partly out of sight on the other side. She was just a vague shape now, spitting and sizzling as flames scorched deep. He wondered if he would only ever remember her like this, a dreadful sight scorched forever onto his brain, into his memory.

Wren stepped forward again to kick the downed man.

Dean reached for his arm, grabbed it. "Wren, step back."

"Dean?" Emma said, aghast.

"She's gone," he said, raising his voice over the flames. "She was gone when she came out of the caves. The crack in her skull. And she *died* lying on the ground. You... you saw that, right? You saw what I saw?"

"We've got to get further away," Alile said. She and Bethan half-lifted Goyo. He struggled to stand, groggy from Wren's punch. Dean had seen him punch someone once before, two men in a bar fight in Chile. Teeth and bloodied spittle had speckled the floor: walking away, Wren said he'd given them about forty per cent. It was amazing the old guy was still awake.

They moved away from the conflagration. Wren backed up, still focused on Goyo.

"You don't want to hit him too?" he asked Dean. "After he did that to Lanna?"

"I know why he did it," Bethan said.

"Because he's a fucking nut-job!" Emma shouted. "And you two bastards came here with him, *helped* him!"

"We had no idea what he was going to do!" Alile said.

Dean could see the truth of that in her face, hear it in her voice. One glance at Bethan was enough to convince him. She appeared shocked and hollowed out. She hadn't even looked like that after that time at the fracking site. He wanted to go to her, then blinked the idea away. That time was past.

"But it's all your fault," Alile said. "Going down there, doing what you did. *Your* fault!"

"It's your friend who just fucking shot and *burned* someone!" Wren shouted.

"Someone you'd all left down in the caves for an hour!" Bethan said. "Explain that, eh?" She looked between Wren and Emma, then her eyes settled on Dean. "Explain that."

"So why?" Dean asked. "Why did Goyo just shoot my dead friend and try to kill himself?"

"He didn't try to kill himself," Bethan said. She breathed hard, helping Alile half-drag, half-carry the injured man between them. Wren had stepped away and walked on ahead after Emma. Dean didn't think that meant the danger from him was over.

"Looked like that to me," Dean said.

"He wanted to disable both vehicles, and then…" Bethan trailed off and looked ahead at where Emma and Wren had stopped by a scatter of large boulders. Emma sat back on one, shaking her head at something Wren said to her.

"And then see it through?" Dean asked. "What did that mean exactly?"

"Dunno," Bethan said. She and Alile set Goyo down against a rock. His breathing was uneven, filled with pain, and he looked down at his feet, as if concentrating hard on not puking or passing out. "Maybe we're all lucky he lost the gun in there," Dean said, nodding at the wrecked Discovery. Goyo didn't raise his head, but Dean got the impression he was listening, not quite as groggy as he was making out.

Dean saw something in Wren's face that brought him up short. Anger, yes, but more than that. He wasn't sure he'd ever seen the big man looking afraid.

"What's happening?" Wren asked Bethan. "What does he know?"

"Right," Emma said. "What does he think we've been exposed to?"

"What *exactly* did *you* see?" Bethan asked, turning the question back on Emma. "I mean, the truth. The actual thing that scared you all so shitless you ran and left your friend behind?" She looked at Dean as she spoke.

"Even back in the cave, she was changed," Dean said. "She... wasn't herself anymore." He expected Wren and Emma to counter him, but their silence was an agreement. They'd all seen it, and with what had happened her reappearance and strange actions took on new meaning.

"There was something alive down there," Wren said.

"*What* alive?" Alile shouted. "Just be straight!"

"I don't know!" Wren shouted back.

"Fuck's sake!" Bethan said. She glared at Dean.

"Something moved," Dean said. "One of those old bodies, thousands of years old and mummified down there. It moved, but no, it wasn't alive. It *can't* have been."

"Heat from our thermal guns," Emma said. "That's all it was. Panicked you, Wren, and you ran and the panic spread and—"

"I don't... fucking... panic," Wren said, and Dean had never heard him using that tone with Emma before. "I *saw* it move. It wasn't just shifting 'cos we'd heated it up. There was..." He frowned, shook his head.

"Purpose," Dean said softly, remembering.

"In a dead fucking body?" Emma asked.

"Lanna moved too," Wren said, quieter now. "After she'd died and we covered her, and before he..." He nodded at Goyo, still slumped against the rock. "She moved."

Something exploded in the blazing vehicles. Glass shattered outwards, and a limb of fire and sparks arced an object out across the landscape. Whatever it was spat and sizzled in the grass, harsh smoke swirling in the breeze caused by the conflagration.

"I think Goyo believes she'd been exposed to some sort of infection," Bethan said. "It's something he's been looking for, something that terrifies him."

"Like Broughton Haze?" Dean asked.

"Maybe worse than that," Bethan said. She seemed about to elaborate, but then she shook her head instead.

Bethan stood between her friends, and Dean with his. She'd tucked Wren's gun into her waistband after knocking it from his hands. Dean figured Wren could have easily wrestled it back, but the shock of all this was settling on him as well as the rest of them.

"What sort of disease?" Wren asked. That fear again, shimmering just behind his eyes. Dean felt it too. It smelled of smoke and roasting flesh. It looked like Lanna's eyes as she'd emerged from that cave and came for them.

"Old," Goyo croaked. He sat up, shivering.

"Old," Emma said. "That's it?"

"I… don't know," Goyo said. "But something bad. Unknown, maybe."

"You don't know? You've done all this…" She gestured at the burning vehicles, their situation. "…on the strength of that?"

Goyo only shook his head, coughing.

"We need to treat these wounds," Alile said.

"Fuck his wounds," Wren said. "He needs to tell us what he knows."

"That's it," Bethan said. "He doesn't know much. But he's seen stuff, learned enough over the years to convince him that there are old diseases lying around just waiting for us."

"And the world's changing," Alile said.

"Right," Bethan said. "And you assholes are pushing that change, trying to capitalise on it. It's places like this that hold the most threat."

"We've got to go," Alile said. "Our medical kit was in the Discovery. Goyo needs—"

"We should stay here for a few days, make sure no one else is infected," Bethan said.

"We can't stay," Wren said.

"Why not?" Bethan asked.

"Because your prick friend destroyed our camping gear, comms, most of our food and water, spare clothing—" Emma shouted.

"Okay, okay."

"Where's yours, Bethan?" Dean asked.

She blinked. She didn't need to say. Dean looked past his old friend at the burning vehicles. Nothing could be salvaged from there. The fuel had gone up and the fire was entrenched now, consuming the upholstery and plastics, the clothing and equipment. Everything they needed to survive.

"This place is fucking *desolate*!" Emma said. "The nearest community is Joyce Sound, and that's over thirty miles away. We'll have to hike it."

"No!" Goyo snapped. He tried to stand, pushing himself half-upright against the rock. He was shivering with shock, his eyes wide, but his voice was strong. "We can't go back. We have to stay here like Bethan says. Make sure no one else is infected."

"I'm not sitting here and dying just on the off chance," Wren said.

"Couple of our backpacks survived," Emma said. "Got some ration bars, bit of water, some tools and foil blankets. I'm for walking."

"Me too," Wren said. "Live off the land."

"Thirty miles across this landscape?" Bethan asked. "Geysers, sinkholes, quicksand, polar bears, toxic clouds coming up out of the melting ground … we'll be dead in ten."

"Who says you're coming with us?" Emma snapped.

"And we'll be dead sooner, if Goyo has his way," Dean said. "Come on, Bethan, Wren's right. We can't stay here and wait to die, just on the off chance. The nights are cold out here. The land is dangerous, unpredictable. Why'd you think we came here in the Stallion?"

"Because you can afford to," Bethan said.

"Thirty miles across this terrain will take us three days minimum," Emma said. "Lanna can't have been exposed to anything for more than a couple of hours before… whatever that was that happened. If there is an infection of some sort, it has a short incubation. If any of us has what you think she might've had, we'll know soon enough."

"And then what?" Bethan asked.

Emma shrugged.

"We'll deal with that if it happens," Dean said. "One step at a time."

"Really, Dean?" she snapped. "You'll deal with it, will you? All on your own? Seems to me you need someone to hold your hand when you're—"

"Let's not forget the crazy old bastard was screaming about seeing it through!" Wren shouted. "Who knows what they'll try, Emma? I don't trust 'em."

"You were going to shoot him," Bethan said. "Before I, you know, took your gun off you."

"He shot Lanna," Wren said.

"She was already dead. You told us that."

Emma glanced at Wren but added nothing.

"I promise I won't cut your throat while you sleep," Bethan said.

"Right," Emma said. "From what Dean's told us, you kill people when they're awake."

Bethan glared at Dean. Her gaze was harsh and hard, knives pressed against his skin. He couldn't remember exactly what he'd told his team about his time with Bethan, nor how much detail he'd revealed, but he shouldn't have been surprised that Emma remembered. It wasn't something anyone could easily forget. He couldn't, and it was why he and his best friend hadn't talked in over six years.

"We're going," Emma said. "Wren? Dean?"

"Yeah," Wren said.

Dean nodded.

Bethan and Alile glanced at each other, and Dean couldn't tell what they'd decided. He guessed he'd find out soon enough, whatever it was. He wanted to defuse the loaded situation, if he could.

"Can we salvage anything from there?" he asked, nodding towards the blazing vehicles. He knew the answer even as he spoke. They all did. Goyo's actions had left them with the clothes they stood in, and a few tools and other items in the rucksacks they'd taken down into the caverns.

"You, me and Wren," Emma said to Dean. "Three days. Like Wren said, we can live off the land."

"Oh, and I'm sure you know how to do that," Bethan said.

Dean remembered what they'd seen of this changing, unwelcoming place during their journey here inside the Stallion, and he imagined that living off the land would be a big ask.

"I used to," he said.

"You know which plants to eat, and those that'll kill you?" Alile asked. "You know the first signs of methane sinkholes? What to do when confronted by a polar bear?"

"I'll work it out," Wren said.

"Oh, 'cos you're a big strong jock?"

Wren bristled, took a step forward.

"We'll be fine!" Dean said. He nodded at Goyo. "It's you guys I worry about."

"Oh, really?" Bethan asked. "Well don't. We're coming with you."

"Er, nope," Emma said.

"Really?"

Silence. Dean looked back and forth between Bethan and Emma. Then he said, "She's right, Emma. Her friend is, too. Safety in numbers. We should stick together."

"First sign of any of us falling ill, we stop," Bethan said.

"Whatever." Emma nodded at Goyo. "You think he'll come with us?"

"More than happy if he stayed," Wren said.

Bethan walked a few steps back towards the burning vehicles, perhaps considering everything they'd lost inside. Dean followed her, feeling Emma's and Wren's eyes on his back.

"What sort of disease, Bethan?" he asked quietly.

"Don't think even he knows. But we have to assume it's something terrible. Don't we?"

"He shot her. Burned her. I can I can smell…"

Dean remembered making love with Lanna the night before, tying the rope around the rock with her, crawling after her into the caves. He remembered her ready smile and cutting wit, and the distracted way she sometimes looked at him that had always, always kept him guessing. Now he'd never know anything for sure.

"I really am sorry about your friend," Bethan said.

"She was more than that."

"Yeah. Guessed." She'd always been able to see through him, that's what had made them such good friends. The fact that she still could now drove a blade into his heart. He guessed not talking didn't necessarily break that bond.

"Bethan—" he said, but she cut him off.

"We've lost too much today to talk about what's past," she said. "Let's just think about how fucked we are in the here and now."

They returned to their people, separately, and assessed whatever belongings they had left. Lanna's backpack was somewhere down in the caves, and Wren's had been run over and crushed when Goyo rammed the Stallion, but Dean's and Emma's were whole. They were high-tech packs designed for close-quarters caving and short-term survival, and expensive though they were, he realised they would be of limited use for a thirty-mile hike. There were energy bars and lightweight ultra-warm blankets, first aid and basic tool kits, true. But the bulk of each pack was taken up with surveying equipment and short-distance communications kits, a small, pressurised oxygen bottle and mask, thin nylon ropes, and storage and analysis kit for the stuff they'd come here to find. The idea was that as soon as they were in the cave and digging stuff out, their packs could begin the analysis process to see if where they were was of financial significance.

Still, there was food enough to last them for several days, rationed well. Three of them at least. If they shared with Bethan and her group, it might be just two days' worth. And those days would be hard work, traversing a constantly changing, treacherous, geologically active landscape. They needed strength, endurance, focus, and the ability to keep their wits about them.

More troubling, most of their water supplies were now hissing away to steam as the Stallion burned.

"So what you got?" Dean called over to Bethan. She glanced up, looked at him and then past him at Wren and Emma.

"Everything we had was in the Discovery," she said.

"What's ours is ours," Emma said.

"Makes for a happy marriage," Bethan said.

"What about him?" Dean asked, nodding at Goyo. Alile was still tending him, and she heard the question.

"He's fine," she said.

"Fine?"

"His nose is broken and he's bruised his chest, and he's got some superficial burns. But he's the strongest man I know," Alile said. "He'll be okay." Dean saw Alile and Bethan exchange a glance, but he didn't push it. He was with Wren on this one—he'd be happy if Goyo decided to stay behind.

"Has he even decided to come with us?" Dean asked.

"Plenty of time," Goyo said. "We've got to walk, and that's plenty of time for any infection to show."

"And if it does?" Emma asked. "You're going to kill us all?"

Goyo smiled and shook his head, groaning in pain.

"Whatever, just keep your fucking distance from me and my people," Emma said. "Let's move out."

EIGHT

In truth, Bethan wasn't sure it was a good idea leaving together. But if they were to make it the thirty miles across Hawkshead Island to the coast and Joyce Sound, it was true that they'd probably be safer in one group. Bethan hoped they'd make seven miles before dark. After the low sun dipped below the horizon, she had no idea what they might do, or where they would shelter. It would be cold, and their thin thermal jackets would only protect them so much. If it rained and they got wet, they'd likely welcome the sunrise with hypothermia. Sharing body warmth with Dean and his friends in some hole in the ground didn't appeal.

Goyo had rallied surprisingly well. His heavy breathing betrayed occasional grunts of pain. Dean had given him some antibiotic cream and gauze from his first aid kit, under Emma's obvious disagreeing glare, and Alile had treated the lacerations and burns on his scalp, neck and right forearm.

"There's really nowhere for us to stay, Goyo," she said.

"Huh." He didn't have to speak for her to understand what he was thinking.

"Spiders and mint," she said.

"Huh." There was a note of humour in his grunt that time, at least.

Alile walked a few steps ahead of them. Thirty feet ahead of her were Dean, Emma and Wren, close together. Wren and Emma were carrying their backpacks and nibbling on energy bars that they'd refused to share. They stayed ahead, and sometimes they talked in low voices. She didn't know what they were saying, whether they were scheming. She didn't know them at all, other than Dean. They presented as much danger as Hawkshead Island.

She hoped they wouldn't have to defend themselves against Dean's group. Bethan knew that Alile carried a knife in a sheath inside her left boot, but she'd never used it in anger. The weight of the gun felt alien in her own belt, and she hadn't grown used to it. Several times she'd considered discarding it into one of the muddy puddles they passed by. She hated guns. But her body had warmed its metal, and though it felt out of place, it was no longer uncomfortable. She hated the sense of protection it gave her, but valued it as well.

She'd hang onto the weapon, just for a little while longer.

Wren seemed to have calmed down somewhat, but she couldn't tell for sure. And Dean had hardly changed physically in the six years since they'd last seen each other. Thinner, maybe, with a peppering of grey above his left ear and in the stubble around his jaw. But he was still mostly the friend she'd once had.

His ghosting of her still hurt if she really stopped and thought about it, so for the past couple of years she'd tried not to. They'd been best friends, a deep rapport uncomplicated by romance. She still remembered the day when, after a few drinks sitting by a local river, he'd told her that she was gorgeous and sexy, and that he did not fancy her in the slightest. She'd been put out for about three seconds, and then she'd laughed, performing twenty embarrassing seconds of orgasmic groaning and screaming that attracted the attention of a group of older folks walking their little yappy dogs. *Harry, meet Sally,* she'd said, and then she'd pushed him down on his back and fallen across his chest, demanding that he yield. *One-ah, two-ah, three-ah!* He'd yielded, and she'd told him that she had never fancied him either. Because he was butt-fucking-ugly.

They'd known each other since the first year of high school and had hit it off over a mutual love of old rock music. He'd bought her a ticket to see Metallica when they toured for James Hetfield's seventieth birthday, and that had sealed the deal. All their friends assumed they'd end up getting together. They hadn't, and for her part it was largely because she hated being predictable. That, and he was butt-fucking-ugly.

Bethan had believed that Dean would always be there for her. The concept of 'friends for life' had never occurred to her, because she wasn't in the habit of looking that far ahead. She'd just assumed he would be there when she needed him, just like she was for him. Until one day he wasn't.

The friendship broke apart after the accident at the fracking plant. It wasn't because of what she'd done, he'd told her in the brief flurry of messages that marked their relationship's end, but because she didn't seem capable of bearing any regret. She'd told him of course she was fucking regretful, but he hadn't believed her. And even if he had, she didn't think he had the complexity of character to ally himself with someone who'd killed other people—

Just cut the line!

He believed she was a killer, and that was something she'd found very hard to deny.

A murderer, the press reports said. Never caught, never suspected, but still it was there behind her eyes every time she blinked. Dean had taken steps to ensure he could blink and sleep guilt-free.

Sometimes she wished he'd had the fucking balls to turn her in.

Now, here he was again, and still when she blinked she saw the faces of the three people who'd died after her sabotage in Alaska. She'd gotten to know their histories quite well, felt sorry for their families and kids, but she'd never really experienced the full weight of guilt. It had been a long way from murder, more an accident, wrong place at the wrong time. The fracking site had been operating illegally, and what they were doing could conceivably have led to hundreds or thousands of deaths further down the line.

As the shadow of that act settled around her once more, so did her sadness over how he had acted afterwards.

She'd tried to get him back, once, but he had not even answered that message. It was the last time there'd been any communication between them. It still smarted like fuck.

Unlike closer to the coast, where they'd seen plains of low-level shrubs and taller copses of trees, the landscape here was harsh and verging on desolate. Wide and mostly flat, with a few mounds of rocks here and there and scattered clumps of skeletal trees, a soft breeze blew west to east, driving sheens of grit across the ground and into their faces. When Bethan breathed in she picked up a chemical taint that reminded her of hot springs. They'd seen those sinkholes and geysers following a fault line on the way here in the Discovery, and she knew they'd likely have closer encounters with them on the way back.

The ground was gravelly, with exposed subsoil and hardy grasses, and here and there hazy mists flittered along with the breeze. She couldn't tell whether it was fog rising from marshy ground in the distance, or water vapour condensing as the sun performed a long slow dive towards its brief night behind them.

The afternoon cold was starting to bite but being active kept them warm. They wore hiking shoes and thermal overshirts, cheap but effective, and as long as an unexpected storm didn't roll in she thought they'd be fine. She looked ahead at where land met sky. The horizons were difficult to place and perceive, distance and perspective blurred and confused by the bland landscape. The rugged terrain could have been a pile of rocks a couple of hundred yards distant, or a small hill several miles further on. It was a disturbing effect that she hadn't noticed so much cocooned inside the Discovery. The moving box, those thin composite and glass walls, had lifted them up and out of this place and into another, ostensibly safer environment, where they breathed conditioned air and weren't subject to the unpredictable extremes of the external environment. Now, they were in the thick of it.

"How you feeling?" she asked Goyo. He did not respond. She looked at Alile, who nodded with a brief smile. *He's not too bad.* She and Alile were quite different people, but in the times they'd worked together they had developed a sort of shorthand in communicating that served them well. A look here, a gesture there. Such connections were made in extremis, Bethan knew, and they had been in a dozen dicey situations together. Bethan had once told Alile she was a gentle soul in a warrior's body.

"So what do you think?" she asked, nodding at Dean and his friends.

"I think they're fucked up," Alile said. "They confronted something they didn't understand. They're scared. They're grieving. All that makes them dangerous. Especially him."

"Wren?"

"Yeah. Mr Macho. Shit to prove."

"Yeah, I don't trust him," Bethan said.

"Don't trust anyone," Goyo whispered.

The others stopped ahead of them, and Bethan and Alile paused beside Goyo. His breath was more settled now, and he seemed to have gathered himself, though she was still worried about any injuries that might not be so obvious. She was also concerned about something that they'd only addressed in passing—could Goyo make this journey in his current state? She'd thought it, and she knew Alile and Goyo had too. Probably Dean and his friends as well, though it would only concern them if he held them up.

But saying it would make it real. If they left Goyo behind on his own, he would die.

"Feeling okay?" Bethan asked again.

"Huh," Goyo said. It seemed his vocabulary was now reduced to insignificant grunts.

"Going to pick us off one by one?" Alile asked.

"Of course not," he said. "But you two…"

"You're in no shape to look after us, even if we needed looking after, which we don't," Alile said.

"Yeah, I know that. But you're my friends. And them…" He nodded ahead at where Dean and the others now stood shielding their eyes and looking at something ahead, across the desolate plain. "They need watching."

"You still don't think we'll make it, do you?"

"I can't tell the future."

"Isn't that what you've been trying to do for years?" Alile asked.

Goyo chuckled, then he was cut off by a low voice from up ahead.

"Bethan, here," Dean said, urgent but quiet. Bethan glanced at Alile and Goyo, then hurried the dozen yards to where the others were now crouched down low.

"Compass says that way," Wren said, holding his wrist up to show his watch pointing the way. "Low ground, probably marshy in places, leading in between those hills."

"What the compass doesn't show is the polar bear," Dean said.

"Huh?" Bethan squinted, scanning the landscape left to right and back again. Perspective continued to play games with her depth of field, though with the slowly rising ground there was more texture by which to make things out. Close to them, a fold in the land hid a drop, beyond which she could make out the heads of a few trees. To the right and closer to the rising hills, mist hung low across what was probably a marshy area, speckled with startling green growth of fern and heathers, and fed by runoff from the slopes as well as the warming and melting permafrost deeper down. The steepest slope was marked with a wide, bare landslide.

"I see nothing," she said.

Dean pointed the way Wren had indicated. "That's twelve o'clock. Look at eleven."

Bethan looked, and it was then that something moved in the distance, a slight shifting against a motionless landscape. A bear, lifting its head.

"It's got two cubs," Dean said.

"Holy shit."

"What?" Wren asked.

"You ever seen a polar bear before?" Bethan asked.

They shook their heads.

"They almost became extinct a couple of decades ago," Bethan said. "Habitat change, the northern ice sheets melting. Then hunting them was outlawed, and an inoculation programme resulted in a large proportion of the surviving population being tracked, sedated and then jabbed against diseases that were running rife."

"And a result of that was a boost in population," Dean said.

"Right. A success story. But one that means we've gotta go around."

"But that valley's wide enough," Wren said. "We can avoid them."

"Momma bear won't give a fuck we're not looking her way," Bethan said. "She has two cubs and this is her turf. And she's the biggest, meanest land predator there is."

"There are six of us. We'll scare it away."

"Gonna shake your fist and swear at her?"

Wren didn't reply.

"You've still got Wren's gun," Emma said.

"Doesn't matter," Bethan said.

"Why doesn't it matter?"

"Because it's a little handheld pea shooter, and if I shoot her it'll only piss her off more. No, we'll head there, up into those low hills. Even then we need to keep an eye, make sure she doesn't decide to chase us away."

"We'll make sure she doesn't see us."

"She probably already smelled us." Bethan glanced back at Alile and Goyo and saw that they'd come close enough to hear the conversation.

"More plants that way, anyway," Alile said, nodding up at the hills.

"Plants?" Emma asked.

"Potential food," Dean said. "We'll be like a panda."

"Panda?" Wren asked.

"Eats shoots and leaves, right?" Dean smiled at Bethan, and she pressed her lips together to hold in a smirk. Still, he knew. Stuff like that wasn't lost, however hard he'd brought down the shutters between them.

"Prick," she said.

"Here." He handed her an energy bar and a bottle of water. She nodded her thanks and walked back to Goyo and Alile.

"We heard," Goyo said. "Seems right. This was never our land, less so now than ever. Let's give her a wide pass."

"This'll make the next few miles tougher than they need to be," Bethan said.

Goyo looked up at the hills, and she watched him assessing them for a second or two. The slopes were slight, the hills low. But still.

She broke the energy bar into three and passed around the bottle, trying not to meet Goyo's eye. His burns were wet now, painful to the touch and glistening with fluid as the bubbled skin tried to heal itself. His ponytail had survived, but scorched hair had twisted and melted into sculptured scabs that he had yet to pull out. Maybe he'd keep them, like the other scars he carried.

"I'm fine," he said. "Fitter than you think."

"I know how fit you are," she said. She remembered the cliff in Patagonia where Alile slipped and dropped thirty feet, skinning her right hand and cracking a rib before the rope brought her up short. She'd been swinging in space, rope snagged on an overhang, and Bethan hadn't hesitated in sliding down after her. She'd hauled her in, but it was Goyo who'd kept his composure, clipping on and then slowly pulling Alile back up until she could wedge herself safe. She'd seen him swimming against a flooded river's flow in Brazil when they'd had to sling a rope to the other side, and in Chile Goyo had run thirty miles with her on an endurance race, keeping her pace and very often setting it. He was older than her and Alile combined, and as fit as either of them. Bethan knew that fitness was a result of living a life out in the world, moving from place to place to escape not only the occasional wanted notice because of his activism, but also the painful truth of the loss of his ancestral home. Bethan had no idea how she might feel if she'd grown up so fundamentally baseless.

"Let's go that way," Dean said, pointing along a low gulley that might once have been a stream. The landscape changed quickly here—they'd seen that on the way in—and perhaps the ground had been shifted due to some unseen upheaval, diverting this watercourse into another direction.

"You're limping," Alile said. She was looking at Wren, and Bethan saw that she was right.

"Fucking boots," he said.

Bethan checked them out. The boots Wren and the others wore were dirty and scraped from their descent into the caverns, but she could still tell they were all pretty new. Expensive, too. She'd never heard of the brand but knew just by looking that these were five-hundred-buck boots.

"Limping already, not a good start," she said. "Only twenty-nine miles to go. Get some blister pads on sharpish, otherwise you'll be rubbing on raw flesh. After that, bone. You're a big guy, I wouldn't want to see you cry."

She caught the sheepish glance between Wren and Emma.

"Tell me you wore them in before coming here," Alile said.

"New kit," Wren said. "Best of the best, I thought—"

"Dean?" Bethan asked.

Dean shrugged.

"You've grown soft," Bethan said. "So you've got no blister pads?"

"They were in our first aid kits which your friend kindly burned to ash."

"Pack of pads for another energy bar each," Bethan said.

Emma took a step towards her, more out of surprise than threat. At least, Bethan hoped so.

"So we're trading now, eh?" she asked.

"I know what's yours is yours, but—"

"Bethan's right," Dean said. "We've got a long way to walk, and we have to pool resources if we're gonna make it."

Emma glared at him, then turned away. She quickly looked back again. "Blister pads?"

"Yeah." Bethan smiled as she dug into her pocket. *Guess boss woman's got pressure points on her feet and toes too*, she thought.

They applied blister pads and swapped energy bars. Before setting off again, the six of them ended up assessing what they all had between them. Bethan felt Dean glancing at her, but she left it to the end before throwing him a smile. Let him suffer a bit. She wasn't going to make it that easy for him to wheedle his way back in.

This was now, but there was history. She could never forget the hurt she'd gone through, and the pain she'd cast aside. She didn't want to feel anything like that again.

The gulley wound and twisted up towards the hill, and every now and then Alile climbed up its side to check on the polar bear and her cubs. After half an hour they were out of sight, but that didn't make Bethan feel any better. In fact it was worse: while Alile had eyes on the bear, at least they knew where she was.

The gulley ended in a rockfall. Goyo climbed out first, and Bethan saw him wincing with pain. Proving a damn point.

"That way," Wren said, pointing and consulting his watch as he did so. He started walking, glancing back to see if they were all following.

"You okay?" Bethan asked Goyo.

"Going to be a long few days if you keep asking me that every hour or two."

Few days. His vocalising that brought home to Bethan just how much of a task they had ahead of them. Hiking across landscape like this—volatile, treacherous, inimical to humans—was tough enough if they were all fit, ready and prepared. They'd faced places like this before, as a group of three and sometimes with others, and they knew the risks and dangers. But right now they weren't all fit or ready, and they were far from prepared. They had no effective camping gear, other than some foil blankets they'd have to share out later, and she already knew they'd have to huddle together in two or three groups to keep warm through the night. Fire was no problem—she thought even Dean could probably still start a fire in the wild—and their posh backpacks would likely contain lighters, or matches at the very least. But their food and water was limited, and that meant they'd be eating any edible plants they came across, and drinking from streams or pools. Plants were fine if you knew what you were looking for and, more importantly, were aware of what to avoid. If they were lucky, they might even find some fruit bushes.

But drinking wild water without any method to sterilise or filter it was potentially dangerous. Bethan's filtration bottle had been in the Discovery. Alile still had hers, but she'd admitted that the carbon filter was already old, and there was no way it would last long enough to provide safe water for six of them for several days, or longer.

And that was another worry pecking at Bethan. Three days, they'd estimated, but they'd not really examined that assessment. Emma and her companions had different things in mind, like a dead friend, a potentially dangerous contagion, and a guy gone mad and trying to trap them all so that they could die in the cold, harsh darkness.

She knew there was a good chance it would take longer than they thought. They could certainly cover the distance in maybe three days, providing Goyo held out. Dean and his friends might consider leaving him if he started to fall behind, but Bethan and Alile sure as hell wouldn't. He might be cranky and strange, but their friendship bound them tight.

However, their route would not be straight, flat and safe. They'd already seen that. Where there was one polar bear there'd be more. And wolves too, hunting a landscape where few humans were to be found. Animal dangers aside, they'd also have to watch out for threats from the changing and damaged landscape—sinkholes, geysers, poisonous gas, and who knew what the hell else.

In a group where there was already a natural schism and tempers were running hot, even three days was a long time.

She looked at Goyo again. He glanced at her and smiled, and she knew that smile. It was, *Yeah, yeah, things are fucked but at least we're together.* It was as if he could hear her thoughts, sense her cogs turning.

Bethan knew very well that Goyo was thinking the same things.

She checked the time. It was almost eight p.m., and soon the sun would kiss the horizon and dip below for a few hours. Though the nights up here at this time of year were short, they were dark and cold. She could already feel the chill biting through her clothes, made worse because of the sweat she was working up.

"We should camp soon," she said.

"It's still light," Emma said. "Why not do another hour?"

"Because this is a dangerous place," Bethan said. "Just trust that I know what I'm doing."

"And the bear?" Wren asked.

"We'll keep watch. Take it in turns. But I think we're far enough past it now."

"Good place over there, against those rocks," Dean said. "We can check the forecast, hunker down away from any breezes."

"And start a fire," Alile said. "It's going to be fucking freezing soon."

"No meat on you," Wren said.

"You sizing me up to cook and eat?"

"Ain't that desperate yet."

Dean chuckled, and Bethan smiled. She'd always liked that sound.

"I'd eat Dean first," Wren said. "More fat on him. Crackling."

Dean laughed out loud at that, and for a while as they went about selecting a place to camp, Bethan felt the tensions lessen, and a combined purpose brought the group just a little closer together.

"Someone get me some kindling," Alile said. "I will bring fire to you all."

NINE

Goyo had always been good at compartmentalising pain. As a kid, being passed around between different family members and then, eventually, into the Australian foster system, he'd always feared semi-regular dentist visits. For the first seven years of his life his teeth were fine, then when they'd had to abandon their homeland and were set adrift, his body rebelled and his teeth started moving, requiring braces in his early teens and countless dentist visits to fill cavities. He'd fainted a couple of times, and once he'd run away from his foster parents Brian and Paulina rather than have a filling. He'd liked them, and he'd felt bad when a police car picked him up and took him home to their frantic tears. But those dentist visits haunted him.

It was Paulina who'd changed his perspective. He'd never really understood what she did for employment—she said she worked in the health service, though his friends at the time said she was a quack—but she'd sat him down one day and talked to him about his fears. That had happened many times, but this one day it seemed to sink in. *Pain is transitory*, she'd said. *It's there to tell you something is wrong. Nature's warning system, if you like. Take notice of that and look after yourself, and then afterwards the pain goes away and you can't even remember what it was like. And if something hurts at the dentist, it's a good hurt. It's looking-after-yourself pain. And by the time you get home, it'll be gone.*

She'd been right. Goyo spent his next dentist visit focused on the pain rather than trying to escape it, viewing it as research more than anything else. It had hurt, true, but it was a looking-after-yourself hurt. Ever since then, his reaction to pain had been practical rather than instinctive, as much as possible. When he was bitten by a snake in Botswana, the pain told him what was wrong and drove him to the hospital. When he'd had a skin cancer removed in Toronto, the pain was fresh and rich but required no action.

Bethan sometimes called him a fucking robot.

Now, the pain was not a good pain, and it was not transitory, and it was there to tell him that something was wrong. And he wasn't sure how much longer he could fight it.

His forearm wasn't broken, but it was very badly bruised, and he was pretty sure there was deep muscle damage. He was limping a little, but thankfully his ankle wasn't as badly injured as he'd feared. The burns on his forearms and back of his hand were manageable, but the long sleeves of his thermal overshirt were aggravating the raw flesh. It was wet with fluid, and in places dead skin was hardening to a scab. The burns to his scalp and back of his neck stung, but weren't deep. His nose hurt, both from the impact on the steering wheel and then Wren's powerful punch. And his ribs ached with every step he took, and every time he breathed.

Goyo knew that if he was to make it back to Joyce Sound with the others, he'd have to dig deep and accept the pain.

Though he wasn't sure he wanted to make it back. Wasn't sure that any of them *should*. That's why he'd smashed up the vehicles. But in doing so he'd smashed himself up, and he was hurting, confused, unsure. Not certain enough to do anything final. Even if he had still carried Emma's gun, he didn't think he could shoot anyone in cold blood.

Especially not his only two friends in the world.

Deadeye, he thought, thinking back to Lanna and what he'd seen happening to her, and those bodies tied up and hidden away down in the caves. *Deadeye, or close enough to not matter.* He'd been thinking about this as he walked, considering it through the pain. He was trying to disassociate what he'd seen from the stories he'd heard, but it was difficult.

He closed his eyes, took in a deep breath, then relaxed his shoulders and back and opened his eyes again.

Emma and Dean had found some wood from a couple of small trees and Alile had built a fire. It spat and smoked because some of it was still green, but the fire held on and would give them warmth for a while.

Goyo caught Dean watching him. He looked away, and when he looked back Dean was already kneeling beside him with his pack.

"Got some basic stuff," Dean said. "We lost our main first aid kit in the fire, but I've got some more gauze, and that half a tube of antibiotic gel left over from earlier. Also some painkillers. Though I'm not sure they'll be up to the task."

"Thanks," Goyo said. "I can't see the burns too well."

"I can. You okay with me dressing them again?"

Goyo thought about that. He'd put four bullets into this guy's friend, already dead or not. Bethan had told him she believed they'd been lovers. Then he had thrown her body into the flames. And now the guy wanted to kneel behind him with a pair of scissors.

"You don't seem the murdering type," Goyo said.

"Right." Dean smiled without humour. "And we've had plenty of chances before now, you know."

"You believe me?" Goyo asked.

"I believe you believe there was something dangerous down there," Dean said. "And... the Lanna who came out of those caves wasn't the one I knew."

"You saw it well enough."

"I saw something I can't explain," Dean said. "And not for the first time. So, you gonna let me?"

Goyo lowered his head, wincing as the burns on the back of his neck stretched.

Dean knelt behind him, propping his rucksack against Goyo's side. He opened a pack of gauze and then smeared antibiotic cream on its surface, rather than rubbing cream onto the wounds. Goyo appreciated that. Dude didn't even want to cause him pain.

He caught Bethan looking and smiled. She nodded and went back to what she was doing.

"So what else?" Goyo asked. "Ouch!"

"Keep still. Let the gauze settle on the burn for a bit, the cream has some local anaesthetic in it. Won't take away all the pain, but..."

"Pain's there for a reason." Goyo looked at the ground between his feet, breathing deeply to try and hold down the vomit. The wave of discomfort subsided, and he closed his eyes for a few seconds. He heard the others pottering around the camp. Alile tended the fire; Emma and Bethan discussed supplies; Wren stood away from them, surveying the darkening landscape with a small pair of binoculars. He'd said he was going to look for lights of anyone nearby, and Bethan had rolled her eyes but let him. It seemed that for a time, Goyo had Dean to himself.

"So?" he asked.

"So…"

"What else have you seen that you can't explain?"

"Oh. Right." Another rip of a gauze pack being opened. "Er, you okay if I cut—"

"Not the ponytail."

"Sure. I'll leave that old thing hanging there. Source of your strength, right, Herc?"

"That's about right." Goyo didn't push him this time.

"I guess you know a bit about me and Bethan?"

"A little."

"Right, well, I'm not here to defend myself or change your mind, or whatever. She did what she did, which I still think was fucking awful. Can't say my reaction made me feel any better, but for me it was—"

"I didn't ask about you and Bethan. Not my business."

"No, sure. You asked about what else I'd seen that I can't explain. That's a lot to do with Bethan, actually. You know we travelled a lot together, climate activism, all that."

"Got plenty of that in my past, too," Goyo said.

"We were in Brazil this one time, trying to gather evidence against a bunch of illegal loggers," Dean said. "This was just after the government there changed and finally embraced the whole 'don't kill the only planet we've got' ethos. We were in the forests, lying low during the days and creeping closer to the logging camps at night, taking photos and filming, gathering faces and vehicle registrations. All turned out to be fucking useless, but anyway. And one day in the forest, we saw maybe fifty people from a tribe that had vanished forty years before. Just walking, carefree, right on by. Didn't seem to see us, or if they did they chose to ignore us. When they died out, they'd remained virtually uncontacted by the outside world, one of the world's last. Really sad time. And there they were, walking through the forest as if…"

"As if they still belonged there," Goyo said.

"Exactly that." Goyo heard scissors working, and the crunch-crunch of knotted hair being cut away from his burns. It hurt, but he tried not to flinch. Dean was doing his work, and telling his story, and Goyo was grateful for both.

"We described them to each other afterwards. The same thing. We saw exactly the same thing. We heard them brushing past trees and undergrowth, smelled the scent of their bodies and the paint they used as camouflage."

"Photos?"

"This was during the daytime, we were hiding out from the loggers, didn't have our cameras to hand. I'm not sure… not sure they'd have shown up on photos."

"You think they were ghosts."

"I can't say for certain they were really there. I'm not sure that's the same thing."

"Huh." Goyo waited for more, but Dean seemed to have said his piece. And moments later he sat back with a sigh.

"I think that's all I can do for you for now. Got some gauze left, but I'll save that for just in case. You know."

"In case it gets infected."

Dean picked up his pack and stood to go.

"Seems I haven't said sorry yet," Goyo said.

Behind him, Dean froze. "No. You didn't."

"I am sorry."

"Yeah. Me too." Dean walked around past Goyo, dumped his pack with the others, and took a seat close to the fire. Emma handed him half an energy bar, and he sat chewing small bites, looking into the flames.

Goyo was tired and shivering, and he knew he needed rest. He shrugged a survival blanket around him that Wren had handed out, leaned back against a rock, head resting on his backpack, and closed his eyes.

He dozed. He listened to low talk around the camp, whispers and words that followed him into sleep and informed his dreams. Next time he opened his eyes, Alile and Bethan were hunkered down on either side of him, leaning in and offering their warmth. Dean and Emma lay close to the fire, big foil blankets wrapped around them. Wren was nowhere to be seen.

Wonder where he's got to? Goyo wondered, then he drifted from awake to half-asleep again, floating along in that liminal place where senses still worked, carrying their experiences down into shallow sleep. He dreamed, but forgot what he dreamed, and the next time he opened his eyes he saw Wren silhouetted on top of a rock, sitting with knees drawn up and turned away from them. Goyo had the impression the big man was on watch, and that was a good thing.

He tried sleeping again but couldn't. The pain niggled, the cold stirred against his extremities. He stretched, and Alile snored a little and adjusted her position beside him, moving away. Goyo stood, blanket still around his shoulders, trying not to make a noise as his wounds stretched and flexed and started to hurt all over again. He waited for a while, swaying where he stood, until feeling returned to his legs.

Wren glanced at him, then looked away again.

Dean was asleep by the fire, and Emma leaned up on one arm and pushed some more wood into the flames. She knew he was there but didn't acknowledge him.

He headed for Wren, and when he reached the rock he sat upon, he walked around its base and climbed a little so that they were almost level.

"What do you think that is?" Wren asked. He kept his voice low, wary of waking the others. They all knew that rest was as important as movement if their journey was to be a success.

Goyo looked at where he was pointing, squinting in the half-darkness. It was almost a full moon, and the skies were mostly clear, so a low light silvered the landscape, taking away much of the texture and perspective. In the distance something glowed, a soft luminescence far along the valley and gathered close to where two low ranges of hills met.

"Probably not what you're hoping it is," Goyo said.

"Yeah, I figured."

"Geyser," Goyo said. "Maybe active, or could just be an open steam vent. We saw a few on the way in."

"We did too."

"They'd likely catch the starlight," Goyo said.

"Kinda pretty."

They watched together silently for a while, then Goyo offered to take watch.

"No fucking way," Wren said.

Goyo walked back to the fire. Alile and Bethan were now huddled close, so he sat with them, trying not to disturb the others. Staring into the flames, he prepared himself for a long wait, certain that he would not sleep any more that night.

He woke when the camp was hustling, with Dean kicking out the fire and the others getting their gear together. His behind was wet and cold from sitting on the ground, but he'd kept the foil blanket clasped tight around him.

"Good to go?" Bethan asked. She waited for his answer, and he saw how nervous she was at his response.

"Good to go."

Asleep, he felt like he had gathered his thoughts and settled his mind. His plan was loose but it made him feel better. If any of them were infected, they'd know before they ever reached Joyce Sound.

And Goyo would do his best to take care of them.

TEN

For every second Dean had been tending Goyo's wounds, he'd been aware that Goyo had been at his mercy. One stab of the scissors into his ear and Goyo would have been dead. One flick of a blade across his neck, and the man who'd shot Lanna would have met the justice of the wild.

None of these thoughts were serious. However unlikely it felt, Lanna had been dead when Goyo shot her. If the man had been filled with some form of simpering regret, Dean might have been more set on doing the older guy harm rather than helping him by easing his wounds. The fact that Goyo still believed that he'd done the right thing meant that he was a man of his convictions.

What stuck with Dean was that there was no way he could say for sure that it had *not* been the right thing. The Lanna who'd emerged from the cave mouth was not the one he had known. And it was not simply that she'd fallen and banged her head. The fear of what they'd seen and sensed down there, which had driven him up and out and left her behind, had taken Emma and Wren too. And that was another reason Goyo was still alive—they believed that he might just be right.

There were reasons why they'd left Lanna down there for an hour while they argued about how and when to go back for her. That grotesque crouched shape, shifting. The shadows twisting with it. The sound of its head rising, like a handful of dried sticks being twisted and cracked. And Lanna, closer than all of them, frozen—in shock, or perhaps fascination—at whatever was causing that old dead thing to move. Every moment of that had haunted his recent dreams, and when he'd woken staring into the dying flames of the campfire, for a split second he'd believed himself infected by whatever they had disturbed down in the cave, and he'd craved the sting of flames to sear away whatever taint he carried.

"Thanks for helping Goyo last night." Bethan had moved up to walk beside him. Wren and Emma took the lead, following their compass and Bethan's old-fashioned paper map down from the low hills and back into the wide valley. They were keeping an eye out for mother bear and her cubs, but there was no sign of them.

"Not a problem. Interesting guy."

"You don't know the half of it." She was trying to catch his eye, he knew, but he kept his gaze on the ground ahead as they walked.

"Mostly me he asked about, though," Dean said.

"Yeah, that doesn't surprise me."

"You talked to him much about me?"

"Sure I did. We're good friends."

"Did you think I was going to be here when you came?" he asked.

"Thought there was a chance you might be. I mean, it was you who sent me the note, right?"

He held his breath, waiting for the anger, the rage. His heart beat faster. But nothing came.

"Jesus, I'm sorry I brought you all into this," he said.

Bethan just walked. Her frequent silences if they were having a spiky conversation had always infuriated him. He knew they were meant to disarm and make him keep talking, but this time he didn't, because he honestly didn't know what she wanted to hear him say. Estranging himself from her—ending their friendship—had been a matter of self-preservation, because he could not forget or forgive what she had done. Perhaps it had been selfish, but if she'd shown any remorse at what she'd done, he'd have been there to help her come to terms with her crimes. Her lack of emotion had diverted much of the impact and guilt of the fracking site disaster and deaths onto him, rightly or wrongly. Yet still he blamed himself for not trying harder to stop her. He had known how serious she was becoming about their cause. He'd sensed her anger and seen it on enough occasions before the explosions and deaths to have tried to do something about it.

The fact that, whenever he thought about all this, he often ended up feeling more guilty than she ever had just made him more mad.

"Okay, Dean," she said at last. "I get it. But whatever you think of me, it's still good to see you. You know I'm ready to talk about it when you are."

"It?"

"You and me. That day. Everything…"

This time it was Dean giving nothing back when she trailed off. His silence was an invitation, but he also feared what she might say. She'd always been stronger than him. It was only her stubbornness that had allowed him to maintain his stance.

They walked on in silence for a while, and Dean felt that familiar comfort settling between them. There was so much to say, and yet there was also a calmness in saying nothing. Being estranged and spending years apart had not changed that, and it came as something of a shock. A pleasant shock. The weight of unsaid things was heavy, and for the first time he felt them both bearing the load. Maybe that's all he could hope for from her.

The landscape opened up before them, a strange shallow valley that looked as if a giant hand had smashed down and left a ragged impression in the terrain. Its walls were steep but navigable, and they scrambled down towards the wide sunken expanse.

"A slump," Alile said. "Saw a place like this in Russia once."

"Because of the melt?" Bethan asked.

Alile nodded. "The locals called their slump the gateway to the underworld. They said people had gone down and never returned."

"Well thanks so much for that," Emma said from where she and Wren were scrambling ahead. They'd reached flatter ground now, and the sides of the slump appeared taller down here than they had standing on the ridge. The area was miles wide and long, and the idea of skirting around was not mentioned.

Bethan and Dean walked together in silence, and he sensed the same pressure of unsaid things in her that he felt himself. *Maybe we've both left it too long,* he thought. And then the land had its own say.

The ground started to shake. Small stones and larger rocks rolled and tumbled down the steep slope they had just descended.

"Landslide!" Bethan said.

"Don't see anything…" Dean said. She reached for him and grabbed his arm to steady them both.

The shaking went from a low rumble to a violent jarring, and up ahead he saw Emma and Wren stagger back from something happening ahead of them. They were stumbling from side to side, struggling to keep their feet, and the air itself vibrated with the promise of something deeper, heavier. They walked backwards, arms held out for balance, and then Wren tripped over his own feet and slammed down onto his back.

That was what saved him.

As Wren hit the ground and Emma stumbled to her right, an explosion thudded through the earth, seeming to rend the air all around, and a violent eruption of mud, rock, and steam powered up ahead of them. Emma was caught in the blast: Dean saw her head flip back and her arm snap at the shoulder as something heavy struck her full force.

Bethan fell and swept his legs out from under him as she went, shouting something unintelligible as she rolled on top of him and pressed him face-down into the mud. The ground had gone from damp yet solid, to wet and soft, and he felt Bethan's weight sinking him down into the muck, filthy water seeping into his clothes, clogging his mouth and eyes and nose. He shoved up with one hand and rolled her from his back, turning onto his other side to face her and see past her to the eruption. He spat out rank mud and drew in a long, stuttering breath. The stench of sulphur was rich and heavy.

Methane explosion!

The roar of the blast continued, growing louder rather than fading away. A wave of wet heat washed over them. Lying beside him, facing him, Bethan's face creased as she squeezed her eyes closed, and Dean did the same. Something hit them with the force of a rolling rock, sending them spinning apart and sliding across the wet ground. He struck something hard and tried to push away from it, then opened his eyes and saw Alile, a red wound on her forehead leaking blood. She blinked at him, her eyes wide and white in the redness. He reached for her to help but she batted his hands away, angry.

She shouted something, but he still couldn't hear.

The ground flexed and flipped, winding him and sending him bouncing up and down to land awkwardly on his left arm. He cried out and could not even hear himself inside his own head.

Waves of heat came again and again, and as Bethan scampered past him and grabbed his collar he crawled after her, Alile going with them. Goyo was on his feet looking past them, backing away in shock.

"What the fuck is that?" Goyo shouted.

Dean rolled onto his left side so that he could see.

The spewing, roaring torrent of superheated steam from the new geyser seemed to fade as soon as he set eyes on it, the roar turning to a loud whistling sound that sought to burst his eardrums. The ground still grumbled and vibrated, as if moaning in pain at the wound inflicted upon it. Filthy water powered ninety feet into the air and started to fall, drifting away from them towards the west. If the breeze had been in the opposite direction they might have been steam-fried where they lay.

Emma and Wren!

He searched, but there was no sign of them. Steam and water vapour roiled, hiding the sinkhole that had not been there mere moments before. He'd seen Emma struck before she was swallowed from sight, and he feared she was dead. He didn't know about Wren, but even this far away Dean felt his eyes drying, skin stretching from the heat. When he breathed his throat burned, and the rotten-egg stink and taste of sulphur and methane made him want to puke.

"Come on!" Bethan shouted in his ear. "We'll suffocate if we stay here!" She dragged him again, and then together they stood, Dean grabbing Alile and Bethan supporting Goyo as they struggled back along the foot of the steep slope.

"Holy shit!" Bethan said. "No warning, nothing!"

"I saw Emma go," Goyo said.

"I think I saw her hit, yeah, but maybe she—" Dean said.

"I saw… her go," Goyo said, looking right at Dean, struggling with his breathing. "Wren… I don't know."

"Alile?" Bethan asked.

"I appear to be bleeding."

"Well, yeah."

"Let's move back… some more," Goyo said.

"Right," Alile said, "these things can start a chain reaction. We might be standing right on top of the next one."

"How would we know?" Dean asked.

"We probably never would. Come on… uphill might be best."

They walked a small distance up and across the low slope, then took in deep breaths, watching as the violent new addition to the landscape continued to calm. Steam and superheated gases still powered upwards, but with the pressure broken the violence was lessening, until after a few minutes there was only a soft haze rising from the new rip in the land.

Dean scoured the shattered terrain for Emma and Wren. He thought he saw Emma, a splayed shape covered in mud, unmoving, broken.

"We have to go back down," he said. "We can't just leave her there. And Wren. He might be injured. They both might need help!"

"There!" Bethan said. "See that? Is that one of them?"

Dean squinted, and then he saw Wren pushing himself up onto his hands and knees, head hanging low, mud and shale falling from his back and shoulders. He'd been almost buried by debris, and perhaps that had protected him.

"Wren!" Dean shouted, but the big man was too far away to hear, too close to the venting sinkhole. He took a step forward, but Goyo grabbed his arm.

"It's not safe," Goyo said. "He'll come to us."

"He needs help!" Dean said, shrugging Goyo off.

"I got him," Alile said. Before any of them could say anything, she was away, trotting towards where Wren was still trying to get to his feet. He was on one knee now, his other foot pressed to the ground and both hands on his leg, steadying himself, preparing to stand.

His head turned away from them, towards the fracture.

Dean saw movement there.

"What the hell is…"

"Alile!" Bethan shouted.

Wren stood quickly, swaying slightly and staring at the fading eruption, and the new sinkhole it had created.

"No one go any closer," Goyo said, and his voice was loaded with such dread that Dean glanced away from Wren and back at the older man. He was staring past them all towards Wren, as if seeing something dreadful for the first time, or the last.

Dean looked again, and maybe a hundred yards beyond Wren, three strange figures were emerging up out of the fracture.

"Impossible," Bethan said. "Nothing could be alive down there. The steam. The eruption."

"It has let something out," Goyo said.

Alile saw the movement and stopped halfway between them and Wren.

"What *is* that?" Dean asked. "They look like… it's mud. That's all. Boiling mud, forced upwards by the eruption." He said it but didn't think it, and what Bethan said next confirmed his doubts.

"Mud doesn't crawl."

The shapes were dark with muck, shimmering moist, formless and flowing in such a way that suggested thick fluidity. When Dean saw that they were shifting away from the steaming vent, he could not help but identify that as intention. The ground had fallen away some more, leaving a wider hole than he had first suspected, and the shapes were hauling themselves away from it, across rocky wet debris fallen from the eruption. The one on the left seemed to vibrate as it moved, shivering its way towards them like some huge jellyfish. One of the others rolled, a formless mass edging itself along—even slightly uphill, Dean thought—and pulsing as it moved towards them. The third thing remained motionless at the hole's edge for a while.

And then it sprouted limbs.

Dean gasped. He squinted, trying to see past the skeins of mist, wondering whether a shadow had shifted, giving the impression of form where there was only slick, muddy formlessness. Then the two lead limbs lifted, edged forward and pressed down to the ground again, and the shape dragged itself away from the hole, and he was left with no option but to believe his own eyes. It continued to work its limbs up and down into the soggy ground to propel itself away from the place that had birthed it, the movements becoming more regular and concerted.

"We have to do something," Goyo said. "We can't just let them crawl away from here, find somewhere else to spread their disease."

"You don't even know what they are!" Dean said. "Maybe they're animals caught up in the eruption, they might need our help, we can't just..."

As he spoke, he never took his eyes from the crawling, slithering creatures, and he knew that he was wrong. These weren't animals. They weren't anything he could explain. That didn't mean they were something that Goyo *could* explain, but still it filled him with dread.

"That one on the right..." Bethan said, and as Dean looked he realised why that dread was growing. It wasn't because of what Goyo had said. It was because he had seen something like this before.

That movement, the shifting limbs, so unnatural. As they watched, the figure lifted what served as its head, opened a toothless mouth, and vomited a foul stew of muck from deep inside its gut. The torrent splashed across a prone shape that Dean realised was Emma's corpse. Even from this distance he could see that she was dead—her head was misshapen and twisted too far to the side, and there was too much blood. Too much outside what should have been within.

Wren went towards the muddied forms, crouching and pulling an object from a holster on his ankle.

"He had another gun all along," Bethan said. "I wonder why he—"

"Don't go any closer!" Alile shouted. The creature on the left froze a little, then shifted direction and started pulsing, flexing, rolling towards her.

Wren fired three times. The gunshots sounded weak and distant against the vast landscape. He stepped closer to the thing with the raised head and shot it again, point blank. Its head flipped to one side but it didn't stop moving. Wren stood motionless for a second, looking down at Emma's corpse. Then he kicked the thing aside and shot it again.

The third creature froze at the sound of gunfire. Muck dripped from it in thick rivulets, and the warm, steamy air seemed to clear away some of the hot mud it had brought up out of the ground, and Dean realised that it had never been truly formless. He saw limbs, shifting and stretching as they separated from the muddy mass of its body. There was a head, raised and questing, though he could not believe it had eyes to see, ears to hear.

It scurried across the ground towards Wren, and it was only as Wren raised his foot and brought it down on the thing's head, and again, and again, and they all heard the somehow damp sound of crunching bones, that Dean realised what it was.

A person, using arms and legs to scuttle like a blackened crab.

"How the fuck can that be?" he asked.

Wren coughed and waved his hands around his head. A faint hazy cloud speckled the air around him.

"Are those... flies?" Dean asked.

"Alile, back here!" Bethan shouted.

Alile glanced around, turned to run, slipped on the wet ground. She went down on her hands and knees.

Wren saw her fall and saw the thing closing on her. He braced and fired at it, but if the bullet found its mark it had no effect.

Alile kicked, slipping on the slick ground, and as she gained her feet and started running back towards them, the figure accelerated and lashed out with one of its formless limbs.

Hands, Dean thought. *They're arms, and hands, because those fucking things are* people!

Alile fell again. This time she was tripped.

Dean started towards her, and Goyo grabbed his arm, fingers biting into his bicep. Dean actually growled—he didn't think he'd ever made a sound like that before—and when he turned to shout at Goyo it was Bethan whose eyes he met. She might have shaken her head, maybe. He wasn't sure because his vision was blurred, eyes gritty and sore. Then she looked past him and her eyes widened.

As Dean turned back, Goyo still clasping his arm, Wren fired two more shots and Alile cried out.

The shape crouched astride her on thin, insectile limbs, their ends sinking into the wet ground and bringing its face closer, closer to the trapped woman. It tensed to prop itself up, its head hanging heavy and low above Alile's. Mud and water dripped down as she struggled to kick herself out from beneath its horrendous weight.

"Too late," Goyo said, almost too quiet for Dean to hear.

"Get this fucking thing—" Alile shouted, and as Wren dashed in from the right the figure's head—

That's a person, it's a human, it used to be someone!

—switched left, right, and left again, fast and hard as if stuck on both sides by an invisible force. Then it burst. It didn't so much explode as crunch, like an egg forced apart from the inside by a weak but insistent occupant. A flap of skull the size of a hand slumped down and fell away, then other skull and scalp fragments followed, allowing a sickly flow of dark, thick fluid to patter onto and around Alile's face and neck.

"Stay back!" Goyo shouted.

Wren hesitated, looking back and forth between them and Alile. Dean saw something grab his attention then, and Wren looked away towards the new hole in the ground.

Alile shouted, an incoherent roar, and as she took in a breath for another she started coughing and choking. A hazy cloud of dark specks expanded out from the creature's ruined head, some spattering down on and around Alile, others floating in the air, flitting here and there like sparks revelling in some grotesque freedom dance. They broke down and across Alile like a fog of flies settling on something already dead.

"Alile!"

"Too late," Goyo said again, louder this time.

Bethan took a step forward, and this time it was Dean grabbing someone's arm. He had to hold on tight. He remembered how strong she was. They'd never had a fight, not a real one, but he'd always known there was a good chance she'd put him down if they ever did. Sometimes they'd joked about it. *You've got no grrr,* she'd said. *I've got the rage.* Now was not the time to test that theory.

"Maybe Goyo's right," he said.

"What do we do?" Bethan asked. "We can't just…"

"We have to stop them," Goyo said. "Alile and Wren, both of them. We can't help them, it's too late, but we have to make sure they don't get away from here."

"How the fuck do we do that?" Dean asked. He remembered the sound of gunshots and bullets thudding into Lanna's prone body, and he guessed he knew.

"Alile's going nowhere," Bethan said. Her voice broke. Dean squeezed her arm one more time, then let go.

Alile flipped onto her back and started convulsing, and then quickly grew still. Dean thought maybe she was dead.

Every part of him wanted to move forward to help her and Wren, but Goyo's warning held him back. Wren had shot and stomped two of those strange crawling shapes—

People, can they really be people coming up out of there?—

—and the third now hung motionless and broken, still propped astride Alile's motionless body.

"Like a fungus," Dean said. "It's like they've been waiting down there for however long, and now they see people they're doing that. Coming up. Fucking... bursting."

"Sporing," Bethan said.

"Maybe," Goyo said. "I think it's more complex."

"But why here, why now?"

"Intelligent disease," Goyo said.

"How can a disease know what it's doing?"

He didn't answer. Instead he shouted, "Wren! What do you see?"

Wren was standing motionless by the remains of the second crawling body he'd shot and stomped into the ground. He was looking past it and down into the sinkhole.

"We have to go to them," Dean said. "I know what you said, but that's my friend there!"

"That's our friend too," Goyo said. As if she'd heard, Alile moved again, lifelessness lifting from her body as she rolled onto her stomach and stood in one fluid movement. In doing so she shoved aside the creature that had pushed her down, kicking it away with grunts of effort and disgust. Her face was expressionless, her eyes hooded and drowsy.

Stunned, Dean thought. *She's passed out and woken with that thing hanging over her, and now she's—*

"Alile," Bethan said.

Alile tilted her head to one side and frowned, tasting the name but not recognising it. She was panting hard, as if she'd just run a marathon. A trickle of blood ran from her nose and her left eye.

She stood tall and looked around, then when she saw them she grew still for just a second or two. She let out a low, rumbling laugh. Her head tilted again and she frowned, eyes twitching and never settling on one place, one person.

Then her face slackened and relaxed. She gave them a gentle smile, turned, and started running.

Dean couldn't believe how fast she went. From motionless to sprinting, she moved past the edge of the hole and into the distance in the direction they'd been travelling before the methane pocket had erupted.

Wren saw her going, lifted the gun, but lowered it again without firing. *Too far,* Dean thought. *Too fast.* And he was glad, because he didn't want to see someone shot, whatever might be happening to them. But something else niggled at him, too. He'd seen Wren waving a dark mist from around his head, like flies buzzing at him, and he thought perhaps the big man saw no threat in Alile's retreat away from them.

Maybe he, or whatever had infected him, recognised opportunity.

"You have to stop her," Wren shouted over his shoulder, voice loud yet strained.

"Wren," Dean called, but he didn't know what to add.

"You have to stop her," Wren said again. Then, without looking back, he started climbing down into the sinkhole.

"Wren!" Dean shouted again.

A few seconds later a gunshot rang out. It sounded dull, a crump more than a shot, and its fading echo became a full stop, carrying the violence of the eruption and what had come after away with it. Relative silence settled. There was only drifting steam, a haze of moisture in the air, and those three horrible beings that had emerged from the hole in the ground, now still.

Those, and Emma's sad corpse.

"He's taken care of himself," Goyo said. "Now we have to take care of her."

"Take care?" Dean shouted. "You mean kill, right?"

"That's what I mean." Goyo looked at him without emotion.

"Your friends have all gone," Bethan said. "Help us, Dean."

"She can't reach Joyce Sound," Goyo said. "She can't reach anywhere."

"And you're going to run with us?" Dean asked.

"My leg's fine. And burns won't stop me running."

Dean shook his head, as if to expunge the truth of what was happening. The look in Alile's eyes as she'd turned and fled had been the same as he'd seen when Lanna had climbed out of those caves.

As if they had both suddenly seen and known far more.

ELEVEN

Wren paused inside the chasm as his gunshot echoed away. He checked the magazine; nine rounds left.

Call it eight, he thought. The last bullet was his, up through the roof of his mouth and into his brain. No way he was going to be like those inhuman creatures. No way.

The Glock 17 was his personal weapon, one that even Emma hadn't known he was carrying on his ankle. It was for protection, not escalation. That was why he had kept it to himself, even after the old man went mad. Pulling a new weapon when Bethan had taken his, and Goyo was wielding Emma's gun, would have been crazy. Wren prided himself on not being stupid. He forged his own path, and even though most of the time he didn't take the lead—that had been Emma's job, and he was more than happy for her to carry that weight—he remained his own person. He never stepped in any direction he did not like, nor intend.

Like now. Down here in this pit, preparing to move even deeper in pursuit of that shifting, squirming monster he'd seen from the crevasse's edge, this was still his decision. No one else's.

But they're running.

He coughed, shook his head. The stuff he'd breathed in scratched at his throat as he inhaled, scored at his skull when he thought about the others leaving this place. Alile was probably carrying the infection, maybe all of them.

They're running. See what they might be, what everything might become, the beautiful darkness of that distant shore. A dark sea on one side. A whole world breathing like us on the other, smothered with soft pale trees a hundred and fifty feet high, topped with the pregnant wonders of every possible future. Pale yellow trees, and pink, and bright red too, marching from distant hills down towards these shores, leaving only the beach free of their touch. And that dark sea, also awash with possibilities. Ready to spread. Ready to spore when the moment is right. See what they might become. But only if they run and reach, and nothing is certain, they might not get to where they're heading, so you should—

"Deeper," Wren said, and his voice stilled the shadows, hushed those insistent unknown whispers in his head. He willed away the scratching at the edges of his mind. Ignored the itching in his throat.

He was his own man.

But he could tell that the pressure was building, and his time was running out.

He plucked a flashlight from his belt and flicked it on, shining the light around even though it was still daylight up above. He was maybe fifteen feet below ground level now, working his way down the steep, broken and uneven surface of the sinkhole's sides. Rocks shifted beneath him, the ground still fluid and in motion, and the focused beam of his powerful flashlight went some way to lighting his way.

Warm mist hung thick and heavy, but it was drifting on currents from deeper down. These currents carried strange scents and faraway whispers, like uncertain mutterings of a breath held for so long. Wren tried to shut them out, to not hear. He feared what secrets he might bear witness to, were he to hunker down and open himself to them.

No. No!

Alile is running, they're all running, and they might not make it, and if that happens the long wait might begin all over again, the wait to spread our world into theirs, so you have to—

"No!" His shout was loud, so loud that it hurt his throat, but it was a good pain. A human pain. He felt shock deep inside, and he wasn't sure whether it was his, or if it belonged to something else.

He had to follow that creature he'd seen, and make sure whatever had risen was put down again.

Are you sure?

He paused and frowned at the words that came from a stranger with his voice.

"Fuck you," he whispered. He breathed in and smelled something that reminded him of rot, warm and rich and heavy. Sulphur, he guessed, but maybe it was something else as well. Those weird creatures he'd shot and stamped on up above had carried a similar taint, the scent of the land and something else besides. The musk of something once alive, now stirring again.

He smelled that now, on a waft of warm air drifting up from the deeper hollows his torch could not illuminate. Like the breath of the land laughing at him.

A vaguely human figure moved to his left and he aimed the torch that way, tracking with his gun. Shadows danced aside from the light and froze in place. Shadows, or something else. They only shifted again when he moved the light away. He breathed deeply and waited for the fumes to take him, but the sour tang seemed less rich than before.

The scratching inside his skull, at his throat. That would take him first.

More whispers buzzed around him, but they were insubstantial, suggestions of voices from somewhere near or far away, or thoughts he could not identify. They reminded him of the cloud that had risen from the ruined monster's head when he'd stomped it into the mud up above, in defiance of breeze and gravity. He'd breathed it in, while at the same time unsure whether he really saw or felt it at all. Maybe it was just black spots on his vision, ghost floaters in his eyes.

Between blinks his vision grew brighter, not darker. An alien landscape of tall pale plants, built of promise. It terrified him as he inhaled, made him feel at home as he exhaled.

Wren fought against it. He coughed so hard that his throat bled. If he could have reached inside his skull to scrape away at its itchy inner surface—

"That's what the last bullet is for."

With the next step he slipped, his foot skidding down a slope of mud and spilling him onto his side. The shock, jarring through his chest, brought him back to himself. For a second he held on, then the ground beneath him moved and he rolled with it, wrapping his arms around his head and gripping on to the torch and pistol. He could not afford to lose either.

He thudded into a rock, gasping as the breath was knocked from him. As he opened his eyes he saw a shadow retreating, caught in the beam of light and merging with darkness.

Wren struggled upright and aimed the gun, but there was nothing to shoot at. He looked up, but the sky above the sinkhole mouth was obscured by drifting steam. He might have been twenty feet or two hundred feet down into the ground.

Alile, at least. The thought was in his voice but expressing ideas he did not quite know. *Maybe the others, too. If she runs fast and keeps ahead at least she might make it to—*

He growled and stood, shaking his head to clear those thoughts and make his mind his own again. Before him the sinkhole ran deeper, but down the slope to his left he saw a tumble of broken boulders that formed a sort of artificial balcony. Water poured from a dozen places in the fractured walls and flowed into a stream, leading deeper and down into a tunnel at the end of the new hollow in the earth. The shadows seemed to shrug off his torchlight rather than swallow it.

He took a step closer and realised that the tunnel seemed somehow formed from a definite shape. Not random. Not carved and unearthed by the recent violence. It looked as if it had been here forever.

He scrambled down and across the loose sloping wall. He was covered in filth now, soaking wet, cuts and bruises stinging and singing in pain, but the closer he drew to the strange tunnel into which the filthy stream flowed, the more convinced he became that this was something unnatural.

Something made by people.

An arc of worked stone hung above the ragged opening, half-collapsed. Further in, a tumble of rocks were piled against a curved stone wall. Water flowed past and over them, heading deeper into what Wren was now certain was a human-made tunnel formed of arched stone.

"What the actual fuck?"

His only response was the skitter of tumbling stones as the disturbed ground settled all around, and the trickle of flowing water. That, and the scratching at his mind. Claws raked. Whispers insisted. He groaned and pushed them out.

Not yet, damn you, he thought, and the words were his own. He thought of his grandmother back home in Texas, eighty years old and still digging her own vegetable patch each spring, harvesting each autumn. He thought of his brother, and his wife and kids. His three nieces were the angels that watched over him, even though he'd never told them that. Their lives were what drove him, and what guided him back towards the light when he sometimes took darker paths.

Not yet, damn you.

Wren knew what was happening to him, but he would fight every step of the way, with every shred of breath left to him, to ensure it didn't happen to any of those he loved.

He ducked and plunged headlong into the tunnel, aiming the torch with one hand, pistol with the other. His feet sank into deep, wet mud, and he had to tug his boots out with every step, squelching further inside. Shining the flashlight around, he saw that the tunnel had failed in many areas, but the solid ground above retained the shape it had once formed. A pile of fallen blocks displayed old carvings long since blurred by time and water erosion, but he thought they'd once been images of some kind, perhaps ancient hieroglyphs like those they'd found down in the cave. He wondered what they said, and the idea that he would never know made him feel deeply sad. He was a speck on history. He had come and he would go without knowledge of who had made this place. Wren was not prone to such contemplation, and it surprised him.

"It's not me doing all the thinking," he said. That scratching at his throat had spread now, tingling the skin of his neck and jaw. He scratched there and his hands came away covered in blood-streaked mud. He must have grazed himself one of the times he'd tumbled and fallen on his way down here.

The insistent clawing at the inside of his skull, the efforts to penetrate his mind, betrayed no such physical signs.

"Fuck off," he muttered as he crouched and forged deeper into the tunnel. "Fuck off and—"

A figure came at him from out of the muck, rising from dark wet ground and revealing itself like a blur on reality. Wren gasped and aimed the torch and gun, and slick mud slipped from the creature as it shook itself like a wet dog. He saw its form then—long thin limbs that might have been arms and legs but which now were little more than knotted stilts; a thick, bloated body, like that of a fat spider, with leathery skin hanging in loose folds; long hair that was clotted and heavy with filth.

And its face. Wet with mud, a yawning formless mouth, and expressionless save for those eyes, rolling orbs that caught his torchlight and threw it back as an insipid yellow glare.

Wren was frozen in place, and for a long moment the figure regarded him, tilting its head this way and that as if to better make him out with its old, faded eyes.

Not yet, Wren thought, and then he shouted those words too, and he felt a darkness shrinking back inside him at the rage his voice carried.

The figure also heard, and it lowered its head and surged forward.

Wren stumbled back and tripped over the uneven ground, landing on his rump but keeping his hands raised before him, gun and flashlight aimed at the thing's head as it started to change, deform, pulse as if under pressure from something inside eager to get out.

There was a soft popping sound, four or five times in quick succession. Its eyes turned dark, and puffs of some hazy material erupted from where its ears should be.

Wren held his breath and squeezed the trigger. His shot was true, but he also knew that the creature's head was already coming apart. He heard the creak of crunching skull, bone weakened and softened by however long it had been dormant down here in these cold, damp depths, and the tearing of thin skin as its scalp and skull fell open.

This time it was more a thud than a pop, and then the air was filled with a million black specks that danced to their own tune, spinning and spiralling before zeroing in on Wren.

He fired three more times and the ragged, wretched figure slumped down. He coughed and spat, shaking his head, wiping at his ears and eyes. The scratching inside his mouth was harsher now, and with each breath he groaned with agony. It felt like fingernails were scraping his throat, and those same nails worked at his mind, slicing and winnowing their way inside.

"Not... yet..." Wren said. He stood and stomped past the dead thing, which he thought might have been dead even before he shot it and its head split open, and stalked further along the tunnel. He fought with every breath and every thought to remain himself, and he tried to keep count of how many times he had fired, focused on that last precious bullet that would be his saviour.

He touched the roof of his mouth with his tongue, exploring where the bullet would enter, and even there he felt a new stippled surface, like a rash of fresh ulcers. His tongue hurt. His teeth throbbed with each beat of his heart.

Careless now, he found himself walking easier, dodging fallen rocks and marvelling at the way the tunnel walls had held up for—

How long? Ten thousand years? Fifty thousand?

—and the deeper he went, the clearer some of those strange carvings appeared to him. He paused and examined a spread of wall where the damage was contained to only several crumbled sections. He ran his fingers across the carvings and felt rough, abraded hollows and dips, but looking he could see whole designs, entire stories he could barely comprehend. He did not know which lied, his fingertips or his eyes. Perhaps they both told different truths.

Deeper, and the tunnel took a sharp turn to the right. He paused, weak torch aimed at the turning, and wondered what would be revealed beyond.

Go back, go after them, if they catch Alile and stop her it might be up to you to—

"Shut up," he said, soft as a sigh, and he closed his eyes and took in four long, deep breaths. *I am me. I am Wren. I'm in control.*

Squirming, scratching, the other voice fell silent for a while, though he could still feel its physical manifestation spotting the skin of his arms, his throat, the roof of his mouth. He shut that out as well.

For as long as I can.

He turned the corner and ten feet away the tunnel ended in dark, open air. He took in a deep breath— staleness now, the scent of forgotten time and hot water, earth and air stirred by tumult, with only a hint of rot and decay that might have been the memory of a memory— and shone the torch down at his feet. The rough tunnel ended in a chasm. The walls were gone, and the curved roof, and across that dark space the opposing sheer wall was punctured with a ragged continuation of the tunnel, its structure fragmented, stones and larger rocks still falling away. The land seemed to move, shivering and flexing, and he understood that this was a new wound in the earth hacked here as the geyser had erupted, each of these seismic changes linked.

Wren probed the dark depths with his flashlight, but it illuminated only the sheer walls continuing down, down. Way beyond the light's reach he heard the sound of a watery torrent, and steam still misted the air. Where it touched his skin it felt warm and greasy, a living, unseen touch.

Across the ravine he glimpsed movement. He steadied the flashlight and saw wet dark figures shifting in the fallen tunnel, similar to the ones he had just seen and destroyed.

Too far to jump, he thought, and even so he considered the depths, the distance. *If I fall, I might not strike bottom.*

He could just make out the extent of the tunnel across the chasm. It was wider than where he now stood, with a back wall that appeared to be smothered with carvings. A cave more than a tunnel, a place where this passageway had once ended. There were more of those humanoid monsters stirring, shifting, rising from the filth, not truly alive but in motion. One of them scuttled and scratched for purchase before slipping over the edge and disappearing into the darkness without a sound.

Wren held his breath and listened. He might have heard an impact, or maybe not. *Poor thing*, he thought, unsure where the feeling came from. It can't have been alive down here for so long. None of them were alive, especially with what was inside them, what happened to their heads when he was close. Yet he pitied them. More than that; the fate of the one that had fallen made him feel sad.

I don't have very long, he thought, and this time the voice was his own. He was speaking logic from the depths of whatever was happening to his mind, surviving there against the infection already working in his body and striving to take control. There were four or five figures in the small cavern across the cleft in the earth. Most of them crouched, a couple stood on thin and shaky legs, a mockery of humanity. All of them were looking his way. The light caught their eyes and was reflected in the sickly yellowish orbs. None of them blinked. He wondered if they could.

As he lifted his gun, still trying to remember how many shots he had left, they must have understood that in the man who faced them—already touched by their kind and with seeds of their purpose implanted in him—there was still an element of Wren fighting to hold back the inevitable with as much will as he could muster.

One of the beings crouched, and Wren heard the sickly sound of its head crunching open as it spored. Shivering, pushing all of his self forward and into his arm and hand and finger, he focused and pulled the trigger. The bullet passed through a haze of specks dulling the harsh electronic light and exploded the creature's head. After that first shot, the rest came easier. He shifted his aim to the others and continued firing, unsure whether he was actually killing them or not.

It was the taking action that mattered.

When the gun clicked on empty and most of their wretched movement had ceased, Wren went to his knees. He realised he had forgotten to save the last bullet for himself. Instead, he started drifting away into deep, endless darkness.

In its place came the light touch of something else in his mind, and all his pain went away.

On his way back through the ancient tunnels, Wren ran his hands along the walls and heard the stories carved thereon. He felt them with new understanding and they caused him to smile, and he saw the ghosts of those who had carved these images so long ago. That was way back in a time when no word for magic was known, but even so belief in such things made magic the engine of the world. For so long these words, these intentions, had kept the deadly infection locked away from the outside world, put down and made dormant with no promise of release.

It was the bad magic of the modern world that had broken these tunnels and ancient wards, and animated the infection once again.

Wren sensed it inside him, and without. As he climbed up towards daylight, he felt the first stipple of small lumps growing inside his eyelids, and across his cheeks and nose. His throat was no longer raw and pained; in fact, he breathed freer and calmer than he ever had before. He had no worries. His past was someone else's, and the future was one step away from him, and therefore of no consequence. All that existed was the present. In the present, his mind swarmed with the million possibilities of his new, burgeoning potential.

Wren climbed out of the ravine as a new man, into a world alight with possibility. He had fresh horizons to explore and a gospel of infection to spread.

TWELVE

They ran into the afternoon, the sun chasing them and shortening their shadows.

Bethan moved ahead. Her competitive streak had eased over the years, especially since her closest friend and largest rival had ceased contact with her. Now he was back, her need to be in the lead burned bright once more. That, and the look she'd seen in Alile's eyes.

Alile was a gentle person, calm and kind, and sometimes her passivity had frustrated Bethan. She wrote, spread the word, and Bethan had once asked her whether she got frustrated with the feeling that she was shouting into a hurricane.

Lasting change comes from incremental improvements, Alile replied. *You sabotage one illegal logging operation, two more pop up the next month. If what I write changes the mind of three young people, they pass that philosophy along and talk about it with passion to their friends.*

Bethan knew that she was right. She also knew that Alile's patience was born of tragedy, and she'd never understood how that could be. Alile had seen her community in Eritrea destroyed by drought and famine, and like Goyo she had been made homeless by the fucked-up environment. How she remained so level under these conditions, Bethan did not know. Perhaps the alternative was madness.

Bethan had seen a chilling change in Alile's eyes. As she'd turned and run from them all, she had been driven by an urgent and immediate need. That was something Bethan had rarely seen before in her friend.

It made her fear for her. It made her afraid of what she had become.

I've got to keep on track, she thought, and she remembered those creatures rising up out of the mucky crevasse in the ground. *Got to keep level, maintain that distance from what's happening.* Later, she could sit down and cry. Later, she could scream and shout at the unfairness of it all. The horror.

Keep going, he thought. *For Goyo. For Dean.*

A determined Goyo managed to keep pace behind her, and she heard Dean bringing up the rear, panting hard as he struggled to keep pace. Bethan smiled to herself. Dean had always been the strongest of the two of them, and the fastest, a casual fitness that he'd carried from youth and continued into his adult years. Now he sounded out of breath after just a couple of miles. He still looked good, but he'd gone soft in the years they had been estranged.

"You sure she's heading for Joyce Sound?" Bethan asked.

"Where else?" Goyo said. "Deadeye has made her want to spread the disease. That is where the most people are. Makes sense."

"She can outrun us all," Bethan said. Alile was the true athlete of the group. That was something that as yet had gone unsaid, but Goyo would be thinking it as well.

"We can help her?" Dean asked.

"I can try."

"Like you helped Lanna, right? A bullet to the head?"

Bethan glanced back at Dean. He was panting, yes, but he also looked strong and capable. He and his team had all the expensive kit, and now he'd be realising it was all wrong. He wore those strong hiking boots, not spiked running shoes like her and Goyo. His jacket was probably worth a thousand dollars, but she could already tell he was overheating. They'd all got wet and muddy when the ground opened up, but it was above freezing, and their efforts kept the chill away for now.

"You saw those things," Bethan said. "You saw what happened to Alile."

"You're ready to kill your friend," Dean said, talking directly to her. "You're running to catch and kill her."

"We're running to stop her," Goyo said. "We can't let Alile reach Joyce Sound."

Bethan knew Goyo was not only worried about the small coastal town. He was thinking of the boats there, and the larger vessel Dean and his team had arrived on. It was always the big picture with Goyo. The big picture here was this ancient contagion—this Deadeye—breaking out from Hawkshead Island into the wider world.

"Let's save our breath," Bethan said. "I'm warmed up, you?"

"I'm good," Dean said. "What about you, old man?"

Goyo laughed. It was that genuine deep, hearty laugh of his that Bethan loved so much, and she was glad to hear it. That was his only response, but it was all that was needed.

Since leaving the site of the slump and sinkhole and coming after Alile, they had not laid eyes on her. Bethan checked the ground but she'd seen no footprints, and there was no saying they were following her route. Dean was using his compass watch, and they were following the most direct route rather than the easiest. If Alile was not quite herself—if she was being steered by some parasitic infection—Bethan thought that she would be following the same path.

The idea of chasing her friend with the intention of killing her was horrific, and when the time came she would force Goyo to hold back. There would be another way. There *had* to be another way. Goyo was obsessed, and that had already led him to put a bullet into someone's head, whether or not Lanna had already been dead. She wondered if Dean thought maybe she and Goyo suited each other. They had both killed as a result of their passions. Or their obsessions.

They splashed across a marshy area of ground in the long low valley, where small hills rose a mile distant on either side. The landscape here was veined with streams, and a low-growing heather sprayed the ground purple and pink. Bethan wasn't sure, but she thought the heather was not native to this place. Goyo would know, and maybe she'd ask him later. The seeds had likely been brought by birds, something that must have been happening for decades or centuries, but now the conditions were right for the seeds to sprout, grow and spread rather than die in the cold. The warming environment allowed that, and though it was a sign of sudden change, it was also beautiful. The land was adapting and growing as the environment around it altered with the times. She accepted such beauty where it was to be found and revelled in it. She'd always known that, however fast, drastic, and far-reaching the effects of humanity's actions, once people were gone the world would be just fine over time. There was a contradiction here that she was well aware of, but though a part of her considered humanity a blight, her fight was for its survival in the world it seemed so intent on ruining.

Marshland gave way to grassland as the land rose towards a line of low hills, their route aiming them directly towards the shoulder between two rises. The terrain became more treacherous and difficult to navigate, with folds in the land requiring them to slow their pace and shift their bearing towards the north to edge around another wide sinkhole. This one looked old, with hardy shrubs speckling its interior slopes and several small trees growing from the fertile soils within. It was shallow, and Bethan could make out the dark mouths of several caves around its base as they skirted its top edge.

"There!" Dean said from behind her, and she stumbled to a halt, scanning the hole for movement. She'd been waiting for more of those weird human monstrosities they'd seen hauling themselves up out of the ground where the sinkhole had opened up. "No, Bethan. There." He grabbed her arm and pointed, way across the drop-hole and up into the hills.

Bethan saw the movement then, a flash of Alile's blue jacket against the grey hillscape.

"She's taking the direct route," Goyo said.

"Would she do that?" Dean asked. "Those hills look gnarly."

"If she wanted to get there quickly, yes," Goyo said.

Bethan felt a moment of satisfaction at her guessing Alile's intentions, then a sinking feeling in her gut at seeing her friend still running from them. A part of her had hoped it had been panic at what had happened, and confusion, and that they'd find her curled up behind some rocks, upset, but still very much Alile. The longer they followed, the more Bethan realised that would not be the case.

It made her feel sick.

"Are we good?" Goyo asked.

They'd only paused for a minute, but already Bethan was chilled as the soft breeze kissed her wet clothing. Ten years ago it might have been four or even six degrees colder than the current three or four degrees centigrade, and the occasional waft of wind from the north reminded them of that.

"Let's go," Bethan said. "Bit of hard climbing to come, I reckon. You up for this, Dean?"

He laughed and started jogging on ahead. Bethan caught up with him, Goyo still managing to keep pace behind.

"I mean it," she said. "You're not as fit as you were. We can go on ahead if you like, you catch up with us when—"

"I'm fine." He didn't raise his voice, but neither did he look at her. She recognised the undertone of anger because she'd heard it before.

Alile was no longer in sight. Bethan didn't think she could have reached the top of the slope yet, so she was likely hidden in a ravine, behind some of the scattered piles of rocks, or pursuing her course sheltered by one of the wrinkles in the land. Though the landscape was harsh and desolate, there was still plenty of plant life here, and that would also make it harder to spot Alile in the distance.

They forged on, reaching a steeper slope that slowed their climb and forced them into a scramble. Dean caught up with Bethan again and carried on beside her. Goyo brought up the rear. It was still Dean she heard breathing loudest.

"So… how've you been?" he asked.

"You fucking kidding?"

He grunted, pushing hard and scrambling up a smooth slope of shale. "Good a place as any to ask."

"For five years you haven't cared."

"You really think that?"

She shrugged, then realised he was watching his footing, not her. "Dunno."

"I've always cared," he said.

"Weird way of showing it."

"I just couldn't… be around you anymore."

"Oh, God," Bethan heard from behind them, and she grinned. Goyo hated this sort of shit. She'd talked to him about Dean, of course, but his reaction had always been *Pick up the phone if you give a shit.* He wasn't one to dwell on the complexities of human relationships.

"So now you want to know what I've been doing these last five years."

"Just asking."

"If you wanted to know, you should have called."

"You never called me."

"I did, actually," Bethan said, and she remembered it now, the drunken message, her efforts to retrieve it and delete it resulting in a second, more garbled message left on his phone. She'd not been able to recall much about it the next day, and she'd convinced herself that was why she'd not called him again. Embarrassment. Maybe that was a part of it, but there was also pride, and an arrogance in believing that what she'd done was… if not right, then at least not wrong. The accident, the deaths, were an unavoidable consequence of what they were trying to do. She'd never seen their sabotage of the fracking site as one step too far. It had been essential, but sour luck meant it had ended badly.

"I remember," Dean said.

They went on in silence. Bethan concentrated on climbing, relishing the burn in her thighs, calves and Achilles, careful not to overbalance and fall backwards. A colder breeze blew up here, and once they reached the ridge she knew that they'd be exposed to the harsh elements. With no fresh kit, they'd have to put up with the discomfort until they reached Joyce Sound.

"Remember that time in Vancouver?"

Bethan laughed. She couldn't help it. It had been one of their good times together, a drunken evening when their friendship felt solid, secure, and precious. Dean had always said they were no Harry met Sally, and she'd treasured their uncomplicated affection for each other. A night on the town with friends in Vancouver, a few drams of good whiskey in her hotel room, then they'd gone out onto the balcony to share a joint. It had made him almost poetic, and that night his poem had segued into a moment etched on her mind, and obviously his as well.

The moon had been full, their eleventh-floor hotel balcony bathed in silvery light.

"Two souls, adrift and high," he'd begun, continuing through her giggles, and his own. "And relishing in flight, drifting on the moment between moments, whispering secrets on the breath between breaths, affording the weight of... holy shit, that lucky bastard's getting a blowjob!" He'd pointed at their neighbouring building where a bedroom was brightly illuminated, curtains drawn back wide, and two people frolicked naked on top of the bedding in an obvious invitation for voyeurs to have some fun. Bethan had squinted and looked closer, then she laughed out loud.

"Didn't know you were that way inclined."

Dean had burped softly and raised his whiskey glass. "I'll have you know I'm actually quite a big fan of blowjobs."

"From another dude?"

"Huh?" He'd looked closer and seen what Bethan had seen, and they'd both creased in half laughing.

"What happened in Vancouver?" Goyo asked.

"You had to be there," Bethan said. She glanced across at Dean, both of them sweating, both sharing a grin that could only exist between people with deep history.

"I'm sorry it happened that way," he said softly.

Bethan snorted, but it was through her smile. "Doesn't matter now. Not now. Let's… later."

"Yeah, later." Dean laughed again. "So, you think I've gone soft."

"I was only saying—"

"Race you to the top."

"Fuck's sake," Bethan heard Goyo muttering behind them, then Dean was away, and so was she. Her muscles and lungs burned as she tried to reel him in from his two-second head start, and she checked the slope ahead of them, looking for the best line, avoiding places where she might slip and choosing places where rocks or dips in the land offered small steps to give her added power. They climbed that way towards the ridge, taking turns in the lead, and for a few moments Bethan almost forgot what had happened. She was in the moment, living step by step with her heavy breathing as company, and that of Dean alongside.

Then Goyo called out to them and the moment was shattered. The horrific deaths came in again—Lanna, Emma and Wren—and the fact that they were chasing down her friend, infected with some weird contagion they'd taken to calling Deadeye but which in truth was unknown, perhaps unknowable. Nothing about this was right. She had no right to think fondly of the past when the present was so fucked up.

"Hey, you two," Goyo called. Bethan paused and looked back and down, expecting to see him urging them to slow and conserve their energy. He was right, they should be taking it easy, injuring themselves now would do no one—

"Look! *Look!*" Goyo was pointing across the hillside, and when Bethan followed his gaze, at first she couldn't see anything amiss. She wiped sweat from her eyes. It was Dean who saw.

"Oh, now that's just not fair," he said.

Bethan wiped her eyes again, then saw the polar bear shambling across the slope and heading up towards them. It was some distance away, but even so its shape and intention was unmistakeable.

"This one got cubs?" she asked.

"I can't see," Goyo said.

"Er… we should perhaps get moving…" Dean said.

"Yeah, it's pretty far away for now," Bethan said. She felt a tingle of fear. She'd once confronted a polar bear close-up in northern Alaska, and she knew how vicious and powerful they could be if the mood took them. They were the toughest land predator, and advice about dealing with them always amounted to stay the fuck away if at all possible.

"Goyo?" He remained shielding his eyes and watching the bear's approach, frowning. She looked again. It was below them along the slope, and this time she noticed that it was not coming directly at them.

"I think maybe our friendly bear might even be doing us a favour," Goyo said.

"Huh, how's that?" Dean stood beside Bethan, resting one hand on her shoulder as he also shielded his eyes against the low sun.

"Don't look at the bear," Goyo said.

"What the hell's that, standard advice?"

"No, I see now," Bethan said. She leaned into Dean, pointed directly at the bear, then shifted her aim just ahead of it across the slope, and closer to them.

"What the…?" Dean muttered.

"I see two of them," Goyo said. "Maybe three. Moving fast, but not fast enough to get away from the bear."

"What are they?" Dean asked. "Wolves?"

"Not wolves," Goyo said. They watched for a while, trying to make out exactly what the polar bear was chasing. Bethan's stomach sank because she was already pretty sure.

"No, not wolves," she said. "*Them*."

"Those things from the sinkhole?" Dean asked. "How the hell can they have been following us all this time? Didn't Wren stomp on them?"

"These aren't from there," Goyo said. "They've come from somewhere else."

"I don't understand," Bethan said.

"I think I'm starting to," Goyo said. "Come on, let's climb. I don't know what the outcome of this will be. I'd put my money on the bear, but whatever happens we need to be ahead of whoever wins."

Still watching for signs of Alile, they continued climbing, slower than before and staying closer together. Any sense of competitiveness had vanished. Bethan kept glancing back over her shoulder, and down the slope towards the lumbering bear and the two figures it seemed to be pursuing. They scampered ahead of it, sometimes upright, other times moving on all fours, and she was almost certain they were humans, like those strange figures that had come up out of the ground and died at Wren's hands. Or had once been human, at least. They seemed similarly filthy, which made them difficult to make out against the land's background colours, and the bear spared no time closing on them. They appeared to have no element of speed or surprise. Goyo called a halt just a few minutes later. They could not climb and watch at the same time.

And Goyo needed to watch.

The bear lashed out at the first figure it reached, knocking it aside. It sprawled, rolled upright again—Bethan was reminded of a giant beetle on its back, spinning and twisting to gain its feet once more—and then the bear was on it, stomping with its front paws and lowering its head to bite.

It was too far away for them to hear anything, but Bethan imagined the sound of soft, wet crunching as the bear lifted its prey and shook its head. Old flesh, old bone, rank rotten crunching.

"Holy shit, the other one is…" Goyo started, then they all saw the second monster leap at the polar bear. It landed on the creature's back like a large spider. The bear dropped the thing in its mouth and turned in a circle, reaching back with its jaws, and even from this distance Bethan heard the distant *clack-clack* of its deadly teeth meeting as it snapped at its attacker. After several attempts the bear caught one of its limbs and straightened, tugging the arm out at the root. It spat out its prize then turned the other way, and this time when it clasped a trailing leg between its teeth and pulled, the skinny body flipped through the air and slammed onto the ground. The bear roared in triumph, then the mutilated figure raised its head. And it burst like a ripe seed pod.

"Did I just see that?" Dean asked.

The bear stomped on the thrashing monster, then crouched down and bit into its chest. It was still writhing, its remaining limbs waving and clasping, clawing at the bear's fur. The bear lifted it with ease and shook it back and forth several times, and the humanoid beast came to pieces in its mouth. Torn and tattered body parts scattered.

The bear let go and started wandering left and right, stomping down and snapping with its powerful jaws. It roared again, and its voice seemed to fill the whole landscape. Then it slowed, slowed, and came to a standstill for a long moment, head dipped as it stared at the ground. Motionless.

"What's it doing?" Bethan asked. "Is it hurt?"

"Not hurt, I don't think," Goyo said.

"What, don't tell me animals can catch Deadeye too?" Dean asked.

Bethan glanced sidelong at Goyo. He caught her eye and looked away again.

She unzipped her jacket and pulled Wren's gun out from her belt.

"Don't be stupid," Goyo said. "If it does come for us we'll just have to stay ahead, if we can. If we can't, we should keep close together, make as much noise as possible. Scare it off."

"But if it's infected?" Bethan asked.

Goyo shrugged. "If that's the case and it comes for us, it'll spore in whatever way a polar bear might spore. Best way to protect ourselves then is to split up. That way it'll only get one of us at a time. But that's not something I want to be anywhere near."

"Where the hell did those things come from?" Dean asked. "Were there more down in the sinkhole in that slump, do you think? Maybe they came up after Wren went down there and shot himself."

"No, I don't think they were from that same sinkhole," Goyo said. "I've got some ideas about that. But let's get up to the ridge first, see if there's any sign of Alile. She's our priority."

"Staying alive's mine," Dean said.

"No," Goyo said again. "Stopping her. Let's move."

They headed out again, Bethan taking the lead, and she kept one eye on the polar bear. After a few minutes it started wandering away from them, back down the hillside from where it had come. It moved slower now. She wondered why it had been chasing those things in the first place, and where the hell they'd come from.

If Goyo really did have an idea about that, he'd tell them when he was ready.

They soon reached the ridge, still with no sign of Alile. It was the lowest point between the higher hills, and as they crested the top the view over the other side opened up. The lowlands were swathed in mist, and to the west and north were several steaming vents in the ground, the source of much of the moisture in the air.

They scanned the landscape around them, looking for Alile. The slope they'd come up, the wide shoulder between hills on both sides, the rises of those hills, and down ahead of them into the lowlands. They found no sign of her anywhere.

"You really think she made it all the way up here without us noticing?" Dean asked.

"Some shallow ravines over there," Goyo said, pointing towards the northern hills. "Might've made it up and over that way, keeping herself down below our sightline."

"Or maybe she just made it while we were watching the bear take on those things," Bethan said.

"Could be," Goyo said.

"So we head down there," Dean said. "Assume we're still following her, hope we just stumble across her in all that." He nodded down at the wide open landscape ahead of them, much of it swathed in mist.

"We head direct for Joyce Sound," Goyo said. He pointed towards the west. "That way?"

Dean consulted his watch compass and nodded.

Goyo took a drink from the bottle on his belt and nodded at the others that they should do the same. "Just a sip. Damn, this landscape won't make tracking easy."

"Wait, you can track her?" Dean asked.

"Maybe," Goyo said. "Got to pick up a trail to follow it, though." He kicked at the surface beneath his feet. Small stones skittered away, and a tuft of tough grass curled up.

"So what else are we likely to encounter?" Bethan asked. "You said you might have some ideas about those mud monsters."

"They followed us," Dean said. "Gotta be."

"No," Goyo said. "Not gotta be. In fact, unlikely. You saw how they were moving, awkward and slow, and how easily the bear chased them down. I think it smelled them first from some distance, came looking, found them, and beat them."

"So where the hell were they from?" Bethan asked.

"I think… and this is all guesswork. But I think there might be people like them, infected people from fuck knows how long ago, dormant and hibernating in other places across the island. Who knows what happened here in the past, how many caught the disease, and who put them down? You saw those figures in the cave, Dean. Tied up, tied together, so they couldn't move even in death."

"But how would they all wake at the same time?" Bethan asked. "What, they heard us? Know we're here?"

"You've seen when flying ants leave their nests, how sometimes it happens all at the same time, in countless nests spread across miles of terrain?"

"When conditions are right," Bethan said.

"Maybe. But there's also a theory that there's some sort of communication between those nests, some way they know when the time's right, which benefits them all. Millions of ants taking flight all at the same time ensures the chances that hundreds or thousands will survive and initiate new nests." Goyo frowned. "A web of some kind, like a mycelial network maybe. Waking now that it's no longer frozen in the permafrost."

"But these are people," Dean said. "Yeah, I saw them down in the cave, and the one that seemed to shift and move. It was a fucking *person*, maybe frozen or whatever, dormant down there and starting to thaw and shift when the warmth of our torches touched them."

"I saw it too," Goyo said. "It was a person once, but no more. Now these things are vectors for the disease. They're carriers. The disease drives them. Puts them down to sleep for long, long periods—millennia, maybe tens of thousands of years—and now they're waking up. Spreading the disease among the living, even though they're not quite alive. Not in any way that we understand."

"Wait, you're saying…" Bethan paused, unable to verbalise what Goyo was hinting.

"I'm saying the disease is intelligent, even sentient, and that it's finding a way. One or two bodies wake in that cave, and maybe they infect someone to spread the love, maybe not. But if a dozen hibernating vectors rise up in half a dozen sites *at the same time*, the chances of infection and proliferation increases exponentially."

"Why here, and now?"

"I guess it's just been waiting for the right moment."

"And Dean and his friends woke it up," Bethan said. She looked at Dean. "You made the moment right."

"Yeah, well," Dean said, but there was little else to say.

"We need to find Alile," Bethan said.

"I've been thinking about that," Goyo said. "We're flailing around out here, looking for her. If we can find her, that's good. But getting to Joyce Sound has to be our number one aim now."

"Then what?" Bethan asked.

"Then we convince them of everything I've just told you."

Dean looked away again, down across the landscape they had yet to cross.

"And yes, I know," Goyo said. "That might not be the easy—"

"Hang on," Dean said. "There! Am I seeing things?"

Bethan looked to where he was pointing and saw the small blue speck set against the darker landscape. "Alile," she said.

"Okay, Alile," Goyo said. "We good?"

"Very much no," Dean said.

Goyo had already started running. Dean and Bethan followed.

Bethan remembered that night around their campfire between two tributaries of the Amazon, the things Goyo had told them both about what he feared. She'd let herself forget over the years—or more likely she'd willed herself to forget, because what he'd said was so disturbing—but those stories of dreadful histories continued to haunt her now. Goyo believed they were living through an awful story of their own, and she could not help but believe him. He didn't let much phase him. This, here and now, was what he'd been terrified of his whole life.

They hurried downhill towards the wide valley laid out before them, and it might have been beautiful on any other day. The gently sloping hills on three sides were speckled with copses of short spindly trees and swathes of dark, low grasses, and ferns and low heathers grew around tumbled rocks. The low sunlight cast long shadows and enriched the purples and yellows of hardy plants. Here and there a light mist rose lazily from frequent sinkholes until it was caught by the northerly wind shushing over the ridge to their right, casting a low haze across the valley that seemed almost in reach. Bethan was quite certain they had not driven this way in the Discovery, and there were no signs of vehicle tracks in areas of damp ground further down the hillside and across the lowlands. Hawkshead Island was remote, and it was possible that no one had been in this valley for years or even decades.

Close to the base of the slope they were now descending, a blue figure writhed on the ground.

"What's happened?" Goyo asked as they hurried downhill.

"Sinkhole?" Dean asked.

"Quicksand," Bethan said. "The ground's grown soft, water flows down from the hills, and…"

"She would know," Goyo said. "Alile's been in dangerous terrains just like you and me."

"Is that Alile, though?" Dean asked. "I mean, after everything you've been saying?"

No one answered. They kept their breath and concentration for the descent, arms loose by their sides ready to swing out for balance, running from shifting shale to rocks to wet mud, and soon they approached where Alile was struggling up to her waist in black, marshy soil.

"Not too close," Goyo said, and Bethan wasn't sure whether he meant to Alile, or to this part of the land drawing her down.

Alile was facing away from them, and at their approach she ceased her struggles and froze in place. Then she turned around and looked over her shoulder at them, and started moving again. Her movements were weaker than before, slower, and she looked back and forth between them.

"Help me," she said.

Dean surprised Bethan by being the first to approach her stricken friend.

"Just keep still," he said. "Try not to struggle, it'll only make you—"

"Why did you run?" Goyo asked.

"I was… It was horrible, I didn't know what was happening, something hit me on the head and I was confused."

"And now?" he asked.

"Now I'm… glad you're here. Sorry, Goyo."

Bethan frowned. Something was wrong. Or was it those stories Goyo had planted, tales destined to instil paranoia and suspicion?

"We'll take this nice and slow," Goyo said. "Find something to throw to you, a branch or something, that'll support you until we can get you out."

"Thanks," Alile said. Her voice, her tone. She smiled at Goyo. Bethan still thought something was wrong, other than the obvious fact that they were watching their friend sinking, slowly sinking into this land that seemed set on taking them all.

Dean was already looking around for something they could heave out over the wet marshy quicksand. Alile watched him, and it was as if she felt Bethan watching her. She turned and smiled at Bethan, holding her eye, and it was then that Bethan realised what was amiss.

Alile never looked anyone in the eye for more than a second or two. Not even her friends. In any conversation she'd look back and forth between people, or stare over Bethan's right shoulder, or look at her throat. She'd never asked her why. It was just a quirk.

"You okay?" Bethan asked.

"Sure, Bethan," Alile said. "Hunky dory." She smiled, still holding her gaze. Bethan tried to smile back. That was when Alile, or whatever held her in its thrall, realised that she had been seen.

Her smile faltered a little, then fell away. She started struggling again, grunting as she fisted her hands and pushed at the wet ground to get out, get free, get at them.

"Alile, wait!" Goyo said.

"That's not Alile," Bethan said. "Not completely."

"Help me!" Alile said, voice high and pleading, still punching at the ground as if to beat it into submission. "Bethan, please help me!"

"What do we do?" Dean asked. Bethan couldn't answer. She could not bring herself to shoot her friend, because murder was not her thing, whatever Dean might have thought of her over the past few years. And though Alile met her eyes and held her gaze, that was nowhere near reason enough.

"What do we fucking *do*?" Dean asked.

It was Alile who answered for them all.

Her eyes flooded red with blood and started bleeding, slow slick tears that ran trails through the mud on her cheeks. Her mouth dropped open and her tongue writhed swollen, sprouting purple spots that quickly burst in small bloody pops. She shivered where she was stuck in the ground, sending slow thick ripples across the surface of the glimmering mud.

"Bethan, help!" she said again, and this time her voice was loaded with pain and desperation. Filled with Alile.

"Alile—" Bethan said. But it had always been too late.

Alile's head cricked on her neck, bending so far to the right that Bethan heard the crackle of breaking bones. Her left eye popped, sending blood and clear, gelatinous fluid spilling across her nose and mouth. She opened her mouth to scream again, and more blood pulsed from between her teeth and her engorged tongue pressed against them, bubbling and foaming red as the scream died on her lips. Her mouth started working, teeth clacking together straight through her tongue. It dropped into the mud. Her eyes went wide, panicked and pleading.

Bethan pulled her gun.

Dean came at her, shoving her to the ground and grasping for the gun. It fired, the bullet going wide. He landed on her and flailed across her body with both hands, holding the gun and twisting it in his hand until she let go. He rolled from her, sat up and looked back at where Alile still struggled.

"Give it back!" Bethan shouted.

"Wait!" Dean said. "Maybe she..."

"*Look* at her, Dean!"

Alile's eyes were wide open, sightless red ruins. Her head was so strained onto her right shoulder that the skin of her neck had split, and the fluid pouring from her ruptured eye turned dark. As it flowed, part of it seemed to evaporate, speckling the air around her head. A rash of red-raw boils across her throat and neck popped with a sound like bubble-wrap being twisted, emitting small cloudy puffs that looked like flies, but weren't.

Goyo snatched the gun from Dean's hand, aimed, fired once.

The bullet flicked at Alile's ear. She screamed, and Bethan had never heard a sound like it, a wailing screech through blood and her lacerated tongue, filled with anguish and terror and pain, and Goyo's next shot hit Alile beneath her raised right arm. She shuddered, and Goyo fired two more times. Both bullets struck her head, helping whatever sick process was already underway.

The soft wet ground around Alile splashed with gore and shattered bone. The air blurred with a cloud of dark specks.

Bethan sobbed, a coughed exhalation of raw shock and grief.

"This way," Goyo said, grabbing Bethan's shoulder and pulling. "Dean, this way, upwind of her, fucking *upwind*!"

Dean was already scrambling away, and Bethan found her feet and followed, backing across the slope so that she could keep watching Alile. She needed to know she had not shrugged her way out of the quicksand and was now coming towards them.

She needed to know her friend was dead.

"I couldn't let you…" Dean said. He was staring at Bethan wide-eyed, as if seeing someone he'd never seen before.

"Didn't you hear her?" Bethan shouted. "Didn't you see she was hurting? The real Alile, inside, she was fucking *screaming*, and you let her live through that!"

"Not his fault," Goyo said. "Alile. Poor Alile."

Bethan was shaking, heart rate elevated, and even though the air was cool she felt warm and sweaty.

"I just shot my friend," Goyo said.

"She was hurting," Bethan said.

"But I still shot her. I ended her."

Bethan looked away from Alile at last, and directly at Dean. He looked just the same as he had the last time she'd seen him years before—there were no more wrinkles, no grey hairs. It was as if he was a product of her mind, not his own person, there as a subject of her own anxieties and errors. He was back again now, and she had fucked up again.

"So just what the fuck do we do now?" she asked.

Goyo didn't answer. He was looking at Alile, tears in his eyes.

"Goyo?" Dean asked.

"All my fault," he said. "We should have driven back to the coast after I'd sealed the cave. Lanna was finished, but no one else was, not back then. We'd have missed the sinkhole in the slump, probably. Safe and sound in your high-tech vehicle."

"But what if one of us *had* been infected," Dean said. "Don't beat yourself up, Goyo, you did the—"

"What if one of us is?" Bethan asked. She struggled to her feet, pushing away from the two men. Tears blurred her vision. Alile whispered to her, laughed, smiled in her mind's eye. Always smiling. She tried to breathe calmly and settle her galloping heartbeat, but her stress levels were through the roof, adrenaline pumping, senses sharp. Fight or flight was controlling her, not the other way around.

"I think we'd know," Dean said. "Wouldn't we? I mean, I know *I'm* not infected, so—"

"Goyo?" Bethan asked.

Goyo was still looking at Alile. Her body was slumped over in the wet ground, still buried almost to her waist but no longer sinking deeper. It was as if now she was dead, the land no longer wanted her. Blood pooled and speckled the surface of the wet soil, dark and glimmering like a slick of oil. She was leaned forward, forehead touching the ground, hair loose and knotted with clumps of matter that should have been inside her head. *All those beautiful ideas*, Bethan thought, as if Alile's character were visible in the stuff she now saw. Maybe her thoughts and dreams had flown away with those other things from inside her head. The spores, the taints of Deadeye that had used her as an incubator, now lost to the breeze.

"No, I don't think we would know," Goyo said. "Certainly not about each other. Maybe not even ourselves."

"Well, I know I'm okay," Dean said again.

"How?" Goyo asked.

"Because I feel fine."

"People who have terrible diseases often do, to begin with. That's how it gets them. Only makes itself known when it's too late."

"We can't shoot ourselves because there's just a remote fucking chance!" His words hung on the air, unanswered.

Goyo would have, Bethan thought. *When he crashed the vehicles, that's what he was thinking. Sacrifice us all, just because there's a chance.*

"No," Goyo said. "But we can be careful. Bethan, how did you know?"

"Know what?"

"Alile. She was asking for our help, she sounded like herself to me. Wretched and scared, which is something I'm not used to with her. But it was her voice. Her words and thoughts."

"She met my eyes," Bethan said.

"So?" Dean asked.

Goyo nodded and wiped a hand across his face.

"Someone going to explain?" Dean shouted, taking a step back.

"Alile never looked you in the eye when she was talking to you," Bethan said. "At least, not for long."

"That's it?"

"That's enough," Goyo said. "She was still Alile, but something else was steering her. Controlling her. We saw that at the end."

Dean looked at Bethan, eyes wide. *He wants me to see that he's really him*, she thought. She breathed deeply, feeling her heart starting to settle at last. She breathed, and breathed, and realised that none of them could be at ease anymore.

"We should bury her," Dean said. Bethan knew they could not, but it was Goyo who verbalised it.

"None of us can go near her," he said. "We should get away. Keep upwind as we move on. The infection is probably still in her."

"But isn't she... I don't know. Spent?" Dean asked.

"I really don't know," Goyo said, and he sounded so tired. Almost defeated. Bethan hated that.

"But isn't there a test, or something?"

"Don't you think Dean is acting strangely?" Goyo asked.

"He's scared, just like us."

"No. No, I think he's changed. Something's—"

"I'm fine!" Dean said. "I was just asking if there's any way we can test whether there's an infection. Something in the blood, maybe."

And then Bethan realised what Goyo meant. She remembered what he had done when he'd come up out of that cave and seen Lanna lying there dead, covered in a blanket, the others hanging around not really knowing what to do next. He'd said he was going to put a couple of bullets in her head. And then the blanket had shifted as Lanna, dead and still and breathless, had moved.

But it hadn't been Lanna moving. It was whatever had taken her down in the cave.

Goyo lifted the gun and aimed it at Dean's face.

"What the hell?" He backed away, hands held out ahead of him, as if flesh and bone could stop a bullet. "I'm fine, I was just asking—"

"You've got it!" Bethan said. "Step back, step *back*!"

Dean stumbled back, hands still held up, and she hated the fear on his face, and the belief in his eyes that he was about to die. Goyo maintained his aim, Dean protesting.

After half a minute Goyo said, "Reckon if you were infected, you'd have spored if you thought I was about to blow your head off."

"Huh?" He looked from Bethan to Goyo, back again.

Goyo lowered the gun.

"Lanna started moving when I said I was going to shoot her. Even though we all thought she was dead."

"But she didn't spore when you *did* shoot her," Bethan said. "Alile did. Why?"

Goyo shrugged. "Maybe because the infection wasn't fully established in Lanna. She'd only been exposed an hour before. Maybe it takes a good while longer for it to take full control of the body, the mind, and that happened in Alile." He shook his head. "I don't know. I don't know anything."

"I didn't think you were going to shoot me." Dean laughed, nervous and high. "Not really."

"Huh. Then no. There's no test. Unless I shoot you in the gut, see what happens then."

Bethan looked past them both at Alile. *I'm so tired*, she thought. *I'm so sad.*

"I've cut myself," Goyo said. He held up his hand and showed them an angry pouting wound around the base of his thumb. "I thought maybe the blood might be different. Thought I would see something in it, if I was infected."

"Surely we'd know anyway?" Dean asked. "You've got the gun."

"Maybe, maybe not," Goyo said. "I'm guessing that depends on whether you knowing or not benefits the Deadeye."

"But we're learning, Goyo," Bethan said. "Every one of us that dies is another lesson taught. And that's why we have to reach Joyce Sound. Dean, whatever you and your group exposed and released down there, it's spreading. Goyo could put a bullet in our heads and here and now, but the risk remains. Right, Goyo?"

Goyo nodded once. "Wasn't sure what my intention was. Maybe kill us all. Now, you're right. We have to warn Frank and the townsfolk. The islanders need to know. They need to be ready."

"Ready to do what?" Dean asked. He nodded at Alile, slumped and still, and dead. "How can you stop what came out of her? It's like trying to shoot snow."

Bethan went to reply, but realised she had no answer. Goyo was similarly quiet. She took a sip of water from her bottle. She couldn't help looking at what was left of Alile, her friend and companion. *We did her a favour*, she thought, but it would take a good long while for that concept to properly land.

"How far?" Goyo asked.

"Maybe fifteen miles to the coast," Dean said, consulting his watch.

"Tired, old man?" Bethan asked.

"Screw you, youngster."

None of them even smiled.

THIRTEEN

Dean had never felt fully settled with the decision to cut himself off from Bethan—in some ways it had always felt temporary, though he'd not seen a clear route through to it changing—but the more time that went by, the harder it had been to go about changing how things were. Moving into working with Emma and her crew, meeting Lanna, making good money illegally prospecting for rare earth minerals, had all contributed to his sense that he wasn't being true to himself. The values he'd stood up for when he and Bethan travelled and protested together remained, but they'd been tainted by what had happened between them. Even though he pumped most of the money he earned from his expeditions into causes that Bethan would have supported, Dean could never shake the belief that it was he who had betrayed their friendship, not her. That idea bit deep, because it was *her* betrayal that he grabbed onto as being the cause of their rift. Her activism, driven from an honest desire to do good, had resulted in deaths. The moral high ground had been his, yet he had spent the past few years looking upwards for the truth. Calling Bethan to the caves had been his way of finding it again.

As they moved for the coast, he tried to analyse what he thought, what he felt, and whether those doubting thoughts and feelings were all his own. Grief bit deep, for Lanna and Emma and Wren. Horror at what they had awakened, and the many terrifying things they had seen and done. And he had brought Bethan and her friends into the bleeding heart of this horror. How could he *not* feel different and confused?

He was Dean, with his own memories, his own desires and regrets and anxieties, and deep down he still found those things he had never told anyone, ever. These were still his own, private and secret. He found nothing else lurking, no shadowy presence crouching behind those deepest parts of him, yet he had no idea if this meant he was not now a carrier for the strange infection. That old dude Goyo claimed to know more than anyone about it, yet in reality he knew hardly anything. Dean felt more adrift and alone than ever.

He assumed that Bethan and Goyo were going through the same internal dialogues. Or perhaps they were thinking nothing of the sort. Maybe they were both running through moment after moment, bearers of this new and ancient disease, carrying it towards the coast, and beyond.

"I'm me," he whispered as he ran, too quiet for the others to hear. "I am me."

Streams criss-crossed the land, and they headed west, following whatever small waterways carried on to the sea. The gulleys the little tributaries had carved into the land were not yet deep, so the flow was recent. But they were still deep enough to conceal.

Bethan skidded to a halt first, and Goyo ran into her, sending them both sprawling. Dean stopped beside them and immediately caught sight of what Bethan had seen.

A tall figure unfolded itself from behind a rock, like a giant stick insect extending its arms and twisting its head on a thin, ravaged neck. It was human, but beyond that Dean could not tell its age, sex, or how the hell it was still moving. *Still alive?* he thought, but that was a nebulous concept, and he couldn't analyse it too closely. Not now. Maybe later, if and when they got away from this horror. Its skin was dark as old leather, glistening in weak sunlight, hardened, cracked and crazed by the elements around withered muscles and long bones. There was no hair on its body, but its oversized head sprouted thin clots that were knotted and twisted around clumps of mud, casting startling shadows with the evening sun slowly sinking.

"Don't get close!" Goyo shouted as he and Bethan clambered to their feet. Dean almost laughed. What, did he worry that Dean would go and try to shake the thing's hand? He had seen several dead bodies, but none of them had looked more dead than this thing. That made its semblance of life—movement, animation, those small, shrivelled eyes rolling in wide sockets—so much more difficult to accept.

"Shoot it!" Dean shouted.

Goyo was already aiming. He squeezed off a shot that plucked at the strange creature's right shoulder. It shuddered a little under the impact but offered no other sign that it had been hit. Its long leg stretched out, reaching towards them. It paused, swaying as if to get used to the idea of motion. Then it took two steps, two more, moving faster each time. Goyo pulled the trigger again.

Click!

"You're joking!" Dean said.

Click. Click.

"You are *totally* fucking joking!"

Goyo grabbed Bethan and dragged her back, and Dean retreated with them.

The creature started running. It took long, loping strides, arms swinging, sharp elbows pumping at the air, and its head wobbled on its too-thin neck, swaying from side to side. Its face looked like a vague impression in dried mud.

"This way!" Goyo said. "Up the slope towards those trees!"

They had no time to argue. Dean and Bethan dashed after him, running so close that their arms bumped each other.

"Another one!" Dean said. Ahead, standing within the trees, a tall thin figure waited for them.

"We've only got a few seconds," Goyo said. "Across there, see?"

"The stream?" Bethan asked.

There was no time to explain what he was thinking, so Goyo ran, and Dean and Bethan could only trust him and follow. They cut across the slope, and as they neared the stream tumbling downhill Dean heard a long, low keening sound from behind. It sounded like a wounded dog, the voice wet and flat. He risked a glance back.

The tall creature was coming up the hillside towards them. Its legs kicked past rocks as it ran, arms pinwheeling to maintain balance, and whatever drove it seemed not to care about damaging its old body. Shreds of skin and dried flesh scraped from its feet and lower legs, and its head rocked so violently that Dean thought it might fall off.

Its keening came again, and then he heard something much, much worse.

The sound of crunching bone and tearing skin.

Goyo leapt the stream. It was wider than it had first seemed, and steeper, and he sprawled on the other side, clasping onto the rocky ground as his legs trailed in the white water. Bethan went next, Dean just a second behind her. He cleared the stream and rolled, turning his ankle and winding himself as he hit the ground. He struggled upright and glanced back the way they'd come. The thing was closer, and the other one had emerged from the trees and was rushing downhill towards them.

"Dean!" Bethan said. She was pulling at Goyo, and Dean went to help her. They dragged him from the stream. He stood, panting, looking back.

The first monster tried to jump the stream, but its left leg gave way just as it launched itself, spilling it into the water with a splash. Its arms and legs thrashed as it was carried downstream, bouncing from the near shore, striking rocks, rolling. Its head was dented and misshapen, and as it tumbled over a small fall it left behind a dark cloud in the air above it.

"Hurry!" Goyo said. "Across the slope, away from here."

"What about the other one?" Dean asked. "Where the hell is it?" There was no sign of it.

"Doesn't matter, we can run faster," Goyo said. "Even if it—"

"There!" Bethan said. She pointed, and Dean saw the shape moving downhill towards them. He wondered at the level of its intelligence, and how well it could scheme about what it was doing.

As they started running, their pursuer dropped to its knees, thirty feet uphill from them, digging sharp bony fingers into the damp ground as its head flipped back. Its eyes widened and bled a dark, glutinous substance, and its whole head shook back and forth on its weak neck. Its skull split from its left eye socket across its ear and up over its head. This time, the cloud of disease spores flowed apart and drifted across the hillside towards them.

They ran. Dean held his breath for as long as he could, wondering whether the spores might drift with the breeze and land on his clothing or hair, or in his ears or eyes to infect him that way. Bethan gasped in a fresh new breath a second before him, and the three of them continued running until Goyo called a halt.

"We're okay," Bethan said. "You think? We're okay?"

"Can't know for sure," he said.

"I'm okay," she said.

"Me too," Dean said.

Goyo smiled but said nothing.

"Goyo?" Dean asked.

The older man shook his head, looking around them at the harsh landscape, up at the gloomy sky. Anywhere but at their faces.

"We have to trust each other, right?" Bethan asked.

"We can't," he said.

"But—" Dean began.

"We can't! Just trust yourselves, if you can. But there's no telling... I mean, I don't know anything. None of us knows anything! Those things should have been dead centuries ago, millennia. In the face of that, what can we trust? Just what?"

"That this is all my fault," Dean said.

"Fault doesn't matter," Bethan said.

"Well, I trust that I'm okay," Dean said.

His words hung heavy and uncertain. And he knew the truth that Goyo had spoken—none of them could know anything for sure.

FOURTEEN

On their journey inland from the coast, Bethan had viewed the landscape from the safety of the old Land Rover's interior and seen violence, disruption, and damage brought on by the changing environment. Protected by the vehicle's metal shell and glass windows, and one step removed from the realities of outside, her focus had been on how bad things were and the dangers the landscape presented—the marshy ground, ready to swallow them up; the sudden sinkholes and geysers, traumatic signs of the changing land.

Now she could feel the cool breeze against her skin and smell the scents of sulphur and soil-tinted steam given out by the active landscape. She could hear the grumbles of some distant event, like the grating of rocks deep down as a giant turned in its slumber, and the closer song of small birds exploring a landscape that might be new to their breed and still imprinting itself on their race memory. A family of raptors circled high up, parents keeping their chick close with their distinctive calls while they trained it how to hunt. Hoof-prints evidenced a small group of caribou passing by recently, and around a low mound of rocks woodchuck holes punctured the soft ground. Grasses gained a foothold across swathes of land not yet upset by tumults from deeper down, copses of Arctic willow trees spread roots and seeded themselves further afield, and reeds and other marshland plants took advantage of the warmer temperatures and damper ground. On low hills to the north, heathers speckled the landscape purple and yellow.

The violence and upheaval was still there—the danger of this place was a heavy weight in the air all around them, like a pressure that no barometer could measure—but she was also witnessing the land's ability to change and adapt.

Bethan enjoyed being tactile with nature. If she walked in woodland she touched trees, running her hands across rough bark and kneeling amongst exposed roots. When she strolled along a beach, she took off her shoes and socks and kicked through the surf. She welcomed the sting of sharp rain against her skin, hard stones beneath her feet, cold water welcoming her in. Touching nature was to feel it, sense it, and welcome it.

Hawkshead Island was changing with the times and adapting to humankind's toxic influence, and though that gave Bethan some comfort, it also made her feel even more excluded than ever from the world she loved.

A day, a night and another day after Lanna had emerged from the cave and their nightmare had begun, with the sun skimming the horizon towards its nightly slump and temperatures edging below zero, it was Goyo who spotted the light coming towards them. At first Bethan thought it might have been a single flashlight carried by a lone hiker— or someone or something more dangerous—but she soon made out a pair of lights, and their movement quickly identified them as belonging to a vehicle of some sort. Shivering and huddled close with the others to share meagre warmth, Bethan gave silent thanks. After a short debate, Dean took a small flashlight from his belt and signalled several times until the vehicle paused, then turned and continued in their direction.

They slowed to a walk as they waited for it to arrive. It bounced across the rough ground, and as it grew closer Goyo identified the Ford Xtreme that Frank had promised them but failed to deliver.

"If that's Frank, who's going to tell him about his Discovery?" Bethan asked.

"Don't care," Dean said. "I hope he's got some food."

The Xtreme stopped and the electric engine whispered off, lights fading with it. The door opened and Frank jumped down from the cab like someone half his age. He took them in with a glance, then looked beyond them, and around, as if seeking someone else.

"Frank," Goyo said, nodding.

"What happened to the rest?" Frank asked.

"We ran into some trouble," Goyo said. Frank was still looking anywhere but at them, and Bethan noticed two things at once. The first was that he was not just alert, but afraid. She didn't know Frank, but she knew enough about people to recognise the look in his eye, the stiffness of his shoulders. The second thing she noticed was that he held his right hand against his bulging right pocket, and she was willing to bet he had a gun in there.

"Yeah, Wren said as much."

"Wren?" Goyo gasped.

"Wren's okay?" Dean asked.

He can't be okay, Bethan thought. Her stomach dropped. A chill surged through her already-cold body.

Frank locked eyes with her, and there was nothing welcoming there. He nodded back over his shoulder without breaking eye contact. "He's back at Joyce Sound. Got there a couple of hours ago, told me a tale I can't quite get my head around."

"We… we thought he was dead," Goyo said.

"Uh-huh, he said you'd say that."

"What else did he say?" Bethan asked. "Did he get close to you? Does he seem himself?"

"Seeing as I saw him once before for five minutes and never exchanged a word, kinda difficult for me to say," Frank said. His hand clasped whatever was inside that pocket through the material. He was fifty feet from them, giving himself plenty of time to draw and shoot if they came for him.

"Last time we saw Wren he was going down into a sinkhole," Goyo said. "Injured, maybe dying. And now he's made it to Joyce Sound ahead of us?"

"Looks that way. He said you three killed a couple of the others and abandoned him after a deal went wrong."

"That's bullshit!" Dean said.

"Didn't say I trusted him, son."

"He's in the town?" Goyo said. "With everyone else?"

"Not for long. Told us there's some old disease been found, buried out there, and that you're the ones brought it up outta the ground. So he's getting ready to leave the island, and doing his best to persuade some of the islanders to leave with him."

"Oh, no," Goyo said, eyes wide and filled with dread. Bethan saw his terror, and shared it. If Wren sailed on the boat that had brought him in and infected all the islanders who he could persuade to sail with him, by the time they reached civilisation—Baffin Island or Greenland, maybe even Alaska or Canada—there could be twenty or thirty disease carriers on board, maybe more, ready to disembark. Fan out. Move on.

"He can't get off the island," Bethan said.

"They can't leave," Goyo said. "Listen, Frank—they *cannot* leave. Wren was right about the disease, but it's not us that have it. It's more likely him."

"How did he get out of that sinkhole?" Dean asked. "We heard the shot. He was almost certainly infected by those things he killed, we *saw* that."

"Why did you drive out to find us?" Bethan asked.

"Figured I needed to discover the truth for myself," Frank said. "Come out, find you alive or dead, work out what had happened."

"There is a disease," Goyo said. "It's something old and bad and determined to spread, whatever the cost."

"Determined? You're making it sound like it has a mind of its own."

"It has," Dean said.

"No," Goyo said, "its victims are its mind. Its intelligence is in taking them over, and they become the disease. Its will to persist and spread is all settled in the minds of the people it infects."

"Or the animals," Bethan said.

"Huh?" Frank asked. He seemed even more troubled by the idea of animals catching some new, novel infection.

"Maybe," Bethan said. "We don't know yet for sure, but we saw a polar bear tackling some of the infected things and—"

"What things?"

"Carriers. Old bodies."

"Old bodies doing what?" Frank asked. Bethan wasn't sure whether they were persuading him or pushing him further away, and if he started to think they were messing with him, seeking to mislead him with an outlandish tale, maybe he'd be more inclined to believe Wren. His hand lingered by his pocket. He kept his distance.

"Spreading the disease," Goyo said. "Being steered by the infection."

"How old are these... bodies?" Frank asked.

"There's no saying." Goyo nodded at Dean. "But he and his treasure-seekers found a cavern with cave paintings I'd say are tens of thousands of years old. There were a bunch of mummified corpses down there, some of them tied up."

"Long-Gone," Frank muttered, and for the first time he looked away from them, lowering his guard and staring down at the ground between them.

"What's that?" Bethan asked. It had sounded very much like a name, not just two words.

"What do you know about them, Frank?" Goyo asked "The... Longun, you call them?"

"Long... Gone," Frank said, enunciating the words slower. "Old stories. Doesn't matter right now. What matters is keeping my town and my people safe, and you fuckers have come here and put everything at risk. One of you, all of you, don't matter so much to me. I ain't never shot someone. Stabbed a guy once, when I was thirty, though he didn't die."

Bethan could see that he was almost talking to himself now, persuading himself of whatever needed to be done, and she felt their time constricting. She sensed Goyo's muscles tensed, coiled, and she watched Frank's hand, fingers hanging in his loose trouser pocket now as the gun became the centre of his attention and the focus of what he thought he might have to do next.

Dean broke the moment, surprising Bethan by running at Frank and shouting, "Look out! Look out, Frank, behind you!" As distractions went it was uninspired, and if he thought the deception might work, he was wrong. But his movement and sudden shouting startled Frank long enough for Dean to shove him back against the Xtreme. Frank fumbled the gun from his pocket, but it caught on loose cotton and became stuck. Dean held one hand across the man's chest, pressed him to the Ford, and grabbed his forearm with his other hand.

"Come and get the gun, Bethan," he said. His voice was quieter now but shaking with effort.

Bethan darted after him and grabbed Frank's gun from his pocket. It was an old weapon, small enough to fit in the palm of her hand. Dean eased back and freed Frank, and he cringed against the Xtreme, as if expecting her to put a bullet in his head.

"We're not here to hurt you," Goyo said. "We've got to stop Wren. All of us, however we can."

"Right," Bethan said.

"Right," Dean agreed.

Frank looked at his gun which Bethan now held down by her leg. Not threatening, but also not tucking it out of sight. There, still the centre of their encounter.

"Guess I don't have much choice," Frank said.

"How far are we from Joyce Sound?" Bethan asked.

"Couple hours' drive," he said.

"One more thing," Goyo said. "We've got to figure out how to get there without Wren knowing it's us. Otherwise he might spore, and your town and your friends are finished."

Bethan noted that Frank didn't even raise an eyebrow at Goyo's use of the term 'spore'.

"You drive," Bethan said. "Don't suppose you've got any water and food in the car?"

"Yeah, some water," Frank said. "Dried seal jerky, too."

"I'm vegetarian," Dean said.

Goyo laughed. Bethan liked that sound. It made things feel almost normal.

"While we drive, you can tell us what you know of the Long-Gone," Bethan said.

"Ain't none of it good," Frank said.

"Colour me surprised."

"It's just old stories, passed down from generation to generation. Stories are a big part of our lives, and the tales of our ancestors are always on the wind, in the rocks, whispering across the land when we're quiet and attentive enough to hear them. All that got upset when I was a kid and the world began to change. The snow was melting quicker every year, and then by the time I was fifty it hardly came at all, despite the seasons still following on from each other as they always had, and the sun disappearing for a while then coming back again, as it always had. The land wasn't itself anymore. Sinkholes started opening, small at first and only really dangerous to the creatures that lived out here. Then they got bigger, and geysers started to pop up here and there as the permafrost melt accelerated and the methane built and started exploding up and out, and we lost the first of our folk to the land's anger and violence."

Bethan listened with fascination, relishing the warmth where she sat in the car's passenger seat. She hadn't realised how cold she'd been, cold to the bone, until Frank turned on the car's heaters. Goyo and Dean were in the back, and all their clothes stank like wet dog as the heat cut through the chill, raising the scent of sweat and dirt and ground-in terror. Frank had handed them a bottle of water each, and though it tasted old and stale Bethan gulped it down. The seal jerky tasted like old leather and she loved it.

"Those stories began to change, too. When I was young, tales of the Long-Gone were told by kids at night to scare each other, but during the day we laughed at them, if we bothered to remember them at all. There was never any real threat because those things were from the past. They were gruesome, for sure, but never anything that could reach through time and touch us.

"Then when our land and lives started to feel different year by year, so did the stories of the Long-Gone. Stories began to scare us during the day, as well as at night, because now history was coming to the surface. I remember the first time some kids from the village found an old body out beyond the Squealer Hills outside town, they thought someone had been murdered and left out there. Turns out it was a good couple of thousand years old. Could even tell what the bastard had been chewing on when he died. Just brought up outta the ground, preserved for so long, carried up by the changing water table and a methane explosion. And though the Long-Gone remained unseen and unknown, people began to remember more details from these old campfire tales. Some of them, me included, began to fear.

"It's said they were the first people on Earth. Like any old story like this, there are exaggerations and embellishments, or so it's reckoned. But who's to know? Most people can't even agree what happened a hundred years ago, let alone two thousand. Stupid fucking wars are still fought nowadays over those disagreements. When you're considering tens of thousands of years, you're not even talking any form of physical evidence. It's all stories told to the dark, carried on the wind, and brought down to us from our ancestors, mouth to ear, mouth to ear. But sometimes those stories hold so much horror that you just have to fear them, even if they're only ten per cent true."

"All these stories start somewhere," Bethan said, and Frank glanced at her and smiled. She thought he appreciated the fact that she wasn't rubbishing his strange tale. It was dear to him, part of his past and embedded in his soul.

"Sure, and that's the case with the Long-Gone. They roamed these lands tens of thousands of years ago, long before my own ancestors came here. They were the first people, making Hawkshead Island their home when the seas were lower and there was even a land bridge to Coniston Island, long-since sunk beneath the waves. They built shelters and farmed when it was warmer and more lush, and they put down roots, many millennia before it's believed any wandering human clans even thought about doing so. They buried their dead and gave themselves reason to stay, and across Hawkshead several communities developed. It's said they were advanced in hunting and farming methods, working with a symbiotic feel for the land and nature, rather than grinding against it, which is how most people in the world get by today.

"I always thought the lives of the Long-Gone sounded almost perfect. Maybe they really were as successful and forward-thinking as the stories say, and perhaps they were the ancestors we were all meant to have. Who knows what our present, their future, might have been if they'd survived to pass along their knowledge and ways to their descendants. Maybe our now would be a much better place. Could be we'd be living in a world where people are at one with nature, rather than doing their damndest to destroy it and themselves.

"But they never got a chance to find out. Story says they started mining the hills to the north of the island for ores, once they'd discovered metalworking, and they found something worse. Now, you gotta understand this is just how the story goes, but I've started with what I've heard, so there's no advantage to be had in me holding back on this stranger end to their tale. And however far-fetched much of it is, somewhere in these myths... somewhere, there's a truth. I can see that now, with what you claim is happening. A deeper, darker truth.

"They dug down searching for ores and instead found something else. A cavern. The walls of this cave were carved and formed, thousands of years old—many thousands older even than the Long-Gone—and in that place they found three bodies. These weren't human."

"Not human?" Goyo asked from the back seat. "Animal?"

"Who knows?" Frank said. "Story goes that they were gods, but that's just a name given them because none of the Long-Gone really knew who or what they'd found. They were twice the size of a normal person, taller and wider and stronger, and at first those who dug down and found them thought they were natural rock formations, grown there over hundreds of millennia like stalagmites. They soon realised that the three of them held the same shape, so they started to wonder if they were strange statues. Then the statues began to move."

"Shit," Dean muttered, and Bethan looked back at him. His gaze was elsewhere, beyond the vehicle, looking into the horrors of his recent past.

"They shifted, woken from some terrible deep slumber or hibernation, and the way it's said, they... *flowered*. Spread their seed, and their seed was an infection that scoured across the island, hitting every settlement and eventually destroying them all. Some tried to fight back, but little was known about disease back then—certainly any disease like this. It's said that those few who survived the initial rapid spread hid in deep caverns, bringing down walls and rockfalls, trapping themselves in the hallowed bowels of the land they loved and revered so much. They didn't know if they were infected, yet just in case they were they ensured that they'd die down there, and their bodies would never be found, in the hope that their sacrifice would be the end of the strange contagion. Even though it ensured the end of their bloodlines, they did it to protect the future of everyone and everything else.

"And I guess in the time they had alive before the air grew stale or they ran out of food and water, they decided to tell their story on the deep cave walls. Maybe as a warning to the future they would never know."

Frank fell silent, steering the Xtreme across the rough landscape on instinct alone. Bethan could tell that even though he stared through the windscreen, he was considering something much further away in distance and time.

"Pity we didn't heed those warnings," Bethan said, but she wasn't blaming Dean, his team, anyone. It was a statement of fact.

"Are you trying to tell us those things are forty thousand years old?" Dean asked.

"I ain't telling you nothing but the stories I heard and have grown to fear more and more over the years. Things turn up, like I said. Not bodies that old, but still sometimes the more recent dead that should stay buried. You bastards getting here, doing what you've done, you've made it like I've woken into a nightmare. If what you say is true. Make of those old stories what you will, but what of those cave paintings you said you found? What did they show?"

"Maybe you should tell us what your old stories say they might show," Goyo said.

"What, you're testing me now?"

"Just trying to see the truth in things. Stories have a way of bending over time. Expanding and growing. I know that as well as anyone, especially when your people are known as storytellers."

And Goyo can tell a story, Bethan thought. *But nothing like this. Nothing so fantastical.*

"Those paintings were never part of the stories, cos once they went down they never came up again," Frank said. "But I can hazard a guess what they might portray, from all the other tales about the Long-Gone."

"Guess away," Goyo said, and Bethan shivered, because she felt the full weight of those terrible histories settling around them all, lent gravitas by the great gulf of time stretched between then and now. She had not been down into that cavern, but as Frank answered she turned around and kept her eyes on Dean and Goyo, who both had.

"Figures dancing in flames, maybe. That's how they destroyed those who were first infected, after going down into that first mine they dug in the north. Shapes rising with the smoke, like the ghosts of those caught below trying to hide as they escaped. They say that happened sometimes, the infection trying to flee when those on fire... when their heads burst apart. I guess that's the sporing effect you talked about. Good description. Very... evocative. And maybe they painted the moon and stars watching down like living beings, or gods. Because however advanced the Long-Gone might've been, they likely still believed there was a reason for everything."

Dean's eyes were wide with shock, surprise. Goyo's face was slack with resignation.

Dean snorted, then laughed. Bethan recognised it all too well as anger. "Motherfucker," he said. "You've been down there. Set it all up, trying to frighten visitors away from your island." But he trailed off, and Frank did not honour his outburst with a response.

They all knew that was not true, even Dean. He looked at Bethan as if she was already dead and he was mourning her memory. It chilled her to the core.

"So we put it down again," Goyo said.

"What, the same way the Long-Gone did?" Dean asked.

"We stop Wren from sporing." It was not an answer to Dean's question, and Bethan was mostly glad. Right then, she didn't want to hear one.

But we'll have choices and decisions to make, she thought, *and we might not like any of them.*

FIFTEEN

"Is that... Wren?" Dean leaned on Bethan's seat, squinting through the windscreen at the figure lumbering towards the edge of town. Joyce Sound sat on the coast, a haphazard scattering of wooden and metal buildings on the side of a gentle rise, beyond which the land fell down towards the ocean beyond. The harbour was still out of sight, but Dean could see the moonlit ocean merging with the dark skies at some indefinable distance.

"Wren's already in town," Frank said. "When I left he was in Spacey Jane. The doc was checking him over. He was exhausted from his journey, almost unconscious, and they didn't want to move him."

"If he's spored, everyone will be infected," Bethan said.

"I don't think he will have," Goyo said. "Not unless anyone starts to suspect him. He'll want to leave on the ship, and Deadeye will be guiding him to spread as far and fast as he can. The only way he'll spore here and now is if he sees us."

"Whoever that is, they're walking towards the town from the north," Frank said. "And your friend Wren's big, but he ain't that big."

"It's hard to…" Dean said, squinting some more, trying to gauge the figure's shape and size where it was bathed in silvery moonlight. Its gait was awkward. It swayed from side to side as if uncertain of its long legs, arms with heavy hands held out for balance, even though the terrain this close to town was relatively even, levelled by decades of human influence.

The tall figure paused and turned, and as it grew still Dean started to doubt his own eyes. "Is that… a tree?" he asked. "I thought it was moving but maybe…"

"No trees that tall on Hawkshead," Frank said, "at least not this close to…" He trailed off. He could not finish. As they drove nearer none of them could speak, and Dean heard a low, monotone whine. He realised it was coming from his own mouth.

"Holy fuck," Goyo whispered.

"Can't be," Bethan said. "It's impossible. A caribou? Is that a polar bear on its hind legs? Is it?"

"No," Frank said. "And it ain't Long-Gone, neither."

Dean remembered Frank's tale then, and how ridiculous it had all sounded to his ears. Like the ramblings of an old man who'd let his community's stories whispered through the darkness of an Arctic winter cloud his judgement and mess up his head. He'd still doubted, even when the old dude had told them what the paintings might show, and Dean had recalled his own first glimpse of those images, and how they'd made him feel. Disconnected. Like he was viewing something from another world, another time. Something never meant to be seen.

"Then what?" Bethan asked. "What's on the island that could look like…?"

"Nothing," Frank said. "It's one of them that the Long-Gone found down in that first deep cave. It's like me talkin' about them made them…" He'd brought the Xtreme to a halt a couple of hundred yards from the first buildings at the edge of town, two dilapidated storage sheds that had seen better days, roofs and walls slumped and their colours eaten by rust. Bathed in the headlights, the huge creature stood by the first building, its head as high as the structure's eaves, still turned back as if to look at them. Its remaining hair was crazed as stiff wires, protruding in all directions as if caught in a stormy instant, unmoving and frozen in place. Its head was tall and thin, squarish, lacking any discernible features other than random knots and holes like an old dead oak. Perhaps they were eyes, nose, mouth. Its neck merged straight into long thin arms and a body that was only slightly thicker, barely any shoulders at all. Its waist and hips grew wider, and three long legs were each bent at different angles, propping its unnatural height against the rocky ground.

"No," Dean breathed, "no, no, no…"

"Why now?" Frank asked. "I hear that story every year and tell it just as much, but I never really… you know, never really believed… but why now?"

"Flying ants," Bethan said.

"Right," Goyo said. "Dean and his friends woke the first of them, and the others buried here and thereabouts got the message."

"What message?" Frank asked.

"Time to rise," Bethan said.

"Yes," Goyo said. "Time to spore."

"But that thing," Dean said. "It's not…"

"No, son, it ain't," Frank said.

"Not human like we know," Bethan said.

"Not human like anyone knows," Goyo said. "Not anyone from the last forty thousand years."

"What the fuck do we do?" Frank asked, voice softer. He was asking himself as much as them.

"Run it down," Goyo said.

"Huh?" Dean said. "Kill it, just like that?"

Bethan turned around in her seat, looked at him and Goyo. "Fucker's dead already," she said. "We've seen what it's here for. Alile, your friends, all taken by whatever fucked-up disease that's driving it." She turned back to Frank. "So yes. Kill it, just like that."

Frank needed no more discussion. This was his town, they were his people, in danger from a peril he'd heard and shared stories about all his long life. He started forward again, the Xtreme's electric motor purring, tyres skidding as they sought traction and then grinding across the uneven ground, and as they closed on the ancient horror standing close to the edge of town Dean had a moment to absorb the surreality of the moment. In those terrifying few seconds he leaned forward, and his hand met Bethan's as she reached back over her shoulder for him. They held and squeezed, and Dean closed his eyes.

The impact was sudden and violent, the vehicle shuddered with a loud crunch, and he was flung against Bethan's seat. Someone shouted, warning signals chimed from the Xtreme's dash, and then the world flipped and Goyo slammed into him, pushing him back against his door and crushing the wind from his chest. The vehicle jarred and tilted towards

Dean's side, groaned, then rocked and slammed back down onto four wheels. Goyo rolled from Dean across the rear seat, and Dean smacked his head against the window. The Xtreme shuddered and came to a halt, and something spat and hissed from the engine compartment beyond the cracked dashboard.

He heard a groan from the front and realised that Frank and Bethan were both straining against their jarred and locked safety belts.

"Bethan, unclip!" Goyo said.

Bethan fumbled with her belt release. "It's stuck. What did we hit? Where the fuck is that thing?"

The windscreen was cracked and crazed, half of it obscured where the safety glass had shattered in place. Dean could only see out of Frank's side, where a couple of the buildings on the edge of town and the desolate landscape beyond were visible. There was no sign of anything moving.

"Frank?"

He nodded. The side of his face appeared to be a mask of blood from the nose down. He was breathing heavily, staring ahead, right hand working at his seatbelt release. Dean thought of Goyo's busted, bloody face after smashing the into the Stallion.

"Frank!" Dean said again, louder. This time the old islander did not respond. Maybe he was in shock.

Goyo reached forward, a folding knife open in his hands. "Bethan, hold on and I'll—"

The front windscreen shattered inwards. Glass sprayed around them, and Dean covered his eyes. Bethan shouted in shock, and when he looked again Goyo had hacked through her seatbelt. She fell to the side and tried opening her door, but it was stuck fast. She kicked backwards and started forcing herself between the seats. Dean grabbed her beneath the arms and pulled, and Goyo helped drag her into the back seat.

Frank shouted as the monster hauled itself onto the creased bonnet and reached in through the shattered windscreen. Its arms were long, its clawed hand possessing too many fingers. This close Dean could just make out its features—holes for eyes, a slash for a mouth, and a nose that consisted of two cavities in its face in which sharp yellowed bones were evident. He could see nothing in its eye sockets. Its mouth was expressionless, parted an inch to display several tombstone teeth. Yet this close, there was something humanoid about the creature that Dean wished was not there.

Frank punched at it as it clasped for him, knocking out any remaining glass, and Goyo slashed out with his knife. When it connected with a limb it sounded like metal on wood, and the low hissing sound increased in volume and urgency.

Disengaging his seatbelt, Frank shouldered his door, falling outside and hitting the ground out of sight. The grotesque remnant paused, its strange head turning towards Frank then back at them.

Hundreds of small fungi heads stretched the thick leathery skin across the left side of its face, down its neck and across its chest, like boils ready to burst.

"What the fuck, what the fuck…?" Bethan shouted, kicking against the back of the front seats as if to force herself out through the rear of the vehicle, further and further away from this hell.

Perhaps attracted by her voice, the creature scrambled fully onto the vehicle's bonnet, attempting to thrust itself further through the smashed windscreen. As it lunged, its stiff hairs scratched and squealed against the bodywork. And it stank, a fetid aroma that reminded Dean of dank old unearthed remains dripping with wet soil and insects. A stale stench of time, not one of rot.

Goyo tugged at his door handle, but the door refused to open. Bethan was silent, staring at the nightmare made real, and Dean felt a rush of love for her, and regret that they had spent years of their lives not being friends, not sharing in stories and adventures.

He put his arm around her and pulled her close, and she gripped his thigh. With his other hand he dug into her pocket and pulled out Frank's gun.

The awful head loomed over them as it scrabbled further into the vehicle, slashing the front seats with its long fingers as it hauled itself closer to them.

Why doesn't it spore? Dean wondered, and he held his breath as he pointed the gun at the thing's face.

"*Here here here!*" Bethan shouted, waving her hands to draw its attention. It paused for a moment, and in that instant Dean fired. The gun was amazingly loud in the confined space, and his hearing dulled instantly, fading to a distant hum and then a low whine, with Bethan's and Goyo's shouts coming in from the end of a long, dark tunnel.

It jerked back, flinching, and a flicker of an expression passed over its face. It waved one of its spidery hands in front of it as if shooing away a fly, and Dean leaned forward and shot it again, again.

The monster shoved itself back out of the shattered windscreen and fell in front of the car. Its disappearance was so quick that Dean blinked, frozen, wondering if it had ever been there at all.

"Dean!" Bethan said, his hearing fading back in through the heavy low whine. "We gotta go!" She tapped his face and when he turned to her she nodded past him at his door. It now hung open at a broken angle. Outside, Frank stood with a tyre iron in one hand, his face dripping blood from a cut across the bridge of his nose.

Dean scrambled out, Bethan followed, and she turned and reached for Goyo.

"Where is it?" Dean shouted.

As Goyo crawled across the rear seat towards the open door, the creature leapt onto the bonnet and thrust itself back through the smashed windscreen, grasping with its stick hands, kicking with its three legs, scratching and denting the metal as it shoved harder and harder into the vehicle.

Dean fired through the shattered driver's door, aiming for the thing's head and torso. It shuddered and slowed, but its limbs still worked to pull it closer to Goyo. He pulled the trigger again and it clicked on empty.

"Come on!" Bethan shouted at Goyo.

Goyo glanced back at the beast just as its head tilted and a hundred of the boils on its face and neck popped. Each one released a small puff of grey matter, which seemed to hang solid for a second before dispersing, hazing the air and filling the inside of the vehicle like a fog. It stole away the colour, even in the darkness of night.

Goyo turned back to them, eyes wide. He reached out one hand.

"No!" Bethan shouted, and Dean wondered why. He stepped forward to help Goyo, but then the door slammed shut again.

"Come on," Frank said, clasping Dean's shoulder and pulling him back. He stumbled over his own feet and almost fell, then Bethan was dashing past him. He grabbed her arm and held her back, and she span on him, teeth bared, grimacing as if she was ready to bite out his throat.

The Xtreme's engine started, whirring with a broken sound. Goyo was already in the driver's seat, one hand pressed hard against the thing's face as he shoved it away from him, leaning to the right and pushing himself hard against the door, the other hand clasping the steering wheel as he slammed his foot down on the accelerator.

"Goyo, *no!*" Bethan screamed.

"It's too late!" Frank said. "You saw what happened, you know he's breathed it in. Maybe we have too, but your friend, *definitely!*"

The Xtreme was moving away from them, grinding on broken suspension, engine smoking as something inside shorted and burned, and Goyo had already made it impossible for his fate to be in anyone's hands but his own.

Goyo felt a cool grit speckling up across the inside of his mouth, the surface of his tongue, his throat. He tasted it too, stale and old like he imagined thick dust might taste, but with an almost exotic spicy taint. He'd known what had happened the moment he saw those growths popping across the creature's face and neck, and even though he'd held his breath he felt the tingle of the released spores itching at his eyes and tickling the small hairs in his ears.

Goyo had been wondering at the honesty of his own mind ever since he'd come up out of the cave and killed Lanna, and now he knew for sure. Any doubts could be given free rein. Any thoughts that did not feel quite right could be blamed on this infection over which he now had no control.

I'm still myself for now, he thought, but he did not know how much longer that would last. He didn't even know if he'd know when it changed. Such lack of agency over his own life was something he had never experienced. It was curious. It was daunting.

That was why he knew what he had to do. For Bethan. For his son Nathan. And for everyone here in Joyce Sound. They'd encountered this thing on its way to the small town, so perhaps Goyo could prevent it from ever arriving there.

They'd have to sort out Wren on their own.

He pressed his foot to the accelerator, forcing himself almost upright in the driver's seat, one hand gripping the wheel to keep it straight and true, the other batting at the creature's thick branch-like arms and large, many-fingered hands, because he needed his eyes. He had to see because he had a destination in mind. A place he'd seen just a couple of days ago on their arrival here. It had to be the end of the long trail he'd been following throughout his life, thousands of miles and a thousand campfires ending here, at this one point.

I need my eyes, he thought, and something urged him to

open them wide and glare at the ancient creature hanging across the dashboard and into the front seats.

It thumped him around the head, sharp fingers slicing across his ear and opening the skin above his temple and forehead. Blood dribbled down and he blinked it away, because—

I need my eyes.

He shoved harder against the cold, hard head to keep it away, and as it shifted his hand slid down across one of its eye sockets and onto its cheek. He felt those fungi heads popping open beneath his palm, moist and slick, and he clenched his fingers and squeezed tight. He thought he heard a low keening sound as his fingers dug in, and a rank odour made him cough and gag. More fungi heads popped, but it didn't matter anymore—

I'm Goyo, I'm Goyo, I know who I am—

—because soon neither of them would exist in this world as anything other than a memory.

The Xtreme bounced over a ditch and the heavy thud lifted him from his seat, flinging him sideways into the door. His foot slipped from the accelerator and the creature dragged itself further into the car, his hand sliding from its face. He grabbed onto its arm, but it leaned in closer towards him, urging him to—

Look at me—

Goyo squeezed his eyes shut, convinced that he was still himself, and he felt cool alien tendrils creeping into his thoughts, winnowing their way through his self-image, his identity, and starting to strip away that understanding layer by rapid layer.

He tried to remember his mother, but she was gone.

"Goyo, Goyo, Goyo!" he shouted, because she had given him that name and he had always been so, so proud.

He looked again, staring past the thing slashing and ripping at him, jarring his arm back so that he could grip its face again, digging fingers into what might have been its eye sockets and feeling something cold and wet and dead squelching up to his knuckles, and then he saw his destination.

He pressed harder on the accelerator, and in the few seconds before impact, the creature struggled to pull away. It pushed against him instead of punching and cutting him, but his fingers were thrust into one of its eye sockets now, and past the cold wetness there was something hard inside that he curled his fingers around and grabbed on.

Her name was Malia, he thought, and in the second before the Xtreme smashed into the fuel container, despite the fact that he felt a profound change and was already thinking to himself, *Perhaps everything is not so bad,* he remembered his mother's kind smile.

Beneath the creature's sharp fingers shoving hard against his face, Goyo smiled back.

SIXTEEN

Bethan knew beyond doubt that Goyo was dead. The Xtreme, the fuel tank he'd crashed into, and two nearby buildings were consumed by flames that scorched thirty feet into the sky and lit up the town. Even from where she stood with Dean and Frank two hundred yards away, she could feel the sizzling heat stretching her skin. It crackled across the ground, shrivelling heathers and grasses and a small spread of Arctic willow between the edge of Joyce Sound and the more rugged terrain beyond. The monster that had attacked them was also dead. More dead than before. She could still make it out on the vehicle's bonnet, trapped there somehow, contorted and twisted by the intense heat. She could smell burning rubber and plastic, the chemical tang of flaming fuel, and the sickening hint of roasting meat, and in that conflagration was hopefully the ancient Deadeye that thing had risen from its bizarre and inexplicable hibernation to spread once more.

She knew that he was dead, yet she still watched, hoping against hope that Goyo would appear from somewhere, brushing himself down and giving that wry smile that said, *And still I persist*. She'd seen him face up to treacherous situations many times, and some of those times he'd dodged certain death. He'd always said that it was part of a life well lived.

"Hey," Dean said. He stood close beside her and put his arm around her shoulders. "Hey, Bethan."

"Yeah, I know," she said.

"I'm sorry. He was…"

She tried to speak but could not.

"Brave bastard," Frank said. "Come on, if your friend Wren didn't know we were here before, he sure as hell does now."

Bethan felt gut-punched, hollowed out, and every time she breathed she smelled the results of the fire and felt her nostril hairs tingling, and feared that her next thoughts might not be her own. *Will I even know?* she wondered, but right then it didn't seem to matter. Alile was gone, Goyo was gone, and wherever Wren was now he was likely sporing after hearing the gunshots and commotion, infecting the townsfolk and turning them all into something not themselves. Something different.

"Bethan, I—"

"The docks," she said. "Whatever happens here now, we've got to stop anyone from leaving."

"And then what?" Dean asked.

"One thing at a time," she said. She tore her gaze away from what Goyo had done, and by doing so she was finally able to send him a thought that she felt certain was hers and hers alone. *Fly well my friend, and never look back.*

"You're expecting to talk them out of leaving?" Frank asked.

"No, you will. These are your people."

"Hey, gotta tell you, these are no one's people but their own."

"And we want it to stay that way," Bethan said. "I can't have lost Goyo for nothing. I *can't*! We have to stop Wren, but if the worst has already happened, while you're trying to get through to anyone you know who's not yet infected, Dean and I will be sorting out the *Kelland* and any other ways off the island."

"And how do we do that?" Dean asked.

"However the fuck we can," she said. "Frank, you go to the bar, we'll go to the dock."

"And meet up where?" Frank asked.

Bethan shrugged. She hadn't thought that far ahead.

"You look like death warmed up," Dean said to Frank, and Bethan snorted a bitter laugh. Dean was right. Frank's bleeding was slowing, but his face was caked in blood, streaked here and there with sweat and where he'd wiped blood from his eyes. The chance of anyone listening to what he had to say in that state was slight.

"Okay, this way," Frank said. "We can cut through the cemetery and along the main street, bar's down by the dock anyway. Stay together 'til we get there, safer that way."

"With a gun with no bullets," Dean said.

"Frank's right," Bethan said. Dean was close to her, eyes flicking back and forth between her and the fire roaring behind her. A tyre exploded, and he flinched. "Let's stay together." She brought Dean into a brief, hard hug. When they parted her vision was blurred. She wondered if his was too.

They followed Frank past the blazing Xtreme and into Joyce Sound. From a distance the arrangement of one and two-storey buildings appeared haphazard, but as they moved through the shadows between them Bethan realised that the town had been built around and into the landscape, as opposed to forcing the landscape to accept the town. Streams remained undiverted, rocky outcroppings were left alone, and Joyce Sound clung to the edge of Hawkshead Island like a welcome benefactor, not a parasite. Maybe that was how Wren now welcomed the alien presence in his bloodstream and brain.

Maybe it really is alien, she thought. The tall creature which Goyo had killed was like nothing she had seen before, certainly nothing she'd ever heard of. It had been at least nine feet tall, with three strange legs and features that echoed a human's, or perhaps mocked humanity in its likeness. If it was as old as Frank had suggested in his weird tales of the Long-Gone, perhaps whether it was alien or some ancient forgotten branch of humanity hardly mattered at all. Its controlling disease should have remained buried. If Dean and his idiot friends hadn't uncovered it, someone else would have. That was humans—inquisitive and persistent to the point of destruction.

The Long-Gone and their strange past should have remained unseen by modern eyes, unknown by modern minds. Everything that humanity had been doing for the past couple of centuries had led to this haunted past intruding into the present once more.

They passed between several houses, all with doors and windows closed in silence. There was no sign of anyone else on the streets, despite the explosion and fire.

"Where the fuck is everyone?" Bethan asked.

"I think I might know," Frank said. "Come on. Hurry."

A couple of minutes later they skirted around the town's medical centre and school and reached the bottom of a small slope. They followed a gravelled path to its top, and then on the other side their view of the rest of Joyce Sound, including its small busy harbour, opened up.

Bethan's heart sank. It was Goyo she thought of more than anyone else, her friend who had sacrificed himself because he knew what his immediate fate was to be, and she was certain he'd died knowing that she would do everything she could to prevent it from happening to anyone else.

He had died for nothing. She had failed.

They had all failed.

The *Kelland* was heading south and east away from the island, navigation lights illuminated. Nestled against the wooden dock a couple of hundred yards down the gentle slope from them, three fishing boats sat low in the water, just the upper parts of their superstructure and masts showing. A slick of oil darkened the sea and washed against the rocky shore on the steady swell, the waves breaking white and muddy brown. Further out, and no longer moored, several more boats drifted as they slowly sank.

"Wren," Dean said. "You think he's on there? Or did he spore and—"

"Doesn't matter," Bethan said. "Frank, you got a radio here? Internet?"

"You thinking he or they would have left anything working?"

"We gotta look, try to contact someone on the mainland. Warn them what's coming their way."

"Don't even know where they're sailing to," Frank said.

"And you think anyone will believe us?" Dean asked.

"Make something up," Bethan said. "Tell them it's a new virus, something terrible, Ebola or fucking bubonic plague. Just something so that they'll isolate—"

"And find a ship full of apparently healthy people who can put their own spin on the story," Frank said. "No, we can't rely on that. We've got to get out there and stop it."

"And how do we do that?" Bethan asked, pointing at the sunken boats left behind.

"I have a small inflatable boat—an RIB," Frank said. He gestured along the coast at a building with a small boathouse fifty yards up the shore, a smooth concrete ramp leading down from the building to the water. "At my place. Had it in the boathouse for years, maintained it well, pretty sure it'll still work."

"You have a pump?" Dean asked, and the look Frank gave him could have killed.

"What about all those who didn't go on the *Kelland*?" Bethan asked. "I've seen no one, there's no movement in town, but not everyone would have fit on the ship. So if they're left behind they might be hiding, just waiting for someone to come."

"Maybe they killed anyone who refused to leave," Dean said.

Frank's face fell at that, and Bethan realised they were talking about everyone he held dear, either sailing out on the *Kelland* to distant shores, or possibly lying dead with a bullet to their head. She'd lost Goyo and Alile, but Frank was staring at the loss of everyone and everything he knew. He remained cool and calm and logical, but they were witnessing his whole world falling apart. She hoped he could hold on a little while longer.

"Let's just get to my place," Frank said. "We can pause there, take a breath and think things through. Anyone still here in town, infected or not, is already isolated. It's those on the ship we have to—"

"Down!" Dean said. He grabbed Bethan's sleeve and tugged her to the ground. She bashed her knees on the gravelly surface, then he was up and pulling her after him towards the corner of a small storage building attached to the rear of the medical centre, both of them crouched down low. Frank followed, and they hunkered behind the building and peered out at what Dean had seen.

Along the main street, another one of those tall bastards was moving slowly between one building and the next. It was hunched over, like a tree leaning against a strong wind, though there was only a gentle sea breeze. Its limbs lifted one by one, probing ahead and propping itself before the next leg rose and edged forward. Step by slow step, it reminded Bethan of the movements of an old man, and its hanging head only added to that appearance.

Behind the creature, and gathered to either side, fifteen or twenty townsfolk walked at the same pace. There was a sense of reverence in their movements, as if they had no wish to progress ahead of their leader. Several of them helped it, dipping their heads to provide a resting place for its long arms across their shoulders. Bethan didn't think they were holding it up. If anything, the touch of its long arms appeared almost affectionate.

"I know them," Frank said. "I know them all."

"I'm sorry," Bethan said, because she was certain those people were now infected. She'd seen the thing in the Xtreme's smashed windscreen, the boils of spore heads across its face and neck, and even though she couldn't make out any detail at this distance, she was sure this creature had the same. Many of them would be expended now, their spores spreading the ancient Deadeye disease it carried to these poor unsuspecting townsfolk. Used to living in harsh conditions, their thoughts were no longer their own. Their lives belonged to something else. "I'm really sorry."

"If the stories were right, there'll be a third one of those things," Frank said.

"No saying where it might be, or if it's even risen with the other two," Dean said. "You said it was somewhere in the north? How far away? How might these things have come this far? It's only a couple of days since we disturbed those bodies down in the cave."

"I'm going to kill them," Frank said. He was ignoring Dean, perhaps because there were no logical answers to the difficult questions he asked. Bethan could see that Frank was already focused on what was to come. She hoped that his mind was his own. She hoped that hers was, too.

"How?" she asked.

"Got a high-powered rifle in my place, keep it for polar bears. I'll kill that thing, and any others around. Then keep my friends in isolation until help arrives."

What help? Bethan almost asked, but she held her tongue. She guessed Dean was thinking the same thing. Frank needed hope to grab onto right now. His world was breaking down, and he might be the only one left who could do something about it.

"Your place, then," Bethan said. Frank didn't reply so after a moment she tapped his shoulder. He was still looking at the tall thing crossing the street, and the people gathered around it like a crowd following some revered holy person. "Frank. Your place."

He nodded, gathered himself, then pointed downhill.

"Follow me, keep close behind, and we'll reach the shore that way. Then along the beach. That should keep us mostly sheltered from sight from up here."

"What about from anywhere else?" Dean asked.

"Gimme a break, son. I'm doing my best."

Frank headed off, and Dean smiled at Bethan. He offered nothing other than support, and hope, and she was grateful for it.

If Bethan had been asked to describe the inside of Frank's home without ever having been there, it would have been almost exactly what she saw when they followed him in. Lit by one weak bulb, she saw that one large room took up half of the interior, with open doors leading to a small bathroom and kitchen at the far end. A cot against one wall was a mess of blankets and pillows, a large table was covered with books, maps, empty beer bottles, a couple of rucksacks, and what looked like a part-stripped-down motorboat engine. Two easy chairs sat either side of a low table also scattered with various objects, and beside the door was a rack holding coats, with several pairs of boots beneath. Hidden beneath one coat she saw the sheer lines of a rifle.

Frank reached for the weapon and plucked it down, taking it to the table. He cleared some space, careful not to spill anything onto the floor, and placed the rifle flat on its side. As he worked the sliding mechanism several times, he nodded towards a wall of shelving beside his cot.

"Pump's on the bottom shelf, cable's wound around it. Haven't used it for a bit, but we can't risk testing it 'til you're in the boathouse." He paused, then grunted and pointed at the shelves where a mess of wires and plastic sprouted. "Huh. Well, they fucked my radio. Figures."

Frank dug around in one of the table's drawers and brought out a box of loose bullets, selecting a few of the same calibre and laying them beside the rifle. He snicked the magazine from the rifle's underside and started loading it. "RIB's in the large chest in the corner of the boathouse. The chest ain't locked. It'll need both of you to lift it out, half inflate it, then heave it onto the boat trailer that's by the front doors. When it's ready, open the doors, take the brakes off the trailer, give it a good shove and it should... *should* roll down right into the sea. Inflation pressure is printed on the side..." He trailed off, concentrating on what he was doing.

"That's it?" Dean asked. "You're sure that'll work? What if the trailer goes off the ramp and onto the beach?"

"We'll be fine, Dean!" Bethan said. "Frank, what about you?"

Frank didn't reply. He closed the oily cardboard box and lobbed it at Dean, who caught it in mid-air.

"Might find a few rounds for my gun in there," Frank said. "There's also a shotgun same shelf as the pump. Maybe a dozen shells with it. You'll be needing that once you're on the *Kelland*."

Bethan's heart was racing—trying to be quiet, trying to rush, trying to make things better, while the deaths of loved ones hammered nails into her heart, and the threat to another that she loved felt richer and more blood-red than ever before.

"We'll be okay," she said again, and Dean nodded, distracted as he rooted around in the cardboard box for a few precious rounds for the pistol. "Dean." He paused and looked at her. "We'll be okay. When this is over, when we've done what we have to, we'll still be okay."

He smiled, and this time it held every promise she wished from him.

"Whatever happens, we're okay now," he said.

"Get a room, you two," Frank said. He clicked in another bullet, then slotted the small magazine into his rifle.

"It was never like that," Bethan said.

"Jesus, no!" Dean said. "Not my type at all."

"Nope. Butt-fucking-ugly."

"Too tall."

Frank hefted the rifle and went to the window, peering out past faded curtains.

"We good, Frank?" Bethan asked.

He nodded.

"Godspeed," Dean said.

"God?"

"Just a saying."

Frank nodded over at the shelving unit again. "Pump. Shotgun. Get it done." Then he went to the door and cracked it a few inches, peeking out before exiting and closing it again without once looking back.

Bethan went to the shelves, rooted around and found the pump. It was smaller than she'd expected but wrapped in oilcloth and hopefully well maintained. Dean appeared beside her and found the shotgun and a box of cartridges. It was a pump action. He fiddled with the mechanism, turned the gun left and right, tried to slot in a shell and fumbled it, hands shaking. He picked it up and tried again, and Bethan closed her hand over his. They stood that way for a few seconds, looking at each other. Then she released him and he loaded four more shells, slow and smooth. He dropped the two extras into his pocket.

"Ready for this?" he asked. He held out the pistol. "Eight rounds. That's all."

"Absolutely not ready at all, no," Bethan said. "Let's do it anyway."

She turned out the light, opened the door and looked out. There was no one in sight up in the town, not even Frank, but the thirty yards down to his boathouse close to the shore seemed an awful long way. She slipped out, crouched back and down against the cabin's side. Once Dean was beside her, they ran. She feared that their footfalls sounded too loud, or their breathing would give them away. As they reached the boathouse, she realised they didn't have a clue whether or not it was locked, but it was too late to worry about that now. Dean grabbed the handle and pulled it down, and the door opened with a squeal of wood on wood and a groan of hinges. He scanned behind them, shotgun held down by his side.

"I think we're okay," he said, and Bethan slipped into the boathouse ahead of him. She swept the small pistol around the interior, watching for moving shadows. Two dirty windows let in only a little weak moonlight, and she cringed as she turned on a single bulb hanging from a wire. Every time she blinked she saw that monstrous creature's face as it pressed itself through the Xtreme's windscreen, reaching for them, seeking them all. The boathouse was silent and deserted.

Once inside, Dean closed the door and checked from a small window beside the door.

"If anyone saw us, they're keeping quiet about it," he said.

The boathouse was dilapidated, messy, and looked distinctly unused. A rowboat was tucked against the far wall on its side, two crossed oars propping it there. A couple of outboard motors were stacked in one corner, most of their metal parts rusted. Another stood upright on a wooden rack, this one shining with fresh oil. Other boat parts were scattered around. The far end consisted of two wide doors, closed with a wide gap where they met. There was a chain across the gap, and Bethan thought it was on the outside.

Maybe the weight of the trailer and RIB shoved into the doors would break them open. Maybe, maybe…

She located the trunk, and inside was the deflated RIB, curled up like some dormant creature. She tucked the pistol into her belt, Dean propped the shotgun against the wall, and together they lifted it out. She started to unfurl the boat while Dean returned to the window to keep watch.

"Why can't we just inflate it on the boat trailer?"

"Frank said to half inflate it before getting it on there."

"Yeah, but—"

"He knows what he's doing, Bethan."

"He's distracted. Come on, help me, it'll save time."

Dean helped her lift the slack RIB onto the trailer parked close to the end doors, then he returned to his guard duty. As she connected the pump to a plug socket hanging next to the lightbulb and twisted the output tube into the first of the RIB's air cells, a shot rang out.

She froze and looked at Dean. He ducked left and right, shotgun raised. Then glanced back and shrugged.

"Frank?" she asked.

"Guess so."

"Once I switch on this pump, someone will probably hear."

"Maybe," he said. "No choice, though."

She glanced down at the shotgun he held.

"A threat," he said. "That's all. You know I'm not shooting anyone, Bethan."

"Yeah, I know."

"Those things, though…"

As Dean turned back to the window, Bethan hit the switch on the plug. The pump coughed into life. It was so loud that she stumbled back a couple of steps, startled, and looked at the door, sure that someone would come bursting in at any second.

"Keep watch," she said, almost shouting over the pump. "All around. Frank's won't be the only hunting rifle in town, and there's no saying what they'll do if they're all infected."

"If they get us and the *Kelland* reaches the mainland…"

Bethan went closer to Dean and peered from the window. "Yeah. This goes everywhere."

"Where'd you think those things come from?"

"Don't know, but when they arrived here all that time ago, there weren't boats to carry the infection away. Those living here sacrificed themselves to stop it spreading."

"Arrived from where?"

Bethan shrugged.

The pump rumbled, and Bethan began moving the air hose into the different inflatable cells. They said no more about the fate of the old islanders. For as long as she lived— hours or years—Bethan knew she would never forget what Goyo had done. She was hollowed by his death, but he'd also given her a courage she'd never suspected in herself. In truth, he'd been cultivating that for years.

"Another shot," Dean said, though Bethan hadn't heard that one.

"How many bullets did he have?"

"Maybe five in his magazine, few more he dropped into his pocket."

"What happens if he manages to kill those freaky tall fucks?"

Dean was watching from the window, back to her, so she didn't see his face when he replied, "Then I guess it's whether he can do the same to his friends."

I'm me, Bethan thought. She remembered the delight on her mother's face whenever she took her first sip from a fresh cup of tea. Her father's laugh, snorting when he lost control. Her sister's disapproval at Bethan's chosen path in life, and her promise that their dead parents would be sad. The dog

called Jazz they'd had when they were kids. *That's all me.*
Everything inside is mine, no one else's, nothing else's.

"You okay?" she asked, and this time Dean glanced back
when he answered.

"Far as I can tell."

When the boat was halfway inflated, they hefted the
outboard motor from its rack to the boat's rear and went
about hooking it up. She'd done this before a few times
with Goyo, and though the boat and motor models were
ones she wasn't familiar with, the fixing mechanisms were
pretty similar. In a couple of minutes the outboard was
connected, fixed and tipped up ready for its prop to be
dropped down into action. She went around the trailer and
located the brakes applied to its three wheels. They were
little more than friction levers, and she heaved them all
aside. She pushed the trailer and it moved, just a little. Then
she reconnected the air hose to the valves and went about
inflating the final two cells, thumping the boat to make sure
it was solid enough to take them across the heavy swells of
the open ocean.

Dean took a couple of steps back from the window.

"They're coming," he said. He flipped the lock on the door,
and it looked so small and weak.

"Frank?"

"Can't see him. The townsfolk, and another of those
things. Can't make out how many."

"You're sure it isn't the one we just saw?"

Dean shook his head, and his expression told her
everything. *This one is worse.*

"What did you see?" she asked.

"One of those things that doesn't look so much like a sick old man," he said. "And a few of those close to the boathouse were already, you know…"

"Sporing."

"Yeah. What Deadeye does to their *heads*, Bethan! We gotta go. We might not have much—"

Two more gunshots sounded, much louder now that the pump wasn't covering their reports, and then they heard Frank shouting, "Go go go!" He could only have been shouting at them.

Bethan switched off the pump and disconnected.

"We both need to push," she said.

"We're not opening the doors first?"

"Chained closed on the outside."

Dean looked back and forth between the inflated RIB on its trailer and the wide wooden doors. "Let's shove hard, then."

Dean propped the shotgun in the boat and they crouched close together, hands against the trailer's rear, and started to push. It didn't take much to get the boat and trailer rolling down the slight incline, and they dug in their heels and heaved harder, harder, until the RIB's front end struck the doors. They groaned, creaked, and parted with a crunching, splintering of metal fixtures being ripped from their wooden mountings. The boat and trailer forced through and the chain rattled to the ground.

The ramp's slope increased and the trailer picked up a good speed, starting to roll downhill towards the ocean. Bethan and Dean sprinted behind it, then both jumped up at the same time, climbing onto the trailer's rear and into the RIB. Its base flexed a bit too much for her liking, but she could do nothing about that now. Dean snatched up the shotgun and turned to face inland, while Bethan held on to the outboard motor's handle, ready to tilt it down into the water as soon as they hit.

"Start it now!" Dean said.

Bethan tugged on the cord and the outboard fired up first time. She offered a silent thanks to Frank and his servicing skills. The propeller diced the air behind the boat, and then she looked back up the slope. The townsfolk were crowded close to the boathouse, many of them on their knees, some leaning against the building's walls. All of them twisted and contorted as their heads cracked and burst in a haze of blood and infection, and a mist of spores spread and were carried inland on the sea breeze. Bethan found herself holding her breath but she knew it would do no good. If they'd been caught in the sporing, they were infected.

Neither of them could do anything about it.

Behind the sporing, dying townsfolk, as if overseeing them as they writhed and fell, stood the creature Dean had viewed through the window. It was even taller than the one that had taken out the Xtreme, its legs thicker, torso wider and more solid. Bathed in the pre-dawn light starting to wash over the town, it stared down the sloping shore to the launch ramp from Frank's boathouse. Watching them go.

As the trailer splashed into the water and continued rolling, the boat's front end started to dip down. Bethan knew immediately that something was wrong. The RIB slewed to the left, the bow too low, the stern too high, waves breaking against the tough canvas and already splashing into the boat.

"We're stuck on the trailer!" she shouted above the roar of the outboard. "It'll drag us down!" She considered dropping the prop into the water to try and power them free. But if they were truly hooked onto the trailer, that might tip them end over end and spill them into the sea.

Dean had already seen the danger. He dashed to the bow, slipped on the wet deck, crashed down onto his back with a loud grunt.

"Don't fuck around!" Bethan shouted.

He rolled onto his front and went up on all fours, then slumped across the boat's edge where incoming waves were now breaking against it. His folding knife was already in his hand. He pushed forward into the cold water washing into the boat and felt down for whatever had trapped them against the sunken boat trailer.

Bethan glanced back. The tall creature was walking down towards the shore, but slowly, its movements uncertain and pained. The townsfolk around it were all sporing, most of them on the ground, a couple kneeling as their heads jerked left and right, and Bethan could almost hear the crack of breaking bones. The air was filled with the dark sheen of Deadeye spores and a haze of blood.

"Dean!" she shouted. "Hurry!"

Dean leaned further over the boat's bow and put his head almost into the water, feeling with one hand. He paused, then reached down with the knife and hacked at something.

Just cut the line, Bethan thought, the phrase that had marked a change in the course of both of their lives. She wondered what would have happened if she'd heeded Dean's warning back then and slit the fuel line feeding the sabotaged generator. Perhaps no explosion, no dead frackers, and a continued friendship. Their lives over the past few years would have been different, intertwined instead of pushed apart. Maybe that would have meant he and his team would have not come here, found the cavern, disturbed the terrible contagion that was dormant down there.

"Just cut the line!" she shouted, and she wasn't sure whether Dean heard above the sound of water smacking against the boat and breaking over him. He kept sawing and cutting at whatever he'd found, and then the bow snapped upright, flipping him back onto the deck. One of the ropes around the gunwale was tugged through its guide eyes as the trailer sank deeper beneath them, and Dean turned and gave her a thumbs-up.

Bethan lifted the outboard's handle and tipped the prop down into the water. It bit immediately, and she tensed and grabbed on as she was almost tipped back over the stern. The RIB hit a small wave and jumped, and as it landed it felt solid, certain.

"Yes!" Dean shouted. He went to his knees and came back to her, snatching up the shotgun. "Rope was jammed between the trailer struts, we shoulda half inflated it before—"

"Shoulda woulda coulda," Bethan said, steering the boat head-on into the incoming swell.

Dean looked past her at the shore, and she could not resist a glance back.

"Where's Frank?" she asked. "I heard him shouting, he must have been close!" And then she thought she saw him further along the shore, kneeling beside a couple of fallen bodies, looking down at them, motionless. *Maybe he shot them*, she thought, and the idea sent a chill through her. She hoped that wasn't the case. She hoped he was still himself, still the gruff, proud Frank she'd only known for a few hours but had grown to respect.

He glanced up and saw his boat powering away from shore, then he stood and lifted the rifle.

"What if he's…" Dean began, and Bethan prepared to swing the RIB around, left and right, knowing that zig-zagging would likely have little effect at this distance. She knew for sure that Frank would be a good shot with his rifle.

They needn't have worried. He aimed at the tall creature that stood amidst his falling and fallen friends.

Bethan barely heard the report when he fired. The creature's head flipped back on its big shoulders and came apart, like a rotten tree hit by an axe. Bethan saw the dark spatter of wet matter against the boathouse wall, and then the thing slumped to its knees, long legs folding inwards like those of a dead spider. It clawed at the ground with one hand, pushing, almost punching, as if to ward off the feel of the cold earth that had encased it for so long. After a few seconds it relaxed down, motionless.

Frank kept his rifle aimed at the fallen figure.

Bethan released her hold on the handle, slowing the boat and allowing it to slew around so that they were facing shore again.

"Bethan?" Dean asked. "What're you doing?"

"Frank."

"He'll be infected. Look at him. He's amongst them, they're all around him!"

"We can't just…" Bethan said, but she was allowing emotion to overrule her good sense. That had happened before, long ago, when she'd seen sabotage as positive action without understanding the possible implications of what she'd done. If she had questioned her own actions, perhaps she would have made a different choice.

She questioned them now. *They got him*, Bethan thought, and she knew that Dean was right. It had been inevitable. Frank had never meant to leave the island, not with what his family and friends were going through. His intention had always been to buy her and Dean time to do so. She wondered who the bodies slumped around Frank were to him, how many of them he hunted and drank with, how many he loved.

She opened up the outboard and started taking them back towards shore.

"Bethan," Dean said.

"I know," she said. "I know, Dean." She eased off the throttle again just as Frank waved at them. Bethan lifted a hand to respond, then realised that he was waving them away, urging her to turn back out to sea.

Frank looked around at the bodies scattered around him along the shore of Joyce Sound. He walked from one to another, kneeling to check, moving on, and then he stood beside the tall fallen thing—the creature from islanders' campfire tales, a myth given some terrible form of life by the Deadeye it bore—and put another bullet into its head.

Then he knelt among his dead friends and placed the rifle's barrel beneath his chin.

"No!" Bethan shouted, though she wasn't sure he'd hear her from this far out. And if he could, she knew he would not listen.

He waved again. *Go, go!* She realised that he was giving them a chance to not see.

She closed her eyes just as the shot cracked out across the waves. She heard Dean's gasp, and kept her eyes closed for a few more seconds, relishing the darkness that allowed her to deny reality, just for a little while longer—the cold sea breeze against her skin, the tang of the sea on her lips and in her nose, the rocking of the boat as it rode the swell. When she looked again Frank was just another body lying dead on the shore.

Dean was turned around on the boat's bow, watching her. He nodded over her shoulder and back out to sea, and she twisted the throttle and turned the boat around a hundred and eighty degrees. It rocked sidelong to the waves for a few moments, and she aimed into the swell once more. Past Dean she saw the lit-up speck of the *Kelland* on the horizon. It seemed much further away now that she was observing it from sea level.

"We're away," Dean said. "You okay?"

She nodded. She almost asked him as well but knowing wouldn't change anything. He had the shotgun, she had the pistol. If either of them was infected, the Deadeye would lie low, waiting for them to reach the ship until it revealed itself to them. Maybe not even then. Its revelation would depend upon what actions they took once they reached and boarded the *Kelland*.

If they were both infected, at least they would act together as friends.

Bethan hated the idea of her and Dean going against each other again.

They bounced from wave to wave, picking up speed, leaving behind Hawkshead Island and its sad infected bodies, both old and new, strangers and friends. She gripped the outboard's handle. Soon the impacts of the boat against the swell, though violent and harsh, became almost hypnotic. Dean came back and they sat with their arms touching and watched the outline of the ship as it grew closer, closer.

It was cold, and she tasted salt on the breeze.

SEVENTEEN

Behind them, dawn broke across Hawkshead Island in the hour it took them to reach the *Kelland*. For all that time, though they sat close enough to talk, they said very little. They were shivering from the cold, tired, and huddled close enough to share each other's warmth. That felt good. Bethan concentrated on steering them across the ocean's slow, heavy swell, worrying about whether the outboard had enough fuel, the boat's inflation would hold, the Deadeye would creep into her mind and thoughts, sliding insidious fingers into her perception. She kept testing herself—remembering evocative moments from her childhood, important family dates, and things she loved and hated. She persisted in being her, Bethan, while at the same time feeling sure that if she was now a Bethan carrying Deadeye, she would be thinking these exact same thoughts. Its intelligence was far older than her own, and far wiser. In thinking she might fool it, she could very well be deceiving herself.

She focused on one moment and the next, the now, not the uncertain future and unsettling past. The instant that her breath passed through was all that mattered.

They said nothing, but it was a silence that carried the heft of years, and the regret of unsaid things. She knew that Dean would never forgive what she had done, but she hoped that he was as focused as her on the here, the now. The only time that mattered.

Dean sat with the shotgun clasped in one hand, the other holding onto the remaining rope that ran around the edge of the RIB. Every time they skimmed and struck down again he imagined being bounced out of the boat and landing in the water, watching the RIB sailing on without him to leave him cold and destined to die. He didn't know why he thought like that. He knew that Bethan would swing around and scoop him up. But the image persisted, and he gripped so hard that soon his hand was frozen and clawed from the splashing water, and even if he was catapulted from his seat and flung from the boat he'd still be holding on.

He'd heard her shout, back when they were close to shore and being dragged down by the weight of the trailer. *Just cut the line!* He'd almost laughed. He didn't want to let her know he'd heard. Difference was, he *had* cut the line. He had never for a moment considered *not* cutting it, because that would have hauled them down to tragedy. Warming climate or not, he'd be dead in minutes if he fell into the Arctic Ocean.

He wondered about that. He hoped that meant that he was still him, clean and untouched by Deadeye, because his aim remained to stop the ship.

Dean did not find their silence comfortable. Every time he looked at Bethan he thought she was readying to talk, and he also had plenty to say. But the impacts of the boat surfing waves and striking the water, the noise of the outboard motor, meant that any discussion would have to be shouted.

As they approached the *Kelland*, Bethan eased back on the throttle and brought the RIB bouncing into its wake. She slowed them to a crawl, and Dean scanned the *Kelland*'s stern, searching for lookouts. The ride was more unsettled here but approaching from the rear gave them the best chance of remaining unseen. He braced himself, bringing his cold hand up under his armpit to thaw it, ease the pain. The idea of shooting at someone was horrific, but if he had to use the shotgun he'd need the use of both hands. He could see no one, and he breathed a sigh of relief. Maybe everyone on board was passed out, victims of Deadeye relaxing and ready to spore and spread. He had a strange, disturbing vision of the infected townsfolk kneeling around one of those freakish tall creatures—its tree-like torso upright, withered limbs propping it steady against the ship's yawing—offering unholy thanks for the taint it and its kind had bestowed upon them. When he blinked, the image of the thing wore Wren's face.

"What's the plan?" Dean asked, leaning in so that he could talk into Bethan's ear.

"I have no fucking idea. Kinda hoped that's what you've been quietly working on."

"Been quietly working on not falling out and drowning or freezing to death."

"Huh. Well, let's start with the plain facts. One, we have to stop the ship reaching land, anywhere. Two, there might be twenty or thirty people on board, infected with Deadeye. And who knows, maybe the last of those Long-Gone things."

"I don't wanna see another one of those things up close."

Bethan tapped the shotgun in his lap. "Just close enough for that. So, another possibility is, it's just Wren who's infected, and all the others are still fine and think they're fleeing some sort of disease. His Deadeye might be keeping low and quiet, ready to spore when they're closer to land."

"No plain facts there. All I hear are unknowns."

"I was trying to sugar-coat. But whatever, the single fact is we have to stop the ship."

"How? Sink it?"

"I just don't know. All this way out here I've been turning over what to do. If we manage to take control, turn it around, head back to Joyce Sound, I'm not sure we gain anything. We have to assume the infection is still alive. And sooner or later, more people will come to the island. So yes. I really think sink it. Somehow."

The *Kelland*'s stern loomed above them now. As they approached, Dean continued looking for anyone watching them. He saw no one. That didn't mean a thing.

"And if we do that, what happens to us?"

"That's gotta be way down our list of priorities."

Dean knew that without her having to tell him. But given voice by Bethan, the potential outcome of what they were trying here was harsh and stark. He felt sick.

"It's too much," he said. "Too big."

"How do you eat an elephant?"

"Eh?"

"One bite at a time." Bethan smiled. "Our first bite is getting on board, checking the lie of the land. Take it from there."

"There are mining explosives," he said.

She looked at him, eyebrows raised.

"Down in the hold, in one of the transport chests we brought with us. We were going to take some with us in the Stallion but decided against it."

"Part of me wishes you had. We'd have all gone up and…" She shrugged.

"Emma said if we didn't find anything worth mining on Hawkshead Island we might sail on to another place she had some leads on. So, yeah. It's there, with detonators and timers."

"That you can use?"

Dean shook his head. "We've never used them, at least not on any trip I've been on. I think Emma knew. You?"

"I saw Goyo setting some, once. I got the gist." She said no more, and Dean didn't push. He really did not want to know.

"What's the layout of this thing?" Bethan asked.

"It's a basic passenger and equipment transport, though pretty nice. Superstructure is mainly common areas, bridge, that sort of thing. Belowdecks are a dormitory and a dozen private rooms, engine room to the rear, cargo hold amidships, and its bow opens up for vehicle storage. That's how we brought the Stallion."

"Okay," Bethan said. She was focused on the *Kelland* now, bouncing the RIB from its stirred-up wash, and Dean kept his eye on the ship's stern for any movement. There appeared to be no one on deck, but that didn't mean there wasn't anyone inside the two-storey stern superstructure that housed the bridge and control rooms.

As they neared the stern and the vessel loomed over them, Dean scampered to the front of the RIB, still gripping the rope running around its outside to keep himself from being jarred or bounced into the sea. He also kept the shotgun in his other hand. He used that hand to signal to the right, because he could see no way for them to board the ship while still being bounced around in its wake. They'd have to move alongside, and maybe if they crept closer they'd reach a ladder without anyone looking down and seeing them.

And if someone does see us? Dean wondered. *What then? Help us up on board, if they still think they're fleeing a disease? Infect us if they're already all contaminated?* He didn't know: boarding the *Kelland* without any clue about the situation on the ship was just fucking crazy.

But they had no other choice.

Bethan edged the boat around the *Kelland*'s stern, and they thudded and jarred across its rolling wake. Dean felt each impact deep in his chest, and he held on for dear life. The RIB nudged the hull and bounced away, sending Dean spilling onto the boat's wet deck. He kept hold of the shotgun, banging his head, swallowing seawater and scraping his elbows. Turning onto his side he heaved himself upright again, adrenaline the only reason he wasn't shivering from the freezing water. He looked up at the railing.

Straight into the eyes of a woman staring down at them.

"Shit," Dean muttered. He smiled and went to lift his free hand to wave, but realised he was still holding the shotgun. The woman stared from him to Bethan and back again, then disappeared back over the railing.

"Closer!" Dean shouted to Bethan. The boarding ladder was just a few feet away. As the RIB neared he prepared to grab on, standing tense and steady, one foot up on the RIB's side. He glanced up at the railing again, but there was no sign of the woman. "Steady... steady..."

Just as they edged close to the ladder affixed to the ship's side, he glimpsed a shadow passing across the sun—

What's that? A plane? Something else?

—and the woman landed in the front of the RIB, slamming down on her front, limbs spread, smacking her face on the vessel's hard side. Dean heard the distinct crack of bone breaking. She squirmed for a moment, then lifted her head to look at them, blood streaming from her flattened nose. She was expressionless.

"We're here to—" Dean said, voice raised against the RIB's outboard and the roar of the ocean, but he did not finish his sentence.

The woman's left eye burst with an audible *pop!*, fat whiteheads rose across her left cheek and the side of her neck, and she opened her mouth and vomited a stew of blood and something chunky and slick, a thick mess that did not belong inside any body. Her head jerked up and down three times, left side slamming against the RIB's deck, and then Dean heard more crunching bones even above the motor.

"Dean, don't let her—"

Dean held the shotgun in both hands and fired at the woman's torso. She slammed back across the deck, squealing through the blood still pouring from her mouth and nose, and her head cracked open above her right ear and across to her eye socket. Brains, clear fluid and blood flowed out, and Dean shot her again, this time in the face.

Her head came apart.

Dean held his breath.

A sickly mess spread across the bottom of the boat.

The RIB slewed as the starboard cell started to fold and deflate where the shotgun had blasted through the woman and into the canvas.

Bethan grasped his arm and shoved him at the ladder. Dean grabbed on with his spare hand and climbed, reached up quickly and climbed some more, and when he looked back down, he saw Bethan holding on with both hands, her feet trailing in the sea and dragging her at an angle along the ship's side. If he reached for her, he'd fall, so he climbed again and gave her room to haul herself up, hand over hand, rung by rung.

As he made the gap in the railing he glanced along the deck in both directions, saw no one, and swung himself up. Reaching down with one hand, he grasped Bethan beneath the arm and helped her up onto deck. Panting, she shook him off and pulled the small pistol from her pocket.

The RIB had fallen behind, drifting in a wide curve away from the *Kelland* and slowing, falling to the mercy of the sea. The woman's body slid back and forth across the wet deck, now awash with the bloody mess of her insides. The starboard side of the boat was shrivelled, and soon a wave washed over and swamped the vessel. A few minutes, maybe less, and it would sink.

"You okay?" Bethan asked.

"No. I just shot someone."

"She was dead anyway. Which way?"

"Which way to where?"

"The hold." Bethan was calm, wide-eyed, alert, and Dean only wanted to sit against the bulkhead and think on what he had done.

The gun jumping in my hand, the thud against my hip, the hole in her jacket, the red, the red.

"Did you feel like this?" he asked.

"Really? Come on, Dean. We've got to move and make it worthwhile."

"What if some of that stuff from her—?"

"We won't know until we do! And right now I still want to stop them. You?"

"Yeah, stop them."

"Then we're good. For now. The hold. Come on."

Dean took the lead and started along the deck, crouched low, trying to recall the best way through the ship to the hold. Each time he blinked he saw that woman, already sporing and dying, blasted by the shotgun he still held in his hands.

"Dean, we have to assume they're all infected," Bethan whispered as she followed behind.

"We can't just think that!"

"You saw her. We must."

"I'm not going to blast anyone I see just in case!"

She grabbed his shoulder, hard, and leaned in close. "You know what's at stake here, Dean. You know what happens if we fuck up. Imagine these people landing on the mainland. Baffin Island first, then Canada. Each one infects twenty, or a hundred, and then five thousand, and then—"

"Okay!" He nodded. Yeah, he knew. "Okay." The responsibility bore him down. Its weight landed in the gun in his hands.

Wren sat in the *Kelland*'s well-appointed lounge enjoying a decent bottle of red, thinking of what had been and what was yet to come, and he raised a silent toast to a job well done. The others were gone, and he guessed that deep down a part of him was pretty sad about that. But he was a changed man now, and old associations no longer meant so much. They were in the past.

It was new connections that mattered.

The dozen townsfolk from Joyce Sound sat around him. He'd known none of them less than a day before, but now that they had met their risen ancestors, he was closer to every one of them than he'd ever been with anyone in his life. He might not know all their names, but they were brothers and sisters. No, *closer* than siblings. They were like other parts of him. Their joint futures were assured, and so tied into each other that they might as well be one single organism. Like a network of fungi spread beneath a vast forest, their lives touched and interconnected and would never be prised apart, no matter the distance between them.

Him over there, his left leg hurts where he pulled it climbing onto the Kelland. *He doesn't like the taste of fish, and his friends take the piss out of him about that, because he lives on an island in a community that fish for a living. He plays guitar but his wife doesn't like the sound, so she bought him expensive headphones so he can practise. She'd dead now.*

She's one of those we left behind on the shore. But her memory is part of us all.

Wren sipped his wine. The man rubbed his left leg.

And there, that woman sitting close to me, her hobby is wood carving, and she's made furniture for many friends in Joyce Sound. She lost her thumb and the tops of three fingers in a lathe, and she's known as Stumpy. She doesn't mind that. She drinks Japanese single malt and her favourite writer is Stephen King.

He knew what they were thinking, and they all knew his thoughts.

And it's all for the very best, he mused. That was the Wren part of him, still carrying all his memories and character quirks, yet with whole new vistas opened up to view. Coming to Hawkshead Island had been an exercise in profiteering. Leaving this place, he was going to change the world. Spread the love. Open some eyes.

He could not think of a better return for his investment of time, effort, and life.

Wren, the old Wren, knew very well what had happened. His mind remained, but expanded. There was no trace of doubt and no regret, and he only wished the others remained to share this very particular joy with him, especially Emma They'd experienced some interesting times together, but nothing like this. He felt sad that she hadn't survived to live these great moments with him.

He also mourned those others who had not made it as far as the *Kelland*. The tall ones, the forefathers. A shimmy of fear went through him when he thought of them, because they were like nothing he'd ever known before, and what he knew of them now…

That hardly sat well, even in his altered mind.

They should not be, he thought, and that idea butted against everything else that he now was. It was uncomfortable, and he tried to shut it out, but it remained deeper down, hovering close to where other parts of him—the Wren from before; old thoughts, discarded values—lay mostly dead and buried. Mostly.

At least they remained back on the island, probably dead by now. One had been killed by the old man who'd come with Dean's friend. The others had probably fallen and faded as well. They'd been old and feeble, animated by their purpose yet unable to defy the influences that time had wrought over their strange bodies.

Sometimes, when he blinked, Wren caught a glimpse of their deep and dark history, and then his mind would fold and close him out, because it was unknowable to the likes of him. All he knew was they had remained dormant for so long, waiting for their purpose to be fulfilled. And now it was.

Fulfilled in me, Wren thought. *In all of us.* He looked around the lounge, and when he caught someone else's eye— rarely, because the others were deep in their own thoughts, looking at their feet or the carpet but seeing something far more distant in their futures—they swapped a brief acknowledgement of shared wisdom and mutual destiny.

"Fulfilled in *me,*" he muttered, and his words drew no attention. If any of the other silent passengers heard, they'd know what he meant, because he was thinking and speaking for them all.

Wren stood and stretched, finished the wine. He went to the counter and made a mug of coffee, and as he was looking for cream—weird, he'd always taken it black before—he felt a shudder of pain, a warm discomfort in his stomach, and he tasted salt water.

Or blood.

He held the cup halfway to his lips.

Everyone else in the lounge gasped or stood up and grew more alert.

"One of us spored, then died," he said. "Something's wrong on the ship."

"But what?" the wood-carving woman said. "No one else is on board."

"No one that we know about," Wren said. "Spread out, check the ship. I think I know who it might be."

EIGHTEEN

Bethan followed Dean along the deck and through a doorway, pistol held down by her side. She rested a hand on his shoulder so that he knew she was following, gaining comfort from the touch. They were taking things moment by moment, edging towards an ending she really didn't want to consider.

They headed along a short gangway with three closed doors on either side, then through a wider vestibule. Dean paused there, glancing both ways along a hallway running perpendicular to the one they'd come along, then crossed and ducked down a spiral staircase.

At the bottom he paused again, and Bethan raised an eyebrow. He nodded at an open doorway leading into another gangway, and they started for it.

A shadow shimmered on the wall and a man's shape filled the doorway.

Bethan stepped to Dean's right and brought up her gun.

"Oh thank God!" the man said, raising his hands. "Wait, wait, oh thank God, you're here to stop them? You've going to stop the ship?"

"Who are you?" Dean asked.

"My name's Pilip. We have to be quiet! Some of them are… different. Where's Frank? Are you the ones he went to find? What happened to him, we have to be quiet and hide, I know where we can—"

"Shut up!" Bethan said. She took a step closer, gun aimed at Pilip's face. She watched for any change, any twitch. He was talking too fast, throwing too much information their way, not giving her enough time to think.

I should just shoot him and be safe, she thought.

"Where are the others?" Dean asked. "The townsfolk, and Wren, the big guy I came in with?"

"I haven't seen them," Pilip said, "come on, this way, there's a spiral staircase that leads down to—"

"How do you know?" Bethan said. "Haven't you been hiding?"

"Well yes, down the staircase. There's a room down there."

"Why did you leave?"

"Behind you!" Pilip said, and even as she turned around Bethan cursed herself, her reaction, her naïveté. She went down to her knees and twisted back towards Pilip, hearing the first creaking of strained bone as she did so.

Still standing, Dean kicked out and sent Pilip staggering back, tripping over a door sill and onto his back. His head struck the deck, raised, then struck down again, hard enough to crack bone.

Bethan grabbed Dean and pulled him after her.

Dean resisted, aiming the shotgun down at the contorting man.

"No," she said into his ear. "A gunshot will bring them all and—"

From the distance they heard doors slamming open.

"Hold," she said. "Now. Once inside we have to hold them off."

"This way." Dean dashed along the gangway and took a left, and she followed him down a twisting staircase into the bowels of the ship.

There were sounds all around now—hurried footsteps, doors closing or banging open—and she feared they'd be bottled in, trapped, and then a couple of people would spore and that would be it.

She would keep two bullets back for them both.

If she only had one left, it would be for Dean.

A man appeared along the gangway, bumping into the wall and pausing when he saw them.

"Hey!" he said, "thank God you're here, we've got to—"

Dean's blast took him in the throat, knocking him back against the door jamb, blood spattering around him. He slid down, eyes rolling in his head. Then he started to bleed out through the ears.

"Come on!" Dean shouted, voice deep and wretched. He grabbed her arm and they went through another door, which he closed and locked behind them. "The hold's through there." He pointed through a narrow doorway. "Down the stairs, double doors. I think you can lock them from the inside."

"But you're coming with me?"

"I'm going for the radio. I have to warn someone about all of this, *anyone*. We can't put all our eggs in one basket, Bethan."

"We have to stay together!"

"And... and... die together?" He was shaking, sweating, and his eyes quivered. He turned this way and that as if to find something to focus on. Wiped his hand across his brow. Frowning.

Bethan took a step back from Dean and aimed her gun at his face.

"Hey, I'm me... I'm..."

"What's wrong?"

"I just..." He took in a deep breath. No twitching head, no eyes flushing with blood. But still, she kept her gun on him.

"Dean!"

"I just shot two people, Bethan," he said, and she knew his voice, heard the inherent decency there that he'd always carried.

"You saved them. And us."

"Yeah, but I'm not like you, I'm not..."

"A killer?"

Dean sighed. "I'm me."

"How can I be sure of that?"

"Because I know for *sure* you'd shoot me if you thought I was one of them, and I'm still not sporing."

Bethan tensed forward, pursing her lips, looking for any change, any twitch, a darkening of his eyes. *Yes, I would*, she thought, *but it would be to save you as well as me.*

"Go," he said, and instead of flinching back he came closer, drew her in with his free hand and hugged her tight.

Bethan let him, and it felt good, *better* than good. It felt right.

"What's the explosives chest like?"

"Yellow, plastic. Might be locked."

Bethan pulled back and held up her pistol.

"I'll be back," Dean said. He turned, dashed to a narrow doorway, and disappeared through it.

Bethan waited for a second, listening to Dean's footsteps as he hurried up a staircase, then she turned and headed where he'd said. Narrow doorway, two flights of stairs down, then through double doors into the hold. It was smaller than she'd imagined, with a set of closed folding hatches forming the ceiling and large doors at the bow end through which the Stallion must have passed. There were a few pieces of random equipment scattered about, and some storage chests around the edges.

She closed the door first, throwing a thin bolt that would not keep out anyone for long. There was no saying how many other infected townsfolk were on the ship, but she had to assume that she and Dean were running out of time. Their clock had been ticking from the moment she and her friends had arrived at that cave mouth to see Dean, Emma and Wren wasting time as they debated what to do about Lanna.

She found a yellow plastic chest in one corner. The lid was locked, but the padlock was small, and she used the pistol to prise it off with a brief, loud snapping of plastic. She flipped the lid open against the bulkhead. Inside were several sealed packs. She ripped them open. She'd seen Goyo prepping explosives before, but never on this scale, and some of the equipment was unfamiliar. But she recognised explosives, a box of blasting caps, and a control unit, and she'd figure it out.

Bethan went to work. She had no real idea how much would be necessary to achieve what she wanted, so she included it all. Packed in three places against the port bulkhead of the hold, along the line where the floor joined the curve of the hull, she hoped a blast here would open the walls and the hull, taking down the ship. She hoped, but didn't know. She was feeling her way through this moment by moment.

As she attached blasting caps and wound blocks of explosives together with a roll of black sticking tape she'd found in the chest, she thought about Dean, and how he'd said he wasn't like her. That hurt, because the Bethan he still saw when he looked at her was not the real Bethan anymore.

Am I really still a killer?

Doing what she was doing right then suggested that, yes, she was still ready to kill for a cause. While Dean sought out the radio to attempt a more peaceful resolution, she was preparing to blow them all sky-high.

"Fuck it." She shook her head and carried on with her work. The ship rocked gently, buffers softening much of the movement from the violent Arctic Ocean, and cracks and rattles resounded around the hull. She thought of Alile and Goyo, dead back on that island. Her friends for so long, their loss still felt surreal and dreamlike, the impact yet to land. And poor Frank, brave even at the end in the face of people he knew and loved turning on him.

He'd known the dangers they lived with. The Long-Gone and their terrifying history might have been campfire tales in his mind, but deeper down she thought he'd really believed them. He'd certainly faced up to current events without too much doubt. It was almost as if he'd always been waiting for this to happen, and in that way he reminded her of Goyo.

She didn't hear the door open. Didn't sense the man entering the room. The first she knew of his presence was when she heard a deep sigh, then a loud violent retching, and the splattering of bloody vomit striking the deck.

Bethan span around and raised her gun, dropping a blasting cap and stepping away from the pack of explosives she'd been working on.

"Stay still!" she shouted, but she could already see that the man had no intention of doing what she said. She doubted he could even hear her. He was short and thin, skin leathered by a lifetime on the harsh landscape of Hawkshead Island, and his eyes were rolled back in his head, blood leaking from their corners and flowing from his left ear. He let out a curious sound from his throat—*ack, ack, ack*—and she wondered if he was fighting it, and what he was trying to say.

She shot him in the chest. He stumbled back against the wall beside the door, and his head tilted to the right as the trickle of blood from his left ear became a torrent.

She shot him in the chest again, then raised her aim and put a bullet in his head. The round passed through, sparked from the metal wall behind him and ricocheted somewhere around the hold, and the man slid down to a sitting position, head tilting so that his chin rested on his chest.

He stopped moving, and there were no more *ack-ack* sounds. Bethan held her breath. She hadn't seen any hazy spores in the air, but it didn't matter. One way or another she didn't have long left, and she had to finish what she had begun.

She held her breath and edged towards the door, stepping around the fallen man. There was no one waiting outside.

She listened, hearing only the throb of distant engines and the creaking of metal flexing and settling.

For fuck's sake, I should have taken the explosives to the engine room! she thought. The fuel tanks were probably back there. But it was too late now. Anyone else on the ship would have been alerted by the gunfire. She wouldn't see Dean again.

She kicked the dead man's leg aside, closed the door, and this time made sure the bolt was shut all the way home.

Bethan glanced around the hold. She had to finish setting the explosives.

And then make her decision.

Dean saw the shadow in the doorway, and before he had time to react Wren stepped through.

"Hey man," Wren said. He was holding a cup, and he paused and lifted it to his lips. When he lowered it again he had a strange, almost quizzical expression on his face. Dean wasn't sure what it was—not fear, not even surprise. It looked for all the world like some sort of twisted regret.

He's fighting it! he thought. He lifted the shotgun and aimed it at Wren's chest, looking for any signs, any indication that he was going to start to change and spore. And Dean didn't want to see it. He did not want to witness his friend creaking and breaking bones, bleeding, letting out the Deadeye that had penetrated him and taken him over from the inside out.

"Wren, you gotta let me pass," Dean said. "I know you're not you. Not wholly. But you don't have to let it take you. I can see you fighting it, and—"

"Fighting it?" Wren laughed. "Dude, it's the most beautiful thing there is. You've got fear and anxiety and a gun in your hand, and I've got…" He spread out his arms as wide as the gangway would allow, then brought the coffee to his mouth again for another sip. "I got peace," he said. "I got knowledge. I got the certainty that I'm a better man because of what's happened. Can you ever say that about yourself? That you have peace?"

"Peace?" Dean asked. "Are you still going to feel peace when your head cracks open?"

Wren frowned, a strange expression, as if he was listening to a voice Dean couldn't hear.

I've got to get around him, Dean thought, and he thought of Wren in the past, binding their group together with his humour and strength.

"I don't want to shoot you," Dean said.

"And I don't want you to shoot me." Wren smiled. "You don't need to, Dean. Can't you feel it? Can't you sense it?"

Dean took a step back.

Wren glanced over his shoulder and his expression fell into something empty, like the blank template for a human expression.

Dean squeezed the trigger. The shot struck Wren in the stomach and he folded and fell back through the door. Dean dropped to his knees and felt the *whoosh!* of the metal bar passing above his head, heard the loud clanging impact, and he rolled onto his back and shot the woman behind him in the face.

She screamed, a horrible sound that drove Dean to his feet again. *Four shots*, he thought, *I have only three left*. As he heard the cracking of bones and the thrashing and thudding of limbs against metal bulkheads, he knew that his friend Wren had disappeared a long time ago, back when he'd gone down into that sinkhole.

Holding his breath, Dean leapt over the fallen woman and ran for the radio room.

I'm still me, he thought. But the doubt that Wren had planted was already starting to grow.

Bethan continued attaching the blasting caps and trailing the wires towards the detonator control, keeping the gun tucked into her trousers. The barrel felt warm against her belly. She thought of the man she'd just shot, laughing and eating and spending time with his loved ones.

"He was dead already," she whispered. Her voice muttered around the hold, a sibilant accusation.

As she set the last block of explosives against the wall, she heard footsteps beyond the closed hold doors. She snatched the pistol from her belt, then tucked it back in and returned to the wires. She had to splice them into the detonator control, and she thought the door would hold for a while.

She needed five minutes.

As she went to work again something started crashing against the doors. Metal on metal, a violent heavy sound that reverberated around the enclosed space and hurt her ears. She breathed deeply and concentrated on what she was doing.

Perhaps they had Dean. Maybe he'd told them what she was doing. The realisation that she would never see him again made her gasp and freeze, and she thought of all those things that still remained unsaid. Like, *I love you*. They'd said it to each other before the accident and Dean shutting her out, only ever meaning it in a platonic way, but for her that had always been a deeper form of love, and one that should never have been upset. She wanted to say it to him again now.

Clang!

She wanted to hear him say it to her.

Clang!

Bethan shed a tear as she spliced the remaining wires.

Clang-clang-clang!

She set them into the detonator, suddenly worried that its battery wasn't charged or she'd fixed something wrong, and she tried to shut out the loud sounds so that she could run through what she'd done. Explosives, detonator caps, wires leading to—

Two shotgun blasts rang out, the second peppering shot against the outside of the doors.

"Bethan!"

"Dean," she breathed. She took a step towards the door, then paused.

"Let me in!" he said, his voice muffled beyond the door. "Hurry! I just killed Wren, and two more, and I want to be in there with you when…" He trailed off, and she imagined him standing with his hand pressed to the door.

She walked across and reached for the lock.

Don't, she thought. *Don't be fucking stupid.*

But Bethan had always been fucking stupid. She'd known that even before the fracking site accident, and even more after.

"Dean," she said again, quiet so that he could not hear. She held her gun ready, slipped back the bolt, and stepped back.

The door opened slowly and Dean slipped through. He looked scared and sad and there was blood splashed on his face. Even if he was going to be infected—and really, she thought, what were the chances that either of them was still free of Deadeye?—she thought that, right then, he was still the Dean she knew and loved.

Bethan started lowering the pistol, then blinked. *He's been out there a long time. Anything could have happened.*

"Bethan, you okay?" he asked. He tried another smile that did not work. "It's all good. I got through to the Canadian coastguard and told them everything. They're prepping a team to meet the ship, they'll put us in quarantine, find out what the hell this is and—"

"Bullshit."

"Eh?"

"Bullshit, Dean. You've been gone twenty minutes. You killed Wren?"

"Yeah. Yeah." He lowered his eyes. "And the radio room's only a few rooms back, beneath the bridge."

"We're ready to blow." Bethan held up her hand holding the detonator. Her mind scampered, checking through everything she'd done, searching for any reason this would not work. She thought she had everything covered. Death was as far away as her thumb moving half an inch.

"No!" Dean said, louder this time. "You don't need to do this, Bethan!"

"I think I'm okay," she said. "I'm not sure, but *think* I am. I don't feel any… resistance when I rest my thumb here." She touched the detonator's button. Nothing. If she was infected, surely the Deadeye would be telling her not to press? Isn't that how this worked? Staying among the living so that the disease could spread at all costs?

"Well, I *know* I'm okay," he said. "I called, told them everything. I wouldn't have done that if—"

"You'd do that to stop me blowing up the boat. And I don't know you did, for sure."

He looked past her at the packs of explosives lined along the junction of hold and hull. "And I don't know whether you've really rigged that to blow."

"Dean," she said, and she felt her eyes prickling. "I wish you'd... I wish we could do this together. All those adventures, then I fucked it up, and that left us both alone. I'm sorry I lost you, and even sorrier you lost me. I love you, Dean. And I wish we could spend these last few moments *together*. Because it's got to be done. Even if I could believe you—and most of me does—Deadeye will twist the truth. What happens if we're both fine right now, but we're infected before the coastguard gets here, or before we land? What happens if Wren's sporing got you, or left some trace of the disease on your clothing, the hairs on your lips, your hands? We'll live and change and... and give them all the twisted truths we want them to hear, and they won't have a fucking clue what they're dealing with. *We* don't, not really. It just takes one person to walk away—one of the islanders who're probably still on the ship, or you and me—and spore in a big city. A movie theatre. A football game. Somewhere dark and quiet, where no one knows what's happening. One becomes a hundred, then those hundred carry it quietly, covertly, knowing what they are and what they have and choosing the best moment. Ten minutes later, ten years later. Then a hundred becomes five thousand, then a million. And we can't allow even the smallest risk of that happening."

"We won't. You and me, Bethan. We make a good team." He edged forward, shotgun still in his right hand. It no longer swung with his motion. It was stiff, tense, where he readied to raise it.

"Team?" she asked. "That's one thing we haven't been in a long while."

Now, now, I should press it now! But she couldn't. Her will wasn't strong enough. And Dean was closer, the best friend she'd ever had. The friend she had lost.

"Together, we'll make sure it doesn't happen," he said. "Come on. Be with me. Put that thing down." He smiled. "This time, just cut the line. I forgive you, you know that. It's all as it was years ago when we—"

Bethan pulled the trigger. Dean jerked and fell back, stumbling against the bulkhead then collapsing back through the open doorway.

"Oh Dean, you're too stubborn to ever forgive me," Bethan said. Through her tears she shot at him again, then threw down the gun and grabbed the detonator in both hands.

She closed her eyes and wished her greatest wish.

NINETEEN

Bleeding, wounded in his shoulder and cheek, Dean found his feet and stumbled as quickly as he could along the gangway, heading for the stairs leading up to the deck. He'd seen the look in Bethan's eyes, and it was the same one he'd seen at that fracking site years before—determination, and an unswerving belief that she had no other choice. He'd always believed that he and Bethan would have another chance at friendship—

She shot me!

—and that he could persuade her that what she'd done was wrong, and he could dig deeper and find regret in her—

She tried to kill me!

—and that was why he'd lured her to Hawkshead Island. He had been ready for them to cross paths once more. The past couple of days had made him believe that Bethan was ready, too. Now their paths had parted once again, and she'd—

The blast pounded and echoed through the *Kelland*, stealing his hearing, thudding and vibrating through deck and bulkhead alike. He stumbled to one side and the shaking wall threw him off, across the gangway and into an open doorway. He struck some shelving and held on, feeling a violent, almost lifelike vibration hammering through the metal supports as the ship shook from the impact. Blood poured from his ears and he reached up in a panic, but it was only blood, and nothing else happened. His eyes were fine, his head was fine—

Bethan... oh, Bethan...

The ship was already listing to one side. The blast must have taken out a good portion of the hull, and between the creaking and shrieking of tortured metal he could hear the roar of water, smell the sea like an excited creature, surging in to take him down into its freezing embrace.

Dean wished that Bethan could have believed and trusted him one more time.

"I do forgive you!" he shouted. "I do *love* you! You're still my friend and—"

Behind him a door slammed open and foaming, furious water powered through, driven by pressure from below as the ship rolled further and tilted on its eventual, inevitable journey to the bottom of the ocean.

The shock when the water hit him stole his breath and froze his thoughts.

They were sinking. Along the corridor, the staircase he'd been heading for that led up towards the deck twisted and deformed as bulkheads warped. Treads exploded outwards from the stressed structure, one of them whipping past his head and piercing the wall behind him. Another blast ripped through the ship, this one deforming and cracking metal as the *Kelland*'s back broke and the sea poured in to take its greedy fill.

In the distance he heard voices shouting, and then something that might have been the sound of several skulls crunching and sporing, giving their seed to the sea all at the same time in one last desperate attempt to propagate their gift to the world.

Dean knew he would never reach the deck. Water sucked him down, bashing him from walls and ceiling, and as he surfaced briefly, he gasped in a deep breath, wondering why he should, why he didn't just let himself go as Bethan had and join whatever was left of her down here.

It'll be fine, he thought. *A moment of pain before my long peaceful sleep.*

The movement of the shattered ship seemed to ease and slow as it went down, but the violence of the heavy thuds remained. He splashed through a doorway, aided by the flow of water, and managed to prop himself against a fixed cabinet and shove the door closed behind him. He was in a small office, and he hauled himself up onto the top of the cabinet, sloping now as the vessel continued a slow roll onto its side in its death-throes. Lights flickered off and on, then off again, and darkness held him in its cold embrace.

The *Kelland* sank.

The door groaned but remained shut. There was three feet of air at the top corner of the room, maybe a little more. Enough to sustain him for an hour, perhaps, if the air pocket remained. If the cold didn't take him. If his heart did not give out.

Dean's panic subsided and he started breathing slower, calmer.

His body grew cooler. His wounds no longer hurt.

He felt peace.

Soon there was a thud as the ship hit the seabed, and a groaning and shifting as it took time to settle into its new, forever home.

Forever, at least until someone came to answer the desperate radio message he had sent pleading for help: "SOS, we're sinking, our coordinates are…" Then there would be a search, an investigation, and maybe even salvage. Perhaps they would find him in this room, the air pocket all used up and the atmosphere toxic, dried out and mummified in his cold, stale resting place.

It might never happen, and even if it did, the location and salvage might take quite some time.

But a voice inside, soothing and calming, told him that was fine.

It was used to waiting.

ACKNOWLEDGEMENTS

Thanks as ever to the brilliant Titan team, especially my editor Cath Trechman.

And a big thanks to everyone who read this book and provided such wonderful blurbs.

ABOUT THE AUTHOR

TIM LEBBON is an award-winning author of over forty-five novels, and hundreds of novellas and short stories. He's won multiple awards, including the 2023 World Fantasy Award (best collection) for *All Nightmare Long*, his books have been adapted twice for the big screen (*The Silence* and *Pay The Ghost*), and he has several more projects in development. He also writes screenplays, audio dramas, computer games, comics... anything to tell a story. Follow him on X and Instagram @timlebbon. For more information visit his website: timlebbon.net

THE LAST STORM

Tim Lebbon

With global warming out of control, large swathes of North America have been struck by famine and drought and are now known as the Desert. A young woman sets out across this dry, hostile landscape, gradually building an arcane apparatus she believes will bring rain to the parched earth.

A gripping, terrifying road trip through the heat of the post-apocalyptic American desert from the author of Netflix's *The Silence*. This action-packed and thought-provoking eco-nightmare will appeal to fans of Benjamin Percy, Christopher Golden and Josh Malerman.

"*The Last Storm* is a soaring near-future nightmare that breaks all the tired rules of apocalyptic fiction. The story's ambition is only matched by the grim hope of Tim's boundless, humane imagination. His best novel to date."

Paul Tremblay, author of *A Head Full of Ghosts* and *The Pallbearer's Club*

"Grim, dusty Americana, family drama, near-future horror. The best thing he's ever done!"

Christopher Golden, bestselling author of *Road of Bones*

"Tim Lebbon is always good, but this time he's outdone himself."

Joe R. Lansdale, author of the Hap and Leonard series

TITANBOOKS.COM

EDEN

Tim Lebbon

Earth's rising oceans contain enormous islands of refuse, the Amazon rainforest is all-but destroyed, and countless species edge towards extinction. Humanity's last hope to save the planet lies with The Virgin Zones, thirteen vast areas of land off-limits to people and given back to nature.

Dylan leads a clandestine team of adventure racers, including his daughter Jenn, into Eden, the oldest of the Zones. Jenn carries a secret—Kat, Dylan's wife who abandoned them both years ago, has entered Eden ahead of them. Jenn is determined to find her mother, but neither she nor the rest of their tight-knit team are prepared for what confronts them. Nature has returned to Eden in an elemental, primeval way. And here, nature is no longer humanity's friend.

A gripping horror thriller that will lead you into the ruthless, dark heart of nature from the bestselling author of Netflix's *The Silence*.

"A textured, thought-provoking thriller that will make you wonder what the world would be like if humans were to give it back."

Josh Malerman, *New York Times* best-selling author of *Bird Box* and *Malorie*

"Tim Lebbon gives us a near-future as terrifying as it is exhilarating, and—most frightening of all—irresistibly beautiful. Surrender to Eden."

Alma Katsu, author of *The Deep* and *The Hunger*

TITANBOOKS.COM

COLDBROOK

Tim Lebbon

Coldbrook is a secret laboratory located deep in Appalachian Mountains. Its scientists had achieved the impossible: a gateway to a new world. Theirs was to be the greatest discovery in the history of mankind, but they had no idea what they were about to unleash.

With their breakthrough comes disease and now it is out and ravaging the human population. The only hope is a cure and the only cure is genetic resistance: an uninfected person amongst the billions dead.

In the chaos of destruction there is only one person that can save the human race.

But will they find her in time?

"Lebbon takes zombie apocalypse to new levels […] Compelling, humane horror from one of the genre's leading exponents."

The Guardian

"Lebbon's prose is cold, lean and ruthlessly efficient […] the book excels is in the scenes on the parallel world."

SFX Magazine

TITANBOOKS.COM

For more fantastic fiction, author events,
exclusive excerpts, competitions, limited editions and more

VISIT OUR WEBSITE
titanbooks.com

LIKE US ON FACEBOOK
facebook.com/titanbooks

FOLLOW US ON TWITTER AND INSTAGRAM
@TitanBooks

EMAIL US
readerfeedback@titanemail.com